W9-BLA-198

A REALLY CUTE CORPSE

By Joan Hess

The Ozarks Mysteries

MALICE IN MAGGODY
MISCHIEF IN MAGGODY

The Claire Malloy Mysteries

STRANGLED PROSE
THE MURDER AT THE MURDER AT THE MIMOSA INN
DEAR MISS DEMEANOR
A REALLY CUTE CORPSE

The Theo Bloomer Mysteries
(writing as Joan Hadley)

THE NIGHT CEREUS
THE DEADLY ACKEE

A
REALLY CUTE
CORPSE

Joan Hess

St. Martin's Press
New York

A REALLY CUTE CORPSE. Copyright © 1988 by Joan Hess. All rights reserved. Printed in the United States of America. No part of this book may be used or reproduced in any manner whatsoever without written permission except in the case of brief quotations embodied in critical articles or reviews. For information, address St. Martin's Press, 175 Fifth Avenue, New York, N.Y. 10010.

Library of Congress Cataloging-in-Publication Data

Hess, Joan.
    A really cute corpse / Joan Hess.
      p.   cm. — (A Claire Malloy mystery)
    ISBN 0-312-02271-9
    I. Title.
    PS3558.E79785R4   1988
    813'.54—dc19   88-18202
                                                             CIP

First Edition

10 9 8 7 6 5 4 3 2 1

Lisle Library
Lisle, Illinois

m
HES

A REALLY CUTE CORPSE

"O"N"E"

All I've ever wanted to do was mind my own business. However, for a variety of complex and convoluted reasons, no one believes me. My accountant, a spotty old thing who tends to hiss, has pointed out on several occasions that minding my business includes fretting over such details as quarterly tax estimates, misplaced invoices, depreciation schedules, and tons of papers in alphabetical order. The business to which he refers is the Book Depot, a shabby, dusty, disorganized bookstore in the old train depot down the hill from Farber College. But it is *my* shabby, dusty, disorganized bookstore, and I dearly love it, from its balky boiler in the rear to its leaky brick portico on Thurber Street. It provides a modest income and a steady supply of reading material. What more could one ask for—except a modest supply of reading material and a steady income?

My daughter claims that I don't mind my own business, but she actually is alluding to my maternal inclination to mind hers. Caron is fifteen, to put it mildly. Fifteen is a melodramatic age. Fifteen is a gawky, self-centered, pimply, confused age which no one wears gracefully, and Caron is no exception. She has my red hair and freckles, and lately has acquired the beginnings of some of my more mature physical attributes. Said convexities and concavities alarm both of us. We have a reasonably amiable relationship, and avoid major mother-daughter conflicts for the most part. It is, however, somewhat like tiptoeing through the tulips in combat boots.

The third person who continually moans that I do not mind my own business is Peter Rosen. When he so desires, he is a man of great charm and wit. He has curly black hair, a hawkish nose that is quite appealing, and teeth that could star in a toothpaste commercial. His eyes are gentle pools of molasses, deceptively mild and warm. He is moderately persuasive when we are debating the issue of marriage, especially when we're particularly pleased with each other. We do so because he is divorced, I am widowed, we are of a comparable age—and we are intimate when all-of-the-aboves' schedules permit such a thing.

There are moments less magical, however, when he has accused me of meddling, interfering, sticking my nose into his business, refusing to be completely candid, and in general being the cause of insomnia, incipient ulcers, gray hairs, and threatened demotion to traffic control. Peter is a lieutenant in the Farberville CID; I've been able to offer some assistance in a few of his more perplexing cases. Was he grateful? Was he pleased with my sense of community spirit and dedication to truth and justice for all? Was he the first to rush forward with congratulations for my undeniable prowess in exposing heinous criminals? Does the Pope wear a petticoat?

Despite the critics hovering in the wings to contradict me, I really was minding my own business (on all three levels, no less) when Sally Fromberger sailed into the Book Depot, clipboard in hand. She glanced down at the ledger in front of me, shook her head at the smudges and eraser sprinkles, and shot me a calculating smile.

"Isn't this a fantastic day?" she demanded with enough gusto to dust the nearest rack of self-help books. She was not much taller than the rack, but almost as broad and certainly as packed with cheery advice and hints on getting oneself organized. Her blond hair glinted, her eyes sparkled, her skin glowed, and her fingers danced on the clipboard. She reminded me of a tomato about to burst. Into song, applause, or merely splatters of pulp, I was never quite sure.

"The sun is shining, the pollen count is down, and I'm only off a few pennies," I said warily. Clipboards unnerve me.

"The weather's going to be just super this weekend for the Thurberfest. I have a copy of the minutes from the steering committee meeting last night. I spent the morning typing up the reports from all the chairpeople, except yours, of course. We missed you at the meeting, Claire. I hope nothing terrible happened. . . ?"

I gazed over her shoulder at the pedestrians ambling down the sidewalk while I considered a variety of lies. Realizing the futility of the effort, I said, "Sorry about the meeting. I was tied up with a personal situation at home." I did not elaborate on said situation, since it commenced with a headache, courtesy of my Hitleresque accountant, and escalated with Caron's bright idea that it was time for a learner's permit and legal access to a lethal machine. It concluded with scotch and a new mystery novel with lots of old-fashioned gore.

"Oh," Sally murmured, flipping through the papers clipped firmly on her clipboard. "Well, here are copies of the committee reports from public relations, parade, pageant, food and drink vendors, clean-up, arts and crafts displays, secondary vendors, program scheduling, media coordination, music, street performers, treasury, and children's activities. If we had your report on the current status of the Gala Sidewalk Sale, I'd feel a lot better."

"The sidewalk sale is fine. All the merchants understand they can put out racks or tables and sell whatever merchandise they wish for whatever price they wish for as long as they wish. I didn't realize I needed to write it down and turn it in."

"By midafternoon, please, and three copies if you get a chance. I think it's really vital that we stay on top of every detail of the street festival, since it's such a wonderful opportunity to bring the community together for a healthy, family-oriented affair."

She laid down a thick stack of papers, gave me a perky little wave, and sailed away, content in the knowledge that she would have another officious, meaningless paper to retype, copy, and distribute to all the merchants on Thurber Street. All of us filed them in similar cylindrical metal containers, but Sally Fromberger was a happy woman.

Luanne Bradshaw, on the other hand, was not. Later that afternoon she came limping into the bookstore on crutches, her face pale and her eyes glazed with pain. I gaped at the thick tape around her ankle, then came around the counter to make useless gestures. "My lord, Luanne, what happened?"

"Lead me to a chair, a cup of coffee, and a weapon with which to kill our illustrious leader, Sally Fromberger," Luanne said with a grim smile.

"Two out of three in the office." I helped her hobble down the aisle, wondering what had led to her condition and mood. Luanne was one of my favorite store owners on the street (and Caron's, too, although for different reasons). She materialized a year or so ago and opened Second Hand Rose, a used-clothing store that had about as many paying customers as the Book Depot. She claimed to be divorced, disillusioned, and disenchanted with murky family entanglements in Connecticut. We occasionally discussed said delicacies over a pitcher in the beer garden across the street, or over serious calories in the Mexican restaurant up the hill. We never discussed anything in Sally Fromberger's health food cafe—on principle. Clipboards unnerve me. Alfalfa sprouts unhinge me.

"It's the damn Miss Thurberfest beauty pageant," Luanne said, once we were settled in my tiny office. "Go ahead and say that you told me so over and over again. Harp on the countless times you said that I shouldn't have allowed Sally to browbeat me into directing it, that I should have skipped town, that I've lost my mind and deserve everything I get. Go ahead, Claire—rub it in with lots of salt. Just remember I'm in incredible pain and you owe me money for lunch last week."

"What happened to your ankle?"

"I was on stage with the contestants, trying to explain the four steps for the opening number on the preliminary night. We started with something that would have done Fred Astaire proud, but now we're down to a primitive box step consisting of forward, right, back, left. One would think a herd of cross-eyed cows could be trained to take four simple steps."

"It doesn't sound like a choreographic nightmare," I agreed. "Shall I presume that the bevy of would-be beauty queens cannot outstep cross-eyed cows?"

Luanne ran her fingers through her coarse dark hair and sighed. "Presume your heart out. Of the eighteen girls, about half can do the steps, but not to the music. Others lose count long about 'three' and come to a full stop, blinking piteously. The rest then bump into their inert sisters, which results in bruises, tears, and acrimony. We're talking inches from hair-pulling and other forms of sheer brutality. What are they teaching in physical education classes these days?"

"So you stomped up on stage to straighten them out?" I asked, trying to maintain a properly sympathetic expression.

"I did, and was actually getting into it with enthusiasm. Last year's Miss Thurberfest and I were kicking up our heels, she with the abandon of youth and I with a slightly more restrained abandon, when I caught my heel on a protruding nail and nose-dived over the edge of the stage into the orchestra pit. The last thing I remember is the girls peering down at me, their little eyes wide with awe. I came to at the hospital, where the nurses' little eyes were narrowed with sardonic amusement."

"Thus winning the title of first fatality at the Miss Thurberfest beauty pageant. Are you going to sue the theater owner for the damage and humiliation due to negligence?"

Luanne sighed again. "You've never met him, have you? I hobbled by this morning to see how the girls were doing, and he rose from the bowels of the orchestra pit to bawl me out for damaging his stage. *Me,* mind you, the me with a sprained ankle, a slight concussion, and a fanny literally black all over with bruises. I thought he was going to snatch away one of my crutches and beat me over the head with it. I ending up apologizing to him. I think I agreed to pay him for repairs."

"He sounds delightful. How was it going this morning without your supervision and wisdom? If I recall Sally's last hundred-page report correctly, the pageant runs Friday and Saturday nights. The girls still have a few more days to master the essence of the box step."

"Today they were rehearsing their talent acts." She looked at me, and I looked at her. After a moment of silence, she said, "Baton twirling. Singers with a two-note range: flat and sharp. Dramatic recitations, one of which involves a Statue of Liberty costume with a torch that glows in the dark like a great green phallus. Fly casting. Pet tricks. I nixed the trampoline act and the stir-fry demonstration, thus forcing two more renditions of 'The Impossible Dream.'"

"Why are you doing this, Luanne? Don't give me any more nonsense about civic pride and obligations to the Thurber Street Merchants' Association. The civilians don't give a damn and the merchants are in it to feather their cash registers. In any case, such lofty ideals can be demonstrated in less painful ways than directing a flesh display for doting relatives and pubescent boys. One can gaze coldly at Sally Fromberger and just say no."

She stuck out her lower lip and did a fair imitation of Caron Malloy when hearing the odds of signing up for a demolition derby. "I did say no. I also said no thank you, I really can't, I'm awfully busy, I'm terminally ill, I'm into Zen, I'm a militant feminist agitator, I don't have any free time, and please oh please don't make me do this—I'll give you free clothes for a full year. Sally gave me the program for last year's pageant and McWethy's home telephone number so I could book the theater for rehearsals. Let's kill her."

"I suppose we could slip cyanide into her soybean patty, or

suffocate her with tofu, but they'd know who did it." I gave myself a brief moment to savor the scenario, then shook my head. "We're being childish, Luanne. The more adult approach to the abdication of your position of authority is right there on your ankle. Tell her you're in too much pain, then go home and stay there until the street festival is done. I'll come by every night with chicken soup and my very own impressions of the parade, the jugglers, and the Gala Sidewalk Sale."

Luanne leaned down to tidy up an errant strip of adhesive tape. "I did," she said in a low voice. "Want to know what she suggested?"

"I don't think so. How about another cup of coffee and a rousing discussion of the state of the economy in the face of escalating interest rates? Or if you're in the mood for a good laugh, Caron's reasons why she absolutely has to get a learner's permit or be too embarrassed to show her face in public ever again as long as we both shall live?"

"Sally told me to double up on oyster-shell calcium tablets, then said that I needed an assistant for the rest of the week, someone who's taken a less demanding committee chairpersonship and thus has oodles of free time to help with the last minute minutiae."

"She doesn't even know how to pronounce that word."

"Maybe not. But I truly need someone who—"

"A recession might help the economy in the long run, you know. When unemployment goes up as a result of cutbacks in the wholesale manufacturing—"

"A friend who will come to the aid of the Thurberfest, and—"

"Then we're likely to experience a decrease in the prime lending rate because—"

"A good, loyal friend who—"

"The Federal Reserve Board will—"

"Because of my severely sprained ankle—"

"Adjust due to the decline in the gross national product!"

"Handle a few itty-bitty details!"

"What on earth are you talking about?" Caron said as she came into the office and perched on a corner of the desk. "You're both foaming and howling, and making no sense whatsoever. You sound worse than the Math Club voting on the banquet-night entertainment. The trig boys wanted to do a skit about Euclid in the nude. Miss Hoffmaken got her hypotenuse bent out of shape and nearly keeled over. It was *très amusant*."

Luanne cheated by lifting up her ankle for Caron's inspection. "I was wounded in the line of duty, and therefore am obliged to ask your mother for a little bit of help in my hour of need. She's being snotty."

"I am not," I protested. "Beauty pageants offend my feminist sensibilities. They demean women by implying that worth is determined by thigh diameter and bust dimensions. No one, including women, should be judged on physical attributes, and especially by a bunch of slobbery old men. A beauty pageant forces women to parade around in skimpy clothes, pretending they're certified virgins who exist only to please men. Don't you agree, Caron?"

Luanne cheated some more. "Think about it for a minute, honey, while your mother finds a way to climb down from her soapbox without spraining *her* ankle. By the way, I got in a box of forties' cocktail dresses, and one of them is black with incredibly funky beadwork and a darling little skirt. I put it aside for you, and I'll let you have it if you'll sweep out the store before the weekend. I can barely walk."

"Caron's not old enough to wear black," I said.

"And it has a matching purse covered with the same beadwork," Luanne continued, thus proving she was a master in the art of cheatery.

Caron eyed both of us, no doubt weighing the cocktail dress and purse against the obscure possibility of a learner's permit. She probably realized that the dress was already hers and the permit unlikely unless we saw a major change in the weather forecast in hell, because she gave me, her own flesh and blood, a dark look.

"Luanne's supposed to be your friend, Mother, and you're always lecturing me about loyalty and stuff like that. Remember when Inez was invited to Rhonda McGuire's bunking party and canceled our plans to go to the movies? You went on and on about long-term values and character and all sorts of dreary things until I thought I'd absolutely die."

"Inez was treacherous. Friends shouldn't test limits like that."

"Besides," Caron sniffed, "Inez's sister is in the pageant, and she said we could help her with her dress and hair. Inez and I think Julianna is a very strong contender for the title."

"Julianna?" Luanne said, frowning. "Does she do a modern dance routine?"

Caron nodded wisely. "Yes, Inez and I convinced her not to do the scene from *Hamlet* when he's yelling at Ophelia about getting herself to a nunnery. Julianna was going to do both parts, but Inez and I felt she would look silly hopping back and forth on the stage. Besides, she's very interpretive in a leotard."

"What are you and Inez—her agents?" I said.

"Julianna was very grateful for our input, Mother. She's hoping to win scholarship money so she can study neurosurgery at Johns Hopkins."

"But the Miss Thurberfest pageant doesn't offer scholarships!" I crowed in triumph.

Luanne cleared her treacherous throat. "No, but the winner gets a bunch of gift certificates from the Thurber Street merchants, and is asked to appear at some of the other pageants in the state. The current Miss Thurberfest, Cyndi Jay, told me she'd traveled all over the state and made a little bit of money through guest appearances."

"You've met Cyndi Jay?" Caron gasped. "What's she like?"

"She's cute and perky, and is a pretty good performer. She's been cooperative all week." Luanne took a plastic medicine vial from her purse, shook a capsule into her palm, and bravely gulped it down, making sure Caron and I appreciated her stoicism and determination to tough it out despite debilitating agony. She then made a major production of getting to her feet, embellishing it with moans, artistic grimaces, and wounded glances in my direction. "Well, I guess I'd better tell Sally to cancel the pageant, since I can't even manage the steps to the stage. It's a shame. The girls have worked all week, and almost everything is done. If there were just one person to supervise a few rehearsals and see to the judges and press people, we could have the pageant. But noooo."

Caron turned her gasp on me. "Mother."

The word consisted of two simple syllables and was the generic term to describe a biological relationship. Etymologically speaking, it came from the Greek *meter,* the Latin *mater,* or perhaps the Sanskrit *matr.* Caron's inflection imbued it with darkly mystical properties that brought to mind a jury foreman pointing an accusatory finger at a despicable felon destined to swing by the neck for a long, long time—if the jury had its druthers, anyway.

I smiled at Luanne. "I'll get you for this."

She smiled at me. "I know you will."

Caron smiled at everyone.

The next afternoon I stood next to Luanne at the back of the auditorium. Despite her petty victory, she did not look especially happy. I was hardly abubble with glee myself. Tweedlehum and Tweedledrum. On the stage, forty rows of seats down from us, a girl in a stiff pink tutu was trying to coax a recalcitrant Pekinese in a pink clown's hat to leap through a hula hoop. She'd been wheedling away for five solid minutes.

"So what remains to be done?" I asked in a low voice.

"Here's the schedule," she said as she handed me a creased paper. "Today the girls have fifteen minutes each to rehearse, and then they can wander away to pad their bras or whatever. Tomorrow morning is when things get harried. We have the technical, full-dress rehearsal at nine, and I'm hoping we can finish by noon. The girls have a luncheon with the judges at one; it's at Sally's cafe. The parade's at three, although only Cyndi and one of the judges will participate in that. Then we get serious at eight for the preliminary round, which results in the selection of the seven finalists for the grand finale on Saturday night at eight. During the day, the finalists will have to work on the production number for Saturday night, of course, and we'll have to schedule the talent to avoid a fatal dose of monotonality and batons."

"That doesn't sound too dreadful," I said mendaciously. "Who are the judges, when do they appear, and where do we stash them?"

Luanne leaned back against the wall and rubbed her eyes. "It's written down in the notebook somewhere, but it's all done. I'm feeling like hell right now; I think I'm going to limp to the office and lie down for a few minutes. Can you keep the rehearsal moving?"

"Can I order teenaged girls on and off the stage, you mean? You go lie down. We'll zip through this thing and be home in time for cocktails."

She moved past me and went down the corridor on the side of the auditorium. I kept one eye on the contestant on the stage while I glanced through Luanne's notebook. I discovered that the judges were to be State Senator Buell "Steve" Stevenson, who would also serve as emcee; Orkin Avery, the illustrious mayor of Farberville and the local Mercedes dealer when not snipping ribbons and breaking ground; and an unknown quantity described tersely as W. H. Maugahyder. Steve was due to arrive shortly to rehearse; the latter two were slated to appear in time for the luncheon and not a minute sooner, since we had no place in which to stash, alas.

I found two sketchy floor plans of the Thurber Street Theater. One showed the lobby and concession area out front, the two corridors on either side of the auditorium (Luanne had designated spots for ushers), and the stage and rows of seats. The judges were to sit in the front row, with a table in front of them so they could sip water and write down cryptic notes during the pageant. A short flight of stairs on the left side of the orchestra pit led to the basement, and there was a greenroom on the right side of the stage so the girls could pace and shred tissues or whatever would-be queens did in the critical precoronation moments.

The second sketch showed the basement dressing room. Two long, narrow rooms were for the contestants, and I could envision the chaos of clothing, nylons, leotards, hair dryers, cosmetic bags, batons, pooper scoopers, and other paraphernalia that would fill the rooms to waist level at best. One room, no bigger than a breadbox, had a star drawn on it. The reigning Miss Thurberfest, I guessed. Royalty had its reward, even if it was six by six, damp, and apt to be as cozy as a crypt.

"Oooh, bad dog!" squealed a voice from the stage. "Couldn't you have waited five more minutes? Oh, really, Chou-Chou, I could just spank you!"

"Don't bother. I'm going to barbecue the mutt," growled a second voice, although I couldn't determine its point of origin.

The girl snatched up her dog and clutched him to her chest. "Don't you say that in front of Chou-Chou. He happens to have a very, very good pedigree and never peepees on the floor at home. Besides, he's already all nervous about doing his tricks, and I don't want him to be intimidated by some nasty old threat."

"Read my lips. If the damn dog pisses on the stage one more time, he'll never be scared again," the voice continued.

"Ooh, you are so rude!" The girl scampered off stage, her pink ballet shoes leaving damp smudges on the wooden surface. Chou-Chou gazed over her shoulder with an enigmatic expression, perhaps gauging the potential for a vicious attack on someone's ankle.

While I stared, rather amused by the brief scene, a lanky figure appeared from one side of the orchestra pit. In fact, he rose from the depths like a missile from a silo, which gave me a hint of his identity. As I strolled down the aisle to meet the owner of the Thurber Street Theater, he went onto the stage and began to wipe up a puddle with a rag from his back pocket. He was decidedly tall, with light brown hair that needed a trim and a scraggly goatee that needed serious professional attention. His faded work shirt and overalls emphasized exceptionally long limbs, but his movements were brisk and economical.

"I'm Claire Malloy," I said to his back.

"Is that so?" He finished the chore, then tossed the rag into the orchestra pit and started to walk away.

"I'm helping Luanne with the pageant," I persisted.

He stopped and looked back at me. "Then tell that girl I meant what I said about the damn dog pissing on the stage. The uric acid eats the wood, and I've put too much time and money into remodeling this rat trap to have some halfass excuse for a dustmop damage it because of a nervous bladder. Understand?"

"I'll tell her," I said mildly, not yet ready to declare war on the man—although not yet sure I wouldn't change my mind in the immediate future. "I've noticed the theater for years, but it was boarded up. How long have you been remodeling it?"

He cocked his head to one side and gave me what might have been a crooked smile. "I bought it seven months ago, give or take a month. It's a hell of a fine building architecturally, and the structure's still good. It was built back in the forties as an opera house; you can see where the boxes were before some fool plastered over them. It was a movie house in the fifties, an art cinema in the sixties, and a gay nightclub up until about ten years ago, when it was condemned and allowed to deteriorate."

"You've done a remarkable job restoring it."

"It's become an obsession with me," he said, shrugging. "I've tarred the roof, plastered, painted, put down new carpet, reupholstered the seats, and tried everything possible to combat the mildew that seeps up from the basement. I'm hocked up to my armpits with the bank, but I've about got this dame back in shape."

"So you're a professional restorer?" I asked, thinking about a stain on the ceiling my office ceiling that might be symptomatic of roof rot, and therefore overlooking his use of the word *dame,* which was not one of my favorites.

"Now I am. I used to be a local politician before I overdosed on hot air and bullshit." He came across the stage in a few giant steps and held out his hand. "David McWethy—Mac to those with a limited attention span."

I shook the hand that had held the rag that had wiped up the puddle that had come from the dog that had pissed on the stage that Mac rebuilt. "Nice to meet you, Mac," I said with a small nod. "I'm Claire Malloy and I own the Book Depot down the street."

I waited for him to praise my architecture, but he merely grunted and said, "I'm surprised you or anyone else with a brain larger than a wart on a preacher's ass would be associated with this nonsense."

"It falls in the area of civic duty, I suppose. It'll be over Saturday night, and the girls will all wander back to the real world."

"I wouldn't presume they can find it on the first try." He scratched his chin as he gazed in the direction Chou-Chou's owner had fled. "Just when you think you've seen the bottom of the well of human stupidity, someone like that girl comes along to demonstrate that the well has no bottom."

"She seemed fairly typical to me," I murmured, wondering why I felt obliged to defend her—or anything linked with the impending travesty.

"Oh, really?" he said in a shrill falsetto. He then turned on his heel and went through the door to the greenroom. After a moment, I heard a girlish shriek and the pitter-patter of girlish feet in the corridor. The expletives (by necessity deleted) that followed were not at all girlish.

Chou-Chou, it seemed, had done it again. Shame, shame.

"T"W"O"

I sat in the front row and kept my eyes on my wristwatch as a series of girls sang, twirled, recited, leaped around in leotards, and evinced no discernible talent. On the other hand, I discovered I had a real talent for peremptory commands and heartless refusals to give any of them an extra minute in the soon-to-be limelight. Julianna managed to give me a small smile while interpreting "Feelings" from a cassette player, but most of the others were too involved in their performances to acknowledge my presence. I did not allow my hypotenuse to get bent out of shape.

Once we had heard the antepenultimate, penultimate, and ultimate renditions of "The Impossible Dream," I stood up and started to leave. Before I reached the end of the row, a dark-haired girl appeared from the wings and came down to the edge of the stage. "Excuse me," she said, "but how is Mrs. Bradshaw? Will she be working with us now?"

"Mrs. Bradshaw's ankle was bothering her, and she went to lie down in the office." I did not recognize the girl, who had not twirled, sang, recited, or tried to convince an animal to do unnatural things. "Did I skip you on the rehearsal schedule?" I asked. "You may have a turn now, if you wish."

"Oh, that's okay," she murmured, fluttering her lashes above enormous brown eyes. She had a pretty, heart-shaped face and a complexion that would shame a peach. The corners of her mouth turned down for a fleeting second and she gave me an encore of the flutters. "I'm not really into sick people, but I feel just awful about Mrs. Bradshaw. Is there anything I can do for her?"

"I'm going to check on her as soon as we're finished here." I went on to introduce myself and admit my role in the proceedings.

"I'm Cyndi Jay, the reigning Miss Thurberfest. It's really, really nice of you to help Mrs. Bradshaw, Mrs. Malloy. We all feel just terrible about what happened to her—and I feel the worst of all." As she shook her head, several of the contestants drifted out from behind the curtain to gather around her and shake their heads, too.

I looked at the serious expressions and all that shiny, bouncy hair. "Why, Cyndi? Did you trip her?"

"Oh, my goodness, no! It's just that Mrs. Bradshaw was on my mark when she caught her heel on that nasty nail and fell. If she hadn't been showing me how to do the ending, I would have been the one to get hurt." She moved to the center of the stage and pointed at a chalky scrawl. "See? The nail was right there where I'm supposed to be for the touch-kick-touch-two-three-four-kick."

Julianna timidly touched a royal shoulder. "You don't think someone pulled up that nail on purpose, do you?"

"Of course not," Cyndi said firmly. "This building is just old and decrepit; it should be condemned. I'm really surprised it ever passed any wiring or plumbing inspections, and it's a miracle the ceiling doesn't collapse right on top of us. Why, there are probably a million nails poking out of the wood all over the place."

"There are not," came a now-familiar growl from the darkness in the back of the stage. "I checked every nail on the stage last week so none of you girls would stub any of your pretty little pinkies. As for the roof, keep up that caterwauling you call singing and it damn well might collapse. The insurance company will consider it an act of God."

Several of the vocalists stiffened, but Cyndi merely looked pensive for a moment, then came back to the corner of the stage.

"Well, I'm totally sick about Mrs. Bradshaw's ankle, but we are supposed to run through the opening number for tomorrow night. Some of the girls are a tiny bit unclear about the steps."

"So am I," I admitted cheerfully. "Mrs. Bradshaw seemed to think you know what you're doing, however, so why don't you direct things while I go up to the office for a minute or two?"

She wrinkled her nose at the group hovering nearby. "If it's okay with everybody, I can try. We did a similar number at the Miss Apple Festival, and I'll be happy to help everybody so we'll look really, really swell tomorrow night for our moms and dads and boyfriends. And the judges, of course."

At the mention of the dreaded triumvirate, the girls began to scurry across the stage to wherever they were supposed to be. Cyndi asked me to tell Mrs. Bradshaw how really, really sorry she was, and how she really, really hoped Mrs. Bradshaw's ankle wasn't hurting really, really, really bad. Although I doubted Luanne wanted such a hefty dose of reality, I assured her I would convey the essence of the sentiment and went up the corridor to the lobby.

The office door was locked. I tapped, then knocked, and finally pounded with my fist, all the while entertaining ghastly images of Luanne's unconscious form sprawled across the carpet. She had mentioned a mild concussion, I thought worriedly, and was the sort to laugh it off all the way to the morgue.

I was glancing around for a battering ram when Caron and Inez came through the front entrance. Inez Thornton was Caron's best friend (when not at Rhonda McGuire's house) and a perfect counterfoil for my daughter's histrionic approach to life. Inez must have peaked in her prepubescent days, for she was faded at the ripe old age of fifteen. She had limp brown hair, dusty freckles, a lumpy body, and flat eyes behind thick glasses.

The two were an interesting study in contrasts. When Caron wallowed in imprudence, Inez was there to pat her shoulder and offer circumspect analysis. Caron's mildest statements ended with an exclamation mark, Inez's every declaration with an implicit question mark. Caron flung herself off the metaphorical cliff. Inez looked a dozen times before she leaped—or dared to cross the street.

"What on earth are you doing, Mother?" Caron asked sternly. "We could see you from the street—as could Other People."

"Luanne's in there, and the door's locked."

Inez blinked at her best friend's deranged mother. "Maybe she's asleep or wants to be left alone, Mrs. Malloy."

"Then she isn't going to get her wish," I said. "Go find Mr. McWethy and ask him if he has a key. I'm afraid Luanne may be unconscious in there. Now, go!"

"But we're not allowed in the auditorium," Inez said with more blinks. "Julianna said it was off limits to everyone until the actual pageant."

Caron jabbed her. "Come on, Inez—this is an emergency, and we have a perfectly good excuse to go in there and find what's-his-name for Mother. Maybe we'll see Cyndi Jay."

I opened my mouth to reiterate the urgency of the mission, but as I did so Luanne opened the door. I rescinded the order and told the girls to wait for me outside the theater, then turned back to Luanne, who gave me a mildly inquiring smile.

"Good grief," I snapped, "I was about to break down the door and stumble over your lifeless body. In spite of my aversion to reckless driving, I was going to accompany you in the ambulance to hold your flaccid hand in my sweaty one. Caron and Inez were going to sing a duet at your funeral. I was going to visit the cemetery every Sunday afternoon for a year, and twice on Memorial Day."

"Do you want me to go in and expire? It'll only take a second, and you know how much I hate to see you disappointed. It makes your face turn all blotchy."

"It does not. Would you be so kind as to tell me what you were doing in there while I was beating on the door?"

She led me into the office, which was furnished with a metal desk and chair, a small couch, and a large, plastic plant that had defied the laws of nature and died. The wallpaper was bleached with age; whatever flowers had once bloomed were long since withered. Asymmetrical tan circles on the ceiling resembled some I knew down the street in someone's bookstore.

Luanne sat down on the couch and dropped her crutches. "I was in the washroom. The water was running and I didn't hear you."

"What were you doing in there all the time I was creating my Stephen King opus?" I said, still irked but not the least bit blotchy.

"I beg your pardon?" Miss Manners couldn't have done it better.

"Never mind." I sat down behind the desk and idly tugged at drawers. "The contestants have completed their vain attempts at talent and are currently rehearsing the opening number under Miss Jay's supervision. Miss Jay asked me to offer her condolences for your infirmity, since she is devastated by the fact that you were stricken when, in reality, she should have been the one to fall off the stage."

"Did she read something to that effect in her horoscope?"

"She pointed out that you were doing whatever you were doing on her mark. Had you not done it in that precise spot, she would have demonstrated the unsuccessful half-gainer into the abyss. One of the girls asked if the nail had been pulled up intentionally, but our Miss Thurberfest was quite cool in the face of such bourgeoise impudence."

Luanne did not laugh at my whimsical recitation. "I was in a few beauty pageants in my day, and there were some dirty doings among the contestants. Most of them were harmless practical jokes, but—"

"You were in a few beauty pageants?" I interrupted.

"That's part of the reason why I agreed to direct this one. Now, don't get all self-righteous and politically correct about it, Claire. I was in high school and college, and I won enough scholarship money to get through graduate school."

"I'm only self-righteous when I'm blotchy." I gave up on the drawers, which were all locked anyway, and leaned back in the squeaky chair. "We'll leave this startling revelation about your past for another time. You don't think someone deliberately tried to hurt Cyndi, do you?"

While she considered it, I watched Caron and Inez skulk across the lobby toward the auditorium and the heart-stopping possibility of an illict glimpse of the queen. I couldn't think of a valid reason to stop them. They were apt to bump into Mac somewhere in the shadows, which would teach them a lesson far beyond my merely mortal capabilities.

"The girls adore Cyndi," Luanne said slowly, "and I can't imagine any of them wishing her harm. She's not the competition. She's gone out of her way to help them prepare for the preliminary round. I heard her lecturing a group of them on the three B's of the runway—bust out, belly in, bottom under. She's quite a pro."

I tried the three B's, although I couldn't judge the effect since I was sitting down. "Well, you know better than I what goes on at these things, so I'm not going to argue over a nail. She's in good hands with our resident phantom of the playhouse."

Footsteps thudded in the corridor, then Caron burst into the office. "It's Cyndi! She's hurt! You'd better come right this second, Mother!" She sucked in a breath, gave us a wild look, and dashed out the door.

Luanne was fumbling with her crutches as I hurried down the corridor after Caron. I stopped in the arched entrance to the auditorium. The girls were huddled in the middle of the stage, unsettlingly quiet. Caron and Inez vacillated in a shadowy corner.

"What's going on?" I called as I went onto the stage.

Her lips quivering, Julianna stepped out of the huddle and met me. "It's okay, Mrs. Malloy. Cyndi was just frightened, and that man is making her sit with her head between her knees so she won't faint."

"What happened to her?"

"Cyndi was centerstage, demonstrating the cute little kick step she thought we ought to include in the ending. Out of nowhere this weight just plummeted down at her, and missed her by about one inch. If it'd hit her on the head, she'd be dead, Mrs. Malloy. I mean, completely dead." She gulped as her words reached her brain. "I guess it was just one of those scary accidents."

"Maybe." I pushed through the girls and squatted down next to Cyndi, who had her face hidden between her knees. Her shoulders were twitching; her neck and bare arms were covered with goose bumps. Mac crouched on her other side, his expression tight and unreadable. "Are you all right?" I asked the girl softly, rubbing her back.

"She's fine," Mac said. "You'd of thought the damn weight bounced off her head for all the squawking and squealing that went on afterward. I've heard worse from the henhouse when the rooster's on the prowl."

Cyndi looked up with a teary smile. "I'm okay, Mrs. Malloy. I realize I'm being silly, but it came so close I could feel a breeze on my cheek. It hit right by my foot. If it had been a teeny bit closer, it would have—" She broke off and hid her face again. Her shoulders jerked as she tried to control her sobs.

Several of the girls began to pat her head and murmured comforting, if meaningless, phrases. I stood up and gestured at Mac to join me on one side of the stage. "Tell me how that weight happened to fall," I said through clenched teeth, pointing at a small canvas bag that was, I suspected, filled with at least ten pounds of sand.

"Beats me. It's a counterweight for the one of the backdrops." He picked it up and fingered the bit of rope still tied to a leather ring. "Looks like something cut partway through the rope. The

new rope, let me say before you start dithering about my irrespon-
sibility and potential liability and whatever else you plan to dither
about."

"I do not dither, especially when someone might have been
killed." I glowered at him for a moment, then glowered at the vast
blackness above our heads. "I want to see where the weight was
hanging. I presume there is a way to climb up there to adjust
things or whatever."

"There's a spiral staircase that leads to a metal walkway, but I
doubt you want to go up there."

"Then you doubt incorrectly. Are you going to show me the
staircase, or shall I find it without your cooperation?"

He recoiled enough to give me a flicker of satisfaction. "I don't
care if you want to break your neck by climbing around up there.
That's why I've got insurance." He led me to the darkest corner of
the stage and pointed with his thumb at a rusty metal staircase
that almost disappeared in the gloom above our heads. "I replaced
most of the bolts that hold this and the walkway to the wall. It
might hold you."

I grasped the rail and shook it, steeling myself not to react to
the appalling amount of give. "You replaced *most* of the bolts and it
might hold me? How encouraging you are, considering the fact that
someone managed to climb up there and cut partway through your
rope so that your weight almost killed someone in your theater."

"Close only counts in horseshoes. And the rope might have
been gnawed by a rat. Lot of rats up there. Big, skinny, hungry
ones with red eyes."

I will admit I hesitated, but only long enough to decide he was
trying to bully me. No rat worth his whiskers would climb up that
rusty staircase. I beckoned to Caron and, when she came over,
said, "If something happens to me, call Peter and tell him. The will
is in the lockbox. And you and Inez behave yourselves and stay off
the telephone until you've done your homework."

Caron regarded me levelly. "Okay. Can I have your hair dryer?"

"It's going to charity." I began what felt like a descent into hell, except for the paradoxical sensation of climbing upward. The staircase clinked and wobbled, but did nothing more dramatic than that, and I reached the narrow catwalk that stretched across the stage. The catwalk swayed as I moved down it at a turtlish pace while busily wondering what I was doing up there without a flashlight or a parachute. Or a brain larger than a protuberance on a righteous rump.

There were all sorts of ropes and cables dangling like the root system of a plant. I gripped the rail and forced myself to look down at the stage thirty feet below me. The girls were still huddled on the stage, and I could see the top of Cyndi's head in the middle of them. As I watched, Luanne came onto the stage to join in the audible clucking over Miss Thurberfest. Mac was gone from the bottom of the staircase, but Caron was staring upward with her mouth agape. The stage was covered with chalk marks; from my perspective it resembled the mysterious scrawls on the blackboard in a football locker room.

When I reached the middle, I saw an unencumbered rope within a foot or so of the rail. I again made myself look down, and decided it was positioned over Cyndi's mark on the stage. This end of the rope was frayed in much the same manner as the other end. Whether it was in that condition from the attentions of a rat or a knife was beyond me, although I couldn't imagine why a rat would creep to the rail, fling itself into the darkness like a flying squirrel, and cling to the rope long enough to do substantial damage.

But Luanne did not seem to think any of the girls disliked Cyndi, much less had any motive to hurt her. Mac was disinterested in the pageant and its outcome. No one else was allowed in the auditorium. I decided I was behaving in a foolish, reckless, overly imaginative fashion, and carefully made my way back to the staircase.

Luanne hobbled across the stage as I reached the bottom. "What on earth were you doing up there?"

Lisle Library
Lisle, Illinois

"I was checking for rats trained in guerrilla tactics. We can all rest easy. You can do so in the office, or we can send everybody home and seek solace in scotch at my place."

"I do think we'd better quit for the day. This accident has upset all of the girls, including this middle-aged one." She studied me with a pinched expression. "You didn't find anything up there, did you?"

"I found the other end of the rope. Mac said there were rats up there, so I suppose one might have gnawed at the rope enough to cause it to break at an inopportune moment."

"And it was a coincidence that the weight hit one centimeter off Cyndi's mark?"

"It could well have been a coincidence," I said with more confidence than I felt. "Just like the nail. You're the one who's had experience in this milieu. I have no idea to what extremes a girl will go in order to win an utterly insignificant title and a year's worth of appearances at the Miss Applecore festival."

Luanne gazed at the girls, then shrugged and shook her head. "You're right, Claire. It's one thing to steal mascara or splash water in another girl's high heels, but to do something this dangerous is senseless. Cyndi's reign is over on Saturday night. Why would anyone want to hurt her?"

"Beats me," I murmured, quoting the irritating man with the rats. "I suppose I could talk to Cyndi and ask her if she can think of anyone who might want to frighten her. She's too upset now, but I'll have a word with her tomorrow."

"Frighten her—or kill her?"

Before I could answer, she hobbled back to the girls and told them rehearsal was over for the day. Cyndi was on her feet, although Julianna and another girl were clinging to her elbows and the other girls were hovering at a convenient distance should she opt to topple.

"I'm sorry to be so silly," she said to Luanne. "I mean, it's not like it actually hit me or anything. It just scared me."

"What's going on?" boomed a voice from the corridor entrance.

We all turned to stare at the stout woman who marched into the auditorium and onto the stage. She appeared to be in her late fifties, and her tweed suit of the same era. She had peppery hair cut off with no concession to her appearance, a square face, and a chin that hinted of a bulldog in her lineage. Two shrewd eyes regarded Cyndi, then turned on me.

"Why is she white and shaking like an hibiscus in a hurricane?" the woman barked at yours truly.

"A weight crashed on the stage. It came close enough to frighten her, but there was no harm done."

"What weight?"

I pointed to the side of the stage, but found myself pointing at a flat expanse of wood. "It was over there, but someone seems to have moved it. It was just a standard sandbag," I added, resisting the urge to retreat under the woman's beady glare. "Who are you?"

"I am Eunice Allingham—and Cyndi's trainer. I've been out of town at a trade show, but I see now I never should have left her in such incompetent hands. The girl is near collapse, which cannot be good for her. She needs to lie down until the color comes back to her cheeks." The woman went over to Cyndi and assessed her as if she were an item on a sale rack. "She appears to be unharmed, although what emotional damage there may be will surface in time. Her hair, most likely."

Cyndi produced a glittery smile that must have impressed (if not blinded) many a judge. "Oh, Eunice, please don't worry about me. I'm just fine, but I would like to lie down. Perhaps Julianna and Heidi will be sweet enough to help me down to my dressing room?"

Julianna and Heidi nodded enthusiastically, and the three slowly made their way across the stage and down the stairs. The rest of the girls rubbed their hands and muttered among themselves as they wandered away.

Once the queen and her attendants were out of sight, Eunice let out a gusty sigh. "Her hair goes limp when she's upset. The curl just slips out of it until she looks worse than a wet dog. I've tried and tried to get her to put it up like they do in the Big One, but she thinks it looks old-fashioned. Of *course* it looks old-fashioned. That's called tradition. I can't begin to tell you how many times she's limp when a nice curl would have cinched the finals or even the title."

Luanne nodded, thus earning a continuation of the limp hair dilemma. I went over to the place where the sandbag had been and looked around for it. I checked behind the stairs and in the dark corners of the stage, then went over to Caron, who was now gaping at Eunice.

"What happened to the weight?" I asked her in a low voice.

"How should I know? Who is that woman, Mother? She is totally bizarre, and making no sense whatsoever. Did she say she was Cyndi's trainer—as in German shepherds?"

Inez made a small noise. "I think it's more like an agent."

"Just because your sister is in the pageant doesn't make you an expert," Caron said without mercy. "She used the word *trainer,* as in dog tricks. Besides, I think she's crude."

I left them and joined Luanne, who was looking increasingly pale and wobbly as the woman lectured in her face. "You'd better go back to the office and sit down," I said, ignoring Eunice. "If you don't, you'll end up with your head between your knees."

She nodded, then hobbled away, leaving me to smile vaguely as Eunice muttered, "We can't have that sort of thing. Bad for the complexion. Bad, bad, bad, bad, bad."

"You're Cyndi's trainer?" I asked, not sure what was bad for the complexion and not wanting to find out at length. "What does that entail?"

"I manage her career, and see that she makes as many of the local and regional pageants as possible. We've got our eye on the

Big One, but she needs more work before we take a run at it. I may let her try the first round this year."

"I don't know what you're talking about," I said politely.

"Are you the pageant director?" Eunice huffed.

"Luanne Bradshaw is the official director. I'm helping out because of her ankle—and I have no experience with beauty pageants. I've never been to one, and I'm afraid I don't understand the jargon."

"You're an amateur? How on earth do you plan to run a good pageant with no experience in the necessary details? Why, even the little local ones require diligence, hard work, and attention to an incredible number of issues. Last year this utterly incompetent woman tried to stage the Miss Chicken Drumstick with no idea— no idea at all—about the problems she would encounter. It was a nightmare from the judges' luncheon to the final scoring. She even had someone use low-wattage lightbulbs in the dressing rooms, if you can imagine. It wasn't even worth our time."

"Well, this one will be a shambles," I said with a bright smile. "Luanne was in a couple of pageants years ago, but neither one of us knows what she's doing. It's somewhat of a lark for us."

Eunice snorted at my charming candor. "We shall see. I'm going down to the dressing room to check on my gal, then I'll come back here so you and I can discuss what's been done and what needs to be done. You go fetch a notebook and a pencil; I'm sure I'll have a long list for you and that other woman. Exactly which pageants was she in?" Her voice fell to a chilling whisper. "She surely never made five, did she? Her cheekbones are unruly."

"Five what?" I hissed back.

"The top five finalists." Eunice turned and stomped across the stage, no doubt appalled by such ignorance. Once she had vanished down the stairs, I told Caron and Inez to go home. I then stopped at the office and repeated Eunice's threat to help those of us who were deficient in the language and clearly unlikely to make the top five. Luanne grabbed her coat and locked the office door. As we reached the small lobby surrounding the box office, we heard Eunice's booming voice.

"What's this about a nail?" she demanded loud enough to be heard anywhere in Farberville, or perhaps the immediate county.

I went home.

"T" "H" "R" "E" "E"

When I picked up Luanne the next morning, she was gray about the gills. It took her a long while to find her purse, make sure her house keys were in it, lock the door, and make her way down the sidewalk to my car. I hardly expected her to break any hundred-yard-dash records, but each step was tentative and clearly painful.

"You don't have to go to the dress rehearsal," I said. "You can stay home for the day and rest, and then make a grand appearance tonight."

"I'll remain in the office. I have a million telephone calls to make, and my ankle won't feel any worse there than it will at home."

"Maybe Eunice will help you."

"Maybe I'll lock the office door."

I dropped her off in front of the theater, then drove down to the Book Depot and ascertained that the student who'd promised to clerk was clerking as promised. She had everything under control. As I walked the two blocks to the Thurber Street Theater, I noticed that the shopkeepers were all busily setting out racks and tables for the Gala Sidewalk Sale. They were doing so without a report, in triplicate (or duplicate, or even singlicate), from their fearless chairperson.

I increased my pace as I passed Sally Fromberger's cafe, but it did no good. Said proprietor popped out the door, her body covered with a sparkling white apron and her nose with a smudge of what I suspected was stone-ground, whole-wheat flour. No additives or preservatives.

"I'm so glad I caught you, Claire. I still need your committee report. The sale officially begins right after the parade and opening ceremonies. I'm not sure what we can do without the report; it's much too late for an ad hoc."

I waved at the activity on both sidewalks. "Everybody knows what to do, and is in the midst of doing it. I'll write you a letter about it next week, since I'm occupied for the moment with the beauty pageant. It seems someone volunteered me."

She beamed at me with the delight of a kindergarten mommy at graduation. "Luanne is so lucky to have you for a friend. She finally admitted she couldn't handle the pageant without help, and I knew you'd be thrilled to be her assistant. Wait here for a minute and I'll give you the menu report on the luncheon. I think you need two copies—one for the file and one for the notebook."

"You're catering the luncheon?" I managed to say in a perfectly civilized voice.

"Yes, and it'll be simply wonderful. The girls will be bubbling with energy for tonight's preliminary round, and the judges will feel ten years younger. We're having tofu lasagna and a salad of alfalfa sprouts with sesame honey dressing. No nasty carbohydrates to slow us down." She went inside and returned with the copies.

I took them and stuffed them in my purse, reminding myself that I could easily discover a pressing need to dash down to the Book Depot to rescue my clerk from some horrible fate—such as a real live customer—and also find a minute to grab a sandwich and a can of soda. It was too early in the day to ponder the implications of something called tofu lasagna.

Once at the theater, I stopped at the office. Luanne was on the telephone, arguing with an unknown party about flower arrangements and a bouquet of one dozen long-stemmed obligatories that seemed to have increased in price. I left the Xeroxed menus on her desk, picked up the notebook, and dutifully went on to the auditorium with the degree of enthusiasm I usually reserve for sessions with an oral hygienist.

The stage was lit from a row of lights along the ceiling of the auditorium. The contestants stood in a row, their expressions perplexed as Eunice Allingham bellowed out instructions and demonstrated a series of kicks. Her short, thick legs, sturdy shoes, and sensible hemline made the scene macabre—at best.

"You can," she puffed, lapsing into a less demanding box step, "all learn this if you concentrate. You must learn to concentrate if you wish to succeed." She stopped and slapped her hand across her bosom until she caught her breath. "There is no room in the finals for gals who cannot concentrate," she added with a stern look. "You must be prepared to follow instructions from the first moment you're chosen for the honor of representing your town or organization in a pageant. There's no time for shirking your obligation to train, train, train. Cyndi follows a strict regime for one month before each pageant. She diets, works out, sleeps twelve hours a day, and keeps a healthy distance from any male distractions. I trust you girls have prepared with equal seriousness for the Miss Thurberfest pageant?"

There was a great deal of shuffling and averted eyes. Faces were studiously guileless, hands clasped, necks red. Eunice marched over to the group and put her hands on her substantial hips. "So we haven't prepared, I see. Some of you will have limp hair tonight, and others of you will be trying to disguise dull complexions. Your eyes will not glitter with excitement, and your voices will lack that vivaciousness the judges look for in a winner. You, for instance" she said, pointing at Julianna, "have you concerned yourself with cellulite? If I were handling you, I'd put you on celery, water, and three hours a day in the gym. Let me see you walk across the stage."

Julianna lifted her chin and produced a tremulous smile as she took a few steps. "My God, no!" Eunice shrieked, sending several girls into the back wall. "You must glide. Roll your hips but don't stride; this is not a football field. Look up and out, and keep your chin level to the floor. Relax those shoulders to downplay your shoulder blades, but don't slouch. And tuck in that derriere if you don't want bad scores for fanny overhang. Now all of you glide. Glide, gals, glide."

Julianna and her sisters were gliding like ice skaters as I went onto the stage. "Thanks for the help, Eunice," I said, striding with the wild abandon of a neckless hulk in a football helmet. "We're scheduled for a technical and dress rehearsal now, so I'll have to ask you to leave. It's a closed rehearsal."

She stared at me as if I'd just suggested she wiggle into a tutu and twirl away. "I shall sit in the front row and take notes. Afterward, we can go over them and make the necessary adjustments. You admitted you have no idea how to run a pageant, my dear Mrs. Malloy. I've spent twenty years training gals for this sort of thing, and my advice will be most valuable." She gave me a modest smile. "I was once Miss Cherry Tomato, although that was years and years ago, when I myself was a mere slip of a gal."

I told myself that the pageant would be history in slightly more than thirty-six hours, which was not an eternity. Any reasonable person could survive for that fleeting number of hours, unless being stretched on the rack or poked with a hot cattle prod. Eunice was a mildly irritating woman, not a hooded rackkeeper from the dungeon. Surely I could bite my lip for the next day and a half, after which Luanne and I could laugh merrily over pretzels and pitchers of beer in the sunny beer garden. It was no big deal, I concluded to myself in a resolute voice.

"Are you going to rehearse in the next millennium?" Mac said from behind me. "As unbelievable as it may seem, I do have more important things to do than to wait around while you broads glide and roll and fret over your fannies."

One broad harrumphed and stomped toward the edge of the

stage. I turned around and smiled. "Did you take the weight that fell yesterday afternoon?"

"Why would I do that?"

"I really don't know," I responded sweetly. "We might need it for evidence, though. Would you be so kind as to search for it instead of lurking around the stage insulting everyone?"

"And miss all the fun?" He strolled away.

Sighing, I opened the notebook and read the outline of the evening's festivities. For those intrigued by the machinations, we were slated to experience (in ascending order of spine-tingling drama): the opening, the swimsuit competition, the talent presentations, and the evening-gown competition, the last in conjunction with the interviews. There would be no respite in the form of an intermission, which meant certain of us would be wasted—if not blatantly unconscious—by the time they announced the seven finalists. Which would take place around midnight, I suspected.

I repeated the schedule for the girls, told them to prepare for the opening number, and went down to join Eunice in the middle of the front row.

"Who is that dreadful man?" she asked loudly.

"David McWethy. He's owned the theater for almost a year, and done an admirable job restoring it. As rude and abrupt as he seems to be, he's a fine craftsman."

"Rude is a mild term." She huffed for a moment, then said, "I've heard of him. He used to be involved in local politics, which gave him an opportunity to offend almost everyone in town. He was most successful in that aspect of his job. A friend of mine tried to get a little bit of cooperation about curbside garbage collection. Cooperation, mind you, not a concession, and this McWethy man practically accused him of bribing a city official. It goes to show you what was on his mind, if you ask me." She stood up and brushed at the wrinkles in her skirt. "We don't have time to gossip. The gals are taking much too long to change, and I haven't even seen Cyndi this morning. Let us go to the dressing room area and hurry them along. If left unsupervised, they do tend to giggle and dawdle rather than attending to more important things."

Having been properly chastised for gossiping, I meekly followed Eunice down the stairs to the basement area below the stage. It was a damp tunnel of unadorned concrete, and reeked of mildew and disuse. A door on each side led to the communal dressing rooms, and from behind the doors we could hear the squeals and squeaks that seemed to be the norm these days. The door on the end was Cyndi's private room, I remembered from the sketch I'd studied. It was adorned with a yellow construction-paper star.

Eunice opened the side doors and barked sternly into each room. The squeals and squeaks stopped. Giving me a satisfied nod, she continued down the hall and rapped on Cyndi's door. "Let's go, my dear. You know how important it is to cooperate with pageant officials with their petty schedules and demands. Besides, I want you to take a nap before the parade. We can't have any squints or droopy smiles on the back of the convertible."

The door opened. Cyndi's face was streaked with tears, and her mascara had left black dribbles down her cheeks. "Oh, Eunice," she whimpered, "I can't go out there like this. There's something you'd better see. You, too, Mrs. Malloy."

Eunice and I crowded into the tiny room. A dressing table took up half of the floor space, leaving room for a chair in front of it and a second to one side. Several cosmetic bags were scattered under the table and clothes hung like meat carcasses from hooks. A battered gas space heater did little to dispel the cold damp air that contributed to the dreary ambiance. On the wall behind the table was a mirror, and scrawled across the mirror in red letters were the words: DEATH TO A ROYAL BITCH!

"Oh, my God," Eunice gasped, stepping on my foot.

I bit back a shriek of pain. "When did you find this, Cyndi?"

"When I first came down to change," she said. She managed to step on my other foot as she turned around to blink at the menacing message. "It's been fifteen minutes or so, but I couldn't move. It was like I was glued to the floor or something like that. I stood here and stared for the longest time, and then I just burst into tears. I can't stand the idea that anyone would be so mean and hateful, Eunice. I've tried so hard to help the girls. They're all such really, really nice girls." She snatched up a wadded tissue from the table and began to sniffle into it. "Someone wants to kill me. I'm so frightened, Mrs. Malloy. What am I going to do?"

The sniffles evolved into wails. Eunice patted the girl's shoulder and offered a few dire words about puffy eyelids and self-control. I leaned over the formidable array of cosmetics and appliances to examine the message. It was printed in lipstick, I realized, and a distressingly sanguine shade. The crude block letters implied no gender. Other implications were harder to miss.

"I'm going to call the police," I said. "Don't wipe it off for any reason."

Cyndi broke off the wails and rubbed her cheeks hard enough to leave scarlet streaks among the black marks. "Oh, please don't do that, Mrs. Malloy," she said earnestly. "That kind of publicity would be awful for the pageant. It's supposed to be a wholesome, family event, not some sleazy carnival show with policemen and armed bodyguards. We don't want to ruin some really nice girl's opportunity to be crowned Miss Thurberfest, simply because a sick person is doing these horrible things."

Eunice leaned forward with a particularly beady look. "As we say, the show must go on. You must think of the gals and all the hard work they've put into their preparation, not to mention the cost of the evening gowns, swimsuits, and talent costumes. They can hardly concentrate if policemen are leering at them every moment of the pageant, or hounding them night and day. We simply can't let them down."

"I have a friend in the Criminal Investigation Department," I said. "I can have a quiet word with him. He'll look around and perhaps speak to Cyndi, but I doubt he'd order us to close down the pageant." I did not add that he'd be laughing too hard to do such a thing. I'd been hoping to get through the pageant without telling him about it, since he was aware of my feminist sensibilities. We'd had lots of invigorating conversations about them.

Eunice was not convinced. Looming even further over me, she said, "We have seen this sort of thing before, even at the most primitive local level. I had Cyndi try a new talent routine at the Junior-Senior Miss Rodeo of the Hills pageant, and one of the contestants stole her hair dryer right out of her bag. It was disgraceful, but no one called the police."

Cyndi wiggled past us and sank down in the chair. "And the girl felt so awful afterward that she apologized and everything. It was so sweet that we just had to hug each other and cry. We became really, really good friends." She picked up another tissue, then let it drop.

"I really think I'd better speak to my friend," I said. "If it's just one of the girls who's overly jealous, we have nothing to worry about beyond a few more tasteless practical jokes. But we can't be sure the nail and the weight were coincidences—and those were dangerous stunts. Luanne's on crutches and you might have been badly hurt."

"Oh, they were coincidences," Cyndi said, although without her former firmness.

"And this?" I gestured at the mirror. "This was done with deliberate malice. Someone wants very much to frighten you. We can't allow this person to work herself up into a frenzy and try to hurt you again." I told Eunice to stay with Cyndi until I returned, then went out into the hallway. The girls were packed in their doorways, silently gaping at the yellow star.

"We heard Cyndi crying," Julianna said solemnly. "Is she okay?"

"Someone wrote a nasty message on her mirror. Did any of you notice anything unusual when you came in this morning? Was there someone down here who shouldn't have been?"

One of the girls, a baton twirler, tittered. "That awful man was down here doing something to the fuse box. He went back up right when I arrived, and he didn't even say good morning or anything. He's spooky."

The Pekinese's owner raised her hand and wiggled her fingers. When I looked at her, she said, "And Mrs. Allingham came in our room and told us to use more padding in our brassieres if we didn't want to look like a bunch of sixth-grade girls."

No one else had anything to contribute. I told them that the dress rehearsal would start in fifteen minutes, and continued upstairs as they returned to their squealing and squeaking. I wandered around the stage, then looked in the greenroom where I found Mac on his hands and knees, a hammer in one hand and a pile of carpet tacks near the other.

"Are you finally ready for the rehearsal?" he said without looking up.

"No, we'll start in fifteen minutes," I said to his rump. "Were you down in the basement earlier this morning?"

"I was down in my basement earlier this morning. Fuse blew, probably from all the damn hair dryers going at the same time. You got a problem with me going down in my basement? I can assure you those dewy-eyed virgins are safe from me, although I'd be glad to make a small wager about the existence of any vestiges of virginity down there."

"We aren't running a competition to select someone to toss in a volcano. Did you find the weight that crashed onto the stage yesterday?"

"I didn't bother to look for it."

I considered a variety of responses, one involving my foot and a convenient area of his anatomy. I finally stopped twitching my toe (and perhaps developing telltale blotches) and said, "Listen, Mac, someone has been pulling some potentially dangerous stunts in your theater. I realize you have insurance, but I doubt you want negative publicity."

"As long as they spell my name correctly, I don't care. Hell, I haven't been on the nightly news in years." He did, however, put down the hammer and stand up. "Then you're convinced the nail and the weight were done on purpose to hurt last year's whatever-she-is?"

"There was a threat written on Cyndi's mirror. I have no idea if it's some girl's idea of a practical joke or a malicious attempt to frighten her. If it was the latter, it was very successful. That rope on the sandbag is the only thing we might be able to examine; a nail's a nail and the message was written in block letters to disguise the handwriting. The police can put the end of the rope under a microscope and tell if it was cut . . . or gnawed."

"But it's disappeared," he murmured, tugging on his goatee as he looked down at me. "Darn shame, ain't it? We may never know if someone's being trying to murder our beloved Miss Thurberfest. If the news people ever get wind of this, they'll fall all over each over to get the scoop. 'Death Stalks the Queen,' or maybe 'Beauty and the Maniacal, Murderous Beast.' It might just make the national news. Be still, my heart."

"Then you'd better go home and change into a suit and tie," I said angrily. I went up the corridor to the office, berating myself for not kicking him halfway across the room when I had the golden opportunity. I stalked across the lobby and into the office, snorting all the way like a moose in a marathon.

Luanne was not in evidence, but the door to the washroom was closed and water was running. Brilliantly deducing her whereabouts, I decided it might be prudent to discuss things with her before I called Peter. I loudly announced my presence and my intentions, and was rewarded with the sound of a toilet flushing.

Someone tapped on the office door. A breathtakingly handsome man in a jacket and turtleneck sweater came into the room. His blond hair, deep blue eyes, and engaging smile were more than enough to seize the dingy room and transform it into an elegant executive office. The dead plastic plant gave a small shudder of life.

The shag carpet snapped to attention. I reminded myself to breathe.

"Hi," he said, showing me pristine white teeth made mortal by the tiniest of gaps between the front two, "are you Luanne Bradshaw?" When I numbly shook my head, he gazed at the washroom door and gave me a comradely wink. "I'm Steve Stevenson, the emcee for the pageant. I'm sorry I was late, but my aide keeps me on such a tight schedule you'd think he took lessons from a slave driver. I never know which way I'm going next. You're. . . ?"

"Claire Malloy. Luanne fell the other day and is on crutches, so I guess I'm her aide." It wasn't clever; it wasn't witty. It was coherent, though, for which I deserved a point or two.

"Well, I hope my tardiness hasn't fouled up the schedule for you, Mrs. Malloy—or may I call you Claire?" I managed a numb nod this time. "Great, then, Claire, and please call me Steve. Would you mind if I made one quick call before the rehearsal?"

The quick-witted woman on the couch managed yet a third numb gesture. While he picked up the receiver and dialed, I considered the possibility that some villain had slipped novocaine in my coffee. Luanne came out of the washroom and stopped in midhobble to stare at our visitor.

He gave her a smile, then said into the receiver, "Pattycake, I just this second arrived at the theater, so we haven't started the rehearsal. I'll send Warren over to pick you up as soon as he drops off a file at Whitley's office. Did you find a sitter?" He paused for a moment. "There's no reason to get upset, honey. I told you that you needn't come to the luncheon or the parade. There are two delightful women right here to make me behave with the beauty queens. Just stay at the hotel this afternoon and let the girls swim or something." He paused once more. "Don't be absurd, Pattycake. We've already discussed that on numerous occasions. You do have a sitter for tonight and tomorrow night, don't you?"

After a few low mutters, he replaced the receiver and went across the room to offer his hand to Luanne. "You must be

Luanne Bradshaw, the pageant director. I'm Steve Stevenson, your obedient and devoted servant for the next two days. Your wish shall be my command."

Luanne finally managed to stop blinking long enough to agree that she was who he'd suspected, and with visible reluctance put her hand back on the crossbar of her crutch. "It's terribly nice of you to help again this year," she said as she made her way to the chair behind the desk. "I realize you're busy with the legislature and your upcoming election."

Once she was seated, he sat down next to me. "I'm busy, but I always make time for my district and those events that make it so special and dear to me. It gives me an excuse to get away from stuffy politicians and meet the people. I had a fantastic time at the pageant last year, and really enjoyed getting to know all those bright, pretty, talented girls. I've already done exceptionally well this time, haven't I?"

We were discussing his luck in meeting the two of us when it occurred to me that fifteen minutes had come and gone about fifteen minutes ago. I stood up and mentioned the schedule. After a promise to come back for a chat with Luanne, Steve opened the door for me and we headed down the corridor to the auditorium. He was regaling me with the highlights of the previous year's pageant when Eunice Allingham came through the arched doorway and almost stumbled into me.

"We are waiting, Mrs. Malloy," she began, then stopped as she saw my companion. "You! How dare you!"

Steve adroitly stepped behind me. "Eunice, how nice to see you again this year. Still keeping your finger in the pageant pie, I see."

"How dare you!" she repeated, advancing until she was breathing on my ear. "After all you've done, you have the gall to come back? I'd have thought you'd have had the decency to stay away this year."

"We both know I had nothing to to do with what happened

because of last year's pageant. Don't you think you're exaggerating?" he said in my other ear.

"Hardly, Mr. Stevenson. Hardly."

It was interesting, but it was doing detrimental things to my long-term hearing and causing condensation on my ear lobes. I sidestepped from between the two of them. "Then you've met?"

While I waited for a response from either of them, Cyndi Jay came out into the corridor. "Eunice, we're running late and I——" Her mouth dropped open as she caught sight of Steve. "Oh, my God," she moaned. Her eyes rolled upward and she crumpled onto the carpet at my feet.

All in all, it was most interesting. Yes, indeed.

"F"O"U"R"

Eunice squatted down and began to rub Cyndi's wrist and slap her face with more enthusiasm than some of us might have considered necessary—or even prudent. Steve hastily announced he wanted to meet this year's lovely contestants, and hustled though the doorway before I could agree that it seemed the politic thing to do. After all, if politicians weren't politic, who was?

Cyndi's eyes fluttered open. Eunice slapped her once more, just to be on the safe side, I supposed, then helped the girl to her feet. "Well," she said in a low, angry voice, "I told you this would happen. I'd like to think you learned your lesson, but this swooning act was hardly a good omen, was it?"

Cyndi glanced at me out of the corner of her eye, then hung her head as if she were a naughty puppy who'd dirtied the carpet for not the first time. "You're right, Eunice. I promised you I'd never see him again, and I haven't. It's just that all those nasty threats and attempts to hurt me have made me nervous. Seeing Senator Stevenson startled me, that's all." She touched her temples with delicately sculptured pink fingernails. "I've just been a wreck these last two days, but I swear I'll settle down."

"I should hope so," Eunice muttered. "God knows I've put enough time and money into you. But you're the one who'll carry us to the top, all the way to the Big One in Atlantic City. I have great expectations, Cyndi, great expectations. I'm going to be right beside you every step of the way, and be watching proudly when they sing, 'There She Is, Miss America.'" Eunice sang the words in a trembling voice, apparently close to tears.

"I know," Cyndi said, nodding earnestly and a little misty herself. "And you've been really, really wonderful, Eunice. I mean, you've been like a mom to me."

It was all so touching that I went into the auditorium. Steve was on the stage, surrounded by the girls and, based on the volume of their squeals, doing an admirable job amusing them. Mac stood to one side, watching impassively. I spotted two ghostly, pubescent forms flitting in the last row of the seats, but I ignored them and went to my post in the middle of the front row.

I clapped my hands and, when I had their reluctant attention, said, "We must get started immediately. The schedule's tight and we're already more than half an hour late. You girls do want to have time to repair your hair before your first meeting with the judges, don't you?"

They deserted their idol and scuttled offstage. Steve dimpled down at me. "You've got quite a flair for this sort of thing, Claire. Can I lure you to the capital to terrify my staff?"

There were ghostly giggles in the distance behind me. "No thank you," I said, refusing to turn my head. "Are you ready to begin? Mac, are you ready to do the lights? Who's going to operate the curtain? What about the audio equipment?"

Mac came down to the edge of the stage. "Those are excellent questions, if I do say so myself. I'm going up to the light booth. Who is going to operate the curtain and the audio equipment?"

"Whoever you've hired," I suggested faintly.

"Hey, I just own the building. I agreed to run the lights, mostly because the equipment's too expensive to trust to some moronic high school boy with zits on his palms. I didn't agree to open a temporary employment agency."

I flipped through the notebook but did not find a list of backstage crew. "I guess Luanne was planning to get around to it yesterday. Is there any way you can do the lights and also—"

"Nope." He put his hands in his pockets and began to whistle a now-familiar tune. And very melodically for such an uncooperative grouch.

Steve shot me another dimple. "When my aide gets back, he can help. It may not be until late in the afternoon, though. I'm sure my wife would enjoy helping, but she couldn't find a sitter for the day. Sorry."

I bowed to the inevitable. "There are two girls skulking in the back of the auditorium," I said to Mac. "Rout them from their hiding place and show them what to do. You do not need to be gentle with them, nor do you need to show them any patience or understanding. For some inexplicable reason, they are not getting their just desserts."

I saw a twinkle in Mac's eye as he nodded and went toward the back of the auditorium. I flapped my notebook at Steve. "Let's get the damn show on the road," I said eloquently.

Eons later Steve and I went back to the office. I was not a pretty picture: my face was pink, my hair ruffled, my eyes dazed, my hands quivering. The notebook was misshapen and tattered from the torture it had received in my lap. Steve settled me on the couch and solicitously offered to bring me a cup of water.

Luanne's pencil clattered on the desktop. "Shall I ask how it went?" she said.

"There are a few problems," Steve said, wincing, "but I'm sure we'll pull it together by tonight. The girls were jittery and the new crew members need practice on some of the technical aspects. A couple of hitches in the talent numbers. A little disorganization during the swimsuit and evening-gown presentations." His fingers tightened on my shoulder for a moment. "It'll be fine tonight. It really will."

Luanne stared at me as if I'd been diagnosed with some fatal tropical disease that would implode me within a matter of seconds. "Dare I ask how the opening number went?"

"Don't ask," I said. "Unless you can book the Guernsey Sisters by eight o'clock tonight."

Eunice came through the door and positioned herself in front of the desk, offering some of us a view of her indignant derriere. "I've been told you have some experience in the operation of a pageant. It is obvious it is currently in the hands of an amateur. Cyndi's more endangered by those hopelessly clumsy girls than she is from some kindergarten child with a tube of lipstick. If she ends up with a scab on her knee, I simply won't be able to have her at the Miss Starley City pageant next week. I realize that it's a minor pageant, but she needs all the experience she can get for the Big One."

Luanne seemed bewildered, so I graciously hummed a few bars of the pageant theme song. Eunice spun around and noticed Steve, who was trying very hard to pass for a throw pillow. "And you," she added with a frigid smile, "you were directly responsible for the disaster at the Miss Stump County pageant, along with the poor gal's collapse this morning. I wouldn't be the least bit surprised if you wrote on her mirror."

"I was not directly responsible," Steve said petulantly.

"Well, directly or indirectly, you—"

"Everybody hush," Luanne interrupted, using her pencil for a gavel. "I will admit I'm temporarily disabled, but I am not someone's dotty old great-aunt in the attic. Someone tell me what's going on!"

Eunice and Steve both looked at me, but I held up my hands and shook my head. "Not me, guys. I only know bits and pieces of what's going on, and they make little or no sense. I suggest we begin with an historical perspective. Eunice can explain Steve's direct responsibility. He can then offer rebuttal for indirect responsibility. I'll do the lipstick."

Luanne blinked at me. "Lipstick?"

"Out of perspective," I said, waggling a finger at her.

Eunice took centerstage. "That man was a judge at last year's pageant. Although he is supposed to be a pillar of society and set a good example for the youth of our state, he allowed his aide to become both emotionally and physically involved with poor little Cyndi, who was quite naive in these matters. The boy sent her gifts, called night and day, took her to parties where alcohol and drugs were in use, and even lured her out of the state on some flimsy pretext. She was so exhausted and bewildered by his attentions that she didn't make the finals of the Miss Stump County and in fact missed two perfectly good pageants in the southeastern part of the state."

Steve tried a dimple, but Eunice froze it off quicker than a dermatologist dealing with a wart. Shrugging, he said, "They're modern kids. Warren was absolutely smitten with the girl, and I'm his boss—not his father. Come on, Eunice, what he does on his own time is his own business."

"What about the trip to Hollywood?" Eunice demanded. "She and that boy flew on your charter, and you paid for their hotel room. She came back to Farberville with all sorts of wild ideas about a movie career. Luckily, I was able to reason with her; otherwise, she'd have thrown a black negligee in a bag and tried to hitchhike back out to that immoral place."

"Cyndi was invited to go as a guest of the state film commission. They always take some of the talent to prove we're not all inarticulate, lice-ridden hillbillies." Steve squared his shoulders. "And I ordered separate rooms for them, Eunice. In fact, my room was between theirs, although I can't swear there wasn't a bit of tiptoeing after midnight. They're normal, healthy kids."

"Cyndi is in no way a normal, healthy kid," Eunice said, squaring her shoulders too. "She is an attractive, vivacious, self-disciplined, determined girl who has a chance to win the Big One—if she works on it. She'll have scholarships, a new wardrobe and accessories, a new car, a kitchen full of appliances, an opportunity to travel all over the country and appear on prime-time television. If I handle her carefully, she should have several hundred thousand in the bank when she gives up her crown. I will not have her chances ruined by your hormone-heavy aide. Last time you refused to do anything more than smirk, but this time you'd better keep him away from her unless the both of you intend to destroy her career over my dead body!"

I wanted to stand up and sing a refrain or two of you-know-what. Instead, I stood up and mentioned that it was almost time for the luncheon. Eunice snorted a farewell and stalked out the door, leaving a wake of righteousness behind her. Steve started to follow, but I caught his arm.

"Just out of curiosity," I said, "do you have the same aide who . . . who was madly in love with Cyndi Jay?"

"Yeah," he said dimplessly.

Once he left, I told Luanne about the message on Cyndi's mirror. She was properly appalled, but neither of us could think of a reason why any of those in the theater would make a threat or attempt to bean Miss Thurberfest with a bag.

Luanne stood up and, with a glum smile, said, "There's nothing we can do, so we'll have to hope Eunice sticks to Cyndi through the finals tomorrow night. At that point Cyndi will become a mortal once more. We'd better head for the luncheon."

"I said earlier that I ought to discuss this with Peter. I'll walk to Sally's with you, then go on to the Book Depot and call him. Maybe he can get away for lunch."

"Do you honestly believe I cannot see right through this civic-minded sham of yours? You aren't frantic to talk to Peter about some silly little words on a mirror. You saw the menu."

I laughed gaily. "I may have glanced at the menu in my official capacity, but I don't even remember what's on it. Besides, Sally is reputed to be a veritable culinary wizard with tofu and vegetables. I happen to be concerned about the events of the last two days, and am willing to make a minor sacrifice in order to ensure Cyndi's longevity and eventual triumph at the Big One."

"Bullshit."

"Goodness gracious, Luanne, I hope you don't use that sort of language in front of the gals. They're much too wholesome to be exposed to profanity. They would be shocked and dismayed. Their ears might fall off right into the tofu lasagna."

"You're stalling, perhaps with the wild notion that I'll forget this vile display of treachery and let you escape the luncheon. Ho, ho, and get your purse." She took a step, then grimaced and closed her eyes for a second. "My ankle's getting worse. It feels as if it's the size of a late-summer zucchini. I don't know how I'm going to make it through the rest of the afternoon, much less the first round tonight."

I studied her, not sure whether she was in pain or pulling my leg via her ankle. Her face had an unhealthy transparent quality and her skin seemed tightly stretched across her (unruly) cheekbones. Dark smudges below her eyes might have come from mascara, but I doubted it. "You look like hell. When you were at the hospital, did you talk to the doctor about your general health?"

"Mac took me to the emergency room. Some twenty-year-old boy pretending to be a grown-up doctor said three or four words to me, fondled my ankle, and then waved me off to the X-ray room. A sweet little student nurse assured me that we had a severe sprain instead of a nasty old break, and proceeded to wrap our ankle in fifty feet of elastic tape, for which I expect to be billed by the inch. But thanks for the compliment."

"You really don't look good," I persisted. "Don't you think you ought to talk to a grandfatherly general practitioner about it? I'll hunt one up and drive you to his office right now."

"For a lecture on sleep and a prescription for vitamins? No, I simply need to elevate my ankle and forget about the half-million telephone calls I didn't get to this morning. The florist has come out of his coma and swears he knows exactly what to do. I arranged for someone to fetch the two other judges and deliver them to Sally's cafe. I've got ushers and concession workers. The press is arranged. However, that's the tip of a very large iceberg, and I haven't talked to the football coach about the escorts, the electrician about the television cables, the trophy store, the parade coordinator, the——"

"Stop this before I go leap off the stage. Get your list of calls that need to be made and I'll drive you home. I'll even fix you a nice sandwich and a cup of tea, then settle you in bed with the telephone. You can stay there until the last moment before kickoff time tonight."

"One of us has to be at the luncheon to introduce the dignitaries and the contestants, see that everyone sits in his or her assigned place, make sure no one chokes on tofu, and keep Sally out of the way."

"Then we'd better hurry," I said. Or snapped.

I told her to wait at the theater while I fetched my car. The lobby was quiet and I heard no squeals from the auditorium, which I cleverly deduced meant that either Eunice or Steve (but not both) had herded the girls on to the luncheon. Caron and Inez had crept away, no doubt to discuss with much adolescent outrage the manner in which Mac had instructed them. It had been the only bright spot in a very gloomy two hours.

A news van was parked in front of Sally's cafe, and a crowd milled nearby. Praying Cyndi Jay had not found a threat written in alfalfa sprouts, I broke into a trot. Once I reached the bystanders, I wiggled my way through. A woman in a suit held a microphone under Steve Stevenson's dimples. A man with a camera balanced on his shoulder moved in to capture every nuance.

"Then despite the results of latest poll, you expect to have no problem in the primary, Senator?" the reporter demanded, clearly willing to risk everything in the name of the public's right to know.

"The primary will be a critical test of my candidacy. My opponent is a good man, but I think my record speaks for itself," Steve said into the camera. He did not, however, allow his record to get in a word edgewise. "As a senator, I've fought for a strong, no-frills educational system. I've helped our area industries receive tax breaks so that they can employ more workers and boost the economy. I've introduced bills to assist the elderly and disabled. As attorney general, I can assure you that I shall demand an immediate investigation into the trucking industry in this area, and continue to——"

I decided he was doing fine without my assistance and went into the cafe. Eunice was chatting with a frail man, whom I recognized from countless photos of ribbon-cutting ceremonies as Orkin Avery. The third judge, a birdlike woman, was reading the menu with a desperate expression. Most of the girls were watching the press conference on the sidewalk, but Cyndi Jay stood to one side. She looked exceedingly grim.

As I walked over to join her, I heard an expletive slip from between her regal lips. Surprised, I said, "Is everything okay?"

She smiled, although it required a visible effort. "Hi, Mrs. Malloy. Everything's just really, really great, and the luncheon's going to be fun. I was thinking about that message on the mirror. That kind of nastiness makes me itchy, but I'm not afraid or anything. I just hate to think one of the girls would be so jealous that she would stoop so low to win. Girls in pageants are always the friendliest things, eager to lend each other safety pins or giggle about their boyfriends. I'm sad that my last pageant isn't as super as I'd hoped."

"Your last pageant?" I echoed. "What about Miss Starley City and the Big One?"

"What I meant was the last two days of being Miss Thurberfest. Of course, I'll have the fun of riding in the parade with Senator Stevenson, and the incredibly big thrill of crowning the new Miss Thurberfest. It's kind of sad, but it's such a special moment and I always cry. It's a pageant tradition, I guess."

Sally Fromberger came out of the kitchen. "I'm glad you're finally here, Claire. The luncheon was supposed to start at exactly one, but this interview is throwing us off schedule. According to Luanne's report, everyone should be seated by now so that she can make the introductory remarks and introduce the panel of judges. She isn't even here."

"I have to drive her home so she can rest," I said. "Otherwise, she won't be able to attend the preliminary round tonight and that'll play total havoc on the schedule. We'll never recover." I produced a worried frown, then clasped my hands and beamed at the woman. "I know how we can avert disaster, Sally—you fill in for me."

"But in the report it says . . ."

"You can fill in for me, because I'm merely filling in for Luanne, who's most likely unconscious by now. Look at the time! You'd better seat everybody at once and get started with your introductory remarks. I'll rescue Steve from the reporter and send him right in."

I left before she could protest and once again wiggled through the bystanders. Steve was still expounding on his record, but when he saw me he broke off and pulled me to his side. "This is our gorgeous pageant director, Claire Malloy. All the girls are terrified that Claire will end up as the new Miss Thurberfest, aren't they, Claire?"

I stared at the flat black eye of the camera, and then at the amused reporter. "I'm not the official director," I said, willing myself not to stammer despite a very real urge to do so. "Luanne Bradshaw is in charge; I'm simply helping her due to a minor accident during rehearsal."

The reporter shoved the microphone at me. "What can you tell us about the second annual Thurberfest, Ms. Malloy? Can we look forward to lots of excitement, music, food, and family entertainment right here in the heart of our community?"

"I suppose so."

After a moment of silence, the reporter stepped in front of the camera and began to tell her viewers about the good fortune in finding Senator Stevenson during his busy campaign season, and how much excitement we were going to find right here in the heart of our community. I whispered to Steve that he was needed inside, and then escaped the crowd and went on to the bookstore.

The clerk assured me that all was well and that she'd handled the sole sale without a problem. I warned her to expect more business once crowds started swarming the sidewalks to the grand Thurberfest parade and ensuing Gala Sidewalk Sale, then went to my car.

Luanne was waiting in front of the theater. After she was in the passenger's seat, with the crutches stowed in the back, she pointed out rather snootily that the luncheon was half over. I assured her that it was in its infancy because of the the press conference, and that Sally Fromberger would put everyone back on a tidy time track.

"What press conference?" she asked. "There's not anything scheduled until tonight, and it's not until the emcee has read the names of the seven finalists. I thought we might rope in a few more relatives and friends if each girl said a few words."

"Our emcee is running for attorney general and so enjoys meeting the people and participating in local events right here in the heart of our community. He wanted to share his feelings with the press."

"Oh," Luanne said wisely. "Then he called the press conference?"

"I don't know, but he was certainly basking in it." Failing to mention other baskers, I stopped in front of Luanne's house and held her arm while she hobbled from the curb to her bedroom. After I'd done everything I promised, and even found a package of cookies in case of a craving, I took out the notebook and studied the immediate future.

"Cyndi and Steve are in the same convertible," I murmured. "I hope she doesn't topple over again. She might be trampled by a junior-high-school marching band or a Shriner. I'm not sure which would be worse."

"You're stalling again," Luanne said from the bed.

"I am not stalling; I am merely pausing to formulate my thoughts so that I won't flounder around all afternoon."

"Then flounder over to theater and make sure the convertible is there. The girls are supposed to go home and take naps, so Steve and Cyndi ought to be the only ones there. The driver is scheduled to pick them up at two-thirty and take them to the stadium parking lot, where the parade will line up."

I raised my eyebrows. "I know all that. It's on page fifty-five of your committee report, which is not especially well written."

"And yours is?"

"It will be." I told her I'd come by after the parade to check on her, then drove back to the theater and parked in the narrow alley in the rear. The heavy metal door was locked, so I went along the sidewalk to the front and found that door also locked. Mac presumably had gone away for lunch, which struck me as a reasonable and desirable idea. As I stood there, trying to decide if I could find a sandwich rich in carbohydrates without passing Sally's cafe, a convertible screeched to a stop in front of me.

The driver, a seedy sort with black hair and red-rimmed eyes, gave me a bleary salute. "Ready to roll, Senator? Where's the queenie and her courtie?"

"The Senator, the queenie, and her courtie are still at lunch."

He took a bottle in a paper bag from under the seat and took a drink from it. "Good, 'cause I picked up the car early. I din't want to be late."

"And you had time to stop by the liquor store on your way?"

He whistled, impressed by my perspicacity. "Right on the button, Senator. After I had a couple beers, I thought hey, Arnie, it's Thurberfest, a nice sunny day, why not make a little party of it? Wanna snort?"

"Not right this moment, thank you." As I tried to figure out what to do about the inebriated chauffeur, I saw Cyndi and Steve leave Sally's cafe and walk toward the theater. Their heads were bent as they talked intently. At one point, Cyndi stopped and waved an envelope under his nose. He shook his head, then caught sight of me and waved.

"Wowsy," Arnie muttered. "The Senator's a good-looking dame. I'd probably vote for her for President. Hell, she can sleep in my white house any time she wants to."

"I'm sorry if we're late," Cyndi called as they crossed the street. "First, Senator Stevenson availed himself of the opportunity to preen in front of the television cameras, thus throwing us off schedule by a good fifteen minutes."

Steve frowned at his watch. "Gee, Cyndi, I didn't think the interview lasted that long. It was just a photo op."

"One of these days we really must teach you how to tell time, mustn't we? Then the woman who introduced the judges was a little bit long-winded. It's already two-thirty, so I don't even have time to go inside and freshen up my makeup. I'll simply have to wing it as is." She stopped beside the convertible and stared at its occupant. When Arnie fluttered his fingers in greeting, she shrank back. "Ooh, he almost mussed me. What's wrong with him?"

Steve grasped the situation without missing a step. "That man is in no condition to drive, Claire. He's likely to run over the pedestrians on the sidewalk and kill some child. We don't want that kind of publicity."

Cyndi tapped on her watch in case I hadn't worked up to a proper sweat (which I had, several minutes earlier). "We really, really have to line up for the parade, Mrs. Malloy. I've been in oodles of them, and it's always chaos for the first thirty minutes or so, until the bands are positioned and the cars in order. It's such an amateurish group that no one has the slightest idea what to do. The junior-high bands are completely out of control, if you know what I mean. If there's a riding club, the horses are all spooked and some kid falls off his pony. It can be just awful."

"I had a pony once," Arnie said. "Cutest little pony in the whole world." He gave us a beatific smile, then fell across the seat and began to snore.

Steve shrugged and gave me a helpless look. Cyndi tapped her watch. Arnie snuggled down in the upholstery and snored more loudly. Somewhere on the campus a bell tolled the half-hour. I mentally cursed Sally Fromberger, Luanne Bradshaw, the idiot who'd thought up the Miss Thurberfest pageant, the idiot who'd thought up anything to do with the Thurberfest, and the pedestrians who were beginning to wander along the sidewalk to find the perfect spot from which to watch the parade. I cursed the weatherman for not producing a violent thunderstorm or a tornado. I saved my most colorful curse for dear Arnie, who made a snuffly noise as he sought a more comfortable position in which to conduct his stupor.

I went around to the driver's side and shoved Arnie hard enough to bang his head on the door handle. I then settled myself behind the wheel and smiled at my passengers.

"Shall we go?" I said.

"F" "I" "V" "E"

The stadium parking lot, known locally as the Passion Pit, was a circus. Junior-high students armed with musical instruments did their best to stampede wild-eyed horses and buckskinned riders. A small child fell off his pony and began to scream. A drill team of miniskirted girls swarmed the convertible to gape at Miss Thurberfest and bat their eyelashes at her companion. Pickup trucks filled with dirty-faced Cub Scouts circled the lot, the drivers apparently unwilling to risk allowing the boys to scramble away. All sorts of people shouted sternly through megaphones. The bands played on. A horse finally bolted, to an acned tuba player's delight. A Cub Scout leaped over the side of the truck and into the coroner's convertible. Cyndi chattered with fans and signed autographs on scraps of paper. Steve shook hands and thanked everyone for their community spirit, which proved that communism would never get a toehole in grass-roots America. Arnie snored steadily.

To my amazement, order triumphed over cacophony. At three o'clock sharp, a police car with flashing lights pulled out of the lot, followed by a marching band abusing Sousa, Shriners on motorized tricycles, a truckload of cheerleaders, and a fleet of antique cars. At some point I was waved into the line of convertibles, each with posters taped on the side doors and dignitaries perched on the tops of the backseat. We ran the gamut from sanitation supervisor to lieutenant governor; my passengers were slightly above average.

I fumbled through my purse for sunglasses. Arnie roused himself long enough to tell me to keep my hands to myself, then flopped back down. I remembered I'd left my sunglasses at Luanne's; therefore I had no hope of disguising myself as we drove past a goodly percentage of Farberville's twenty thousand citizens. That, coupled with my appearance on the local news, was apt to catapult me right into celebrity status. Maybe next year I'd be invited to ride on the back of a convertible, waving and tossing penny candy to children. I could crown the new Ms. Compromised Feminist Sensibilities, the pageant that proved beauty was both ageless and feckless. Whoopee.

We crept around the corner and started down Thurber Street (and my public humiliation). The crowds grew thicker as we reached the theater, and positively thronged the sidewalks in front of Sally's cafe. By the time we reached the Book Depot there was hardly an unpopulated inch of concrete. There were strollers, children, balloons, dogs, and sunglass-clad adults in abundance. Several Farber college faculty members gave me hesitant smiles, no doubt surprised to see me in such a ridiculous role. I heartily concurred with whatever they were murmuring to each other.

Their pompoms aflutter, the drill team paused to perform a routine under the stoplight. I braked, then slouched down and put my hand over my forehead. My attempt to will myself to my apartment failed, however, as did any idle prayer that no one would notice the insignificant driver of such above-average dignitaries.

"Mother!" Caron shrieked from the sidewalk. She and Inez dashed into the street and clutched the side of the car. "I didn't know you got to drive in the parade! This is Very Impressive. Can Inez and I ride with you?"

"Sure," I said expansively, "as long as you don't mind sitting on my friend Arnie. He won't mind; I'm sure of that. Of course I can't promise he won't throw up somewhere along the parade route. I regret to say he's been drinking, which is why I'm driving."

"He's drunk. That's awful," Caron said, thoroughly scandalized. Inez nodded, marginally mortified.

I glanced in the rearview mirror at my passengers, who were both twinkling and smiling so intently their facial muscles were imperiled. Cyndi's waves were vivacious; Steve's were dignified yet steady. At the corner, the drill team ended with a cheer, then fell into formation and started forward to the next crowd of innocent bystanders.

"As much as I have enjoyed our chat, I must run along now," I said to the girls. "I really don't think it would be prudent to sit on Arnie, so you trot back to the sidewalk and cheer for the coroner and the Cub Scouts."

I put the car in gear, but before we'd gone more than a few feet, I heard a peculiar pinging noise from the backseat. As I turned around, mystified, Steve grabbed Cyndi and the two fell across the backseat in a tangle of arms and legs.

"What's wrong?" I demanded.

Steve stared at me through Cyndi's bent arm. "A shot! Someone fired a shot at us! Get us out of here, Claire. For God's sake, drive!"

I saw the black hole in the upholstery above his ear. I jerked the steering wheel to the left and put the pedal to the metal, so to speak. We roared up the sidestreet, bounced over a pothole, bounced even higher over a long-abandoned railroad track embedded in the street, veered around a woman pushing a stroller, and careened around another corner. The tires screamed; the acrid stench of burning rubber caught up with us and made my eyes burn. Cyndi squealed, and Steve loosed a string of colorful expletives. Nearly blinded by tears, I nevertheless missed a jogger as I pulled over to the curb and stopped.

Once I could control my hand long enough to switch off the engine, I leaned back and let my head rest on the top of the seat. I took several deep breaths, then said, "Everybody all right back there?"

"Get off my hair," Cyndi growled.

"I'm doing my best. Your leg is wrapped around mine, and I can't get up. Your elbow is in my throat."

"You're hurting me."

"This isn't my idea of a good time."

Arnie sat up and rubbed his eyes. "Wowsy, that was some ride, Senator. Wowsy." He found his bottle under the seat, took a long drink, then mutely offered it to me.

I closed my eyes. After a few more muttered accusations, the two in the backseat disentangled themselves and sat up. Steve put his hand on my shoulder. "You were great, Claire. Thanks for saving my life. You let me know if there's anything I can ever do for you, anything at all."

"Your life?" Cyndi said incredulously. "That shot was intended for me. It's proof that some madman has been trying to kill me all week."

Steve produced a shaky laugh. "Don't be absurd, Cyndi. No one would try to kill you. You're a great girl and a real pretty one, too, but I'm a state senator. I've made a lot enemies in the six years I've been serving my constituency. One of my campaign promises involves an investigation of union organizers in the trucking industry. Those old boys play rough."

"There have been threats against me all week. Just ask Mrs. Malloy—she'll tell you how the madman tried to kill me right on the stage."

"The teamsters' union has known ties to organized crime."

"This ten-pound weight missed me by one little bitty inch."

"Organized crime means thugs, professional hit men."

"And somebody wrote on the mirror!"

Arnie looked at me. "Sounds like they both want to get killed, don't it?" He took another drink, wiped his mouth on his sleeve, and opened the car door. "I'm not in the mood to fight over the dubious honor of being shot at, so I think I'll just walk, myself. Ciao, Senator. Have a good day." He got out of the car and ambled down the street, stopping every few steps to replenish his strength with a swig, and disappeared around the corner.

Cyndi reiterated all the attempts on her life, while Steve continued to explain the union links to organized crime and New Jersey hit men. I gazed at the sky and wondered if our abrupt exit from the parade had been noticed, or if anyone heard the sound of gunfire and bothered to call the police. I wondered which dealer had loaned the car for the parade. I wondered if the pothole and/or railroad tracks had done dreadful things to the front axle. I did not, on the other hand, wonder who'd fired at whom in the convertible, because it wasn't worth the effort. I had no theories. Not one.

"I'm afraid the bottom line is you're overestimating your importance," Steve said, cutting off Cyndi's third or fourth recitation of the death threat. "Are you able to drive, Claire? We must report this to the authorities as soon as possible. They can contact the FBI. It's a federal offense to attempt to influence an election through terroristic threats or physical coercion."

"I can drive. I suppose we ought to go directly to the police station so they can examine the bullet hole."

Cyndi leaned across the seat and twisted the rearview mirror. "I can't go anywhere until I've had a chance to fix my hair. I look really, really disheveled because someone rolled all over me."

"I saved your life," Steve protested.

She shoved the mirror back and glowered over her shoulder at him. "So now you saved my life. A minute ago I was never in any danger; you were the one half the hit men in the entire state of New Jersey were aiming at. I was just a silly little girl with grandiose ideas."

"Your ideas are pretty damn grandiose," he said coldly.

"That doesn't change things, does it?" She scrambled over the top of the seat and arranged herself next to me. "Could we please stop by the theater for one teeny tiny second, Mrs. Malloy? I just know the reporters and television crews will descend on us when they hear the story, and I'll absolutely die if they see me like this. Please?"

"Every minute counts if the police are to find the sniper," Steve said from the backseat. I noticed in the rearview mirror that he was combing his hair, but I doubted Cyndi wanted to hear about it.

I considered the possibility of catching up with Arnie. We could share his bottle, watch the rest of the parade, and hit the Gala Sidewalk Sale. My passengers could flip a comb to decide which of them was the intended victim and who'd saved whose life. I concluded I was still in shock, and reached for the key.

"We will stop at the theater for five minutes and no longer," I said in my steeliest maternal voice. "Whoever fired the shot is gone by now, so there's no reason to race hysterically to report this to the police. Cyndi can fix her hair in the office while I call Luanne. Steve can watch for hit men. We will then proceed to the police station. Is everybody ready?"

Everybody was ready, so I drove through the back streets to the theater in order to avoid the Thurberfest crowds. The parade was at the far end of the street by now, its flank protected by a police car. There was no indication anyone was the least bit alarmed about our graceless escape from the procession.

We went inside. Steve asked us to hurry and began to pace in the outer lobby, no doubt preferring to be a moving target. Cyndi and I went on to the office. She continued into the washroom while I dialed Luanne's number. After ten rings, I replaced the receiver, uneasily telling myself she was asleep with the bedside telephone unplugged.

It occurred to me that Peter might appreciate some advance notice. It also occurred to me that he might not understand our side trip by the theater so that Miss Thurberfest could repair her hair for the media. Although he could be charmingly spontaneous in certain situations, he was rather a stickler for proper procedure in police matters. What to do, what to do. Had the room been larger, I would have wrung my hands and paced. As it was, I was apt to bump my nose every fifth step.

"Do you think you ought to call the police?" Cyndi said through the washroom door.

If she was mature enough to see the dilemma, I was more than mature enough to grasp it by its horns. I called the police station. I will admit to a flicker of relief when the desk sergeant told me Peter was out of the office, and that he would be pleased to take a message.

He made a few amused noises as I explained that someone had fired a shot at us during the parade. No, none of us were hurt. Yes, there was a bullet hole in the backseat of the convertible. No, I was quite sure it hadn't been there before. No, we hadn't seen anyone with a rifle. No, we hadn't heard the shot but there really and truly was a hole in the upholstery. When I mentioned the political title of one of the passengers, the chuckles stopped.

"Stay there and wait," he said. "It could be dangerous for any of you to go outside, much less drive across town. I'll have a squad car there as soon as they can get through the parade traffic, and an investigative team in ten minutes or so. Lock the doors and stay away from the windows. Don't take any risks."

I hung up and yelled at Cyndi to wait in the office. Steve declined to join her but did agree to pace in the inner lobby. But there was no way to lock the door to the theater without a key, so I dutifully went to find Mac. He came up from the basement as I entered the auditorium.

"You're not supposed to be here before six," he said.

"We had a small problem during the parade. The police are on their way to investigate, and they might want to examine the weight that almost killed Cyndi. Have you found it?"

"I have been trying to repair the audio system for tonight. It seems someone fiddled with all the knobs and all the switches. It sounds great downstairs, but no one up here will hear a thing if I don't undo the damage. If you want me to stop working on it and search the back of the stage, I will. Then none of us will have to suffer through the caterwauling or listen to idiotic jokes and squeals."

I held out my hand. "I think you'd better work on the audio system. I need the key so that I can lock the front door."

"The audience that eager to get front-row seats?"

"No," I said, moving toward him with what I realized was a maniacal glint, "I am following orders from the police. The officer who took my call felt we might be in danger. I need the key. Give it to me."

He retreated a few steps and unclipped a ring of keys from his belt loop. "Sure, but aren't you locking the barn door a little late?"

"Give me the key."

"You want me to get a monkey wrench and stand guard?"

"Give me the key."

He gave me the key. I stalked back up the corridor to lock the door, but the horse was more than gone, metaphorically speaking. The outer lobby was packed to the walls with television interviewers, cameramen, and shrieking reporters. The lights from the cameras and the din of voices were enough to send the horse cross-country and then some. Steve stood on one side of the ticket booth, with a bouquet of microphones in front of him. Cyndi stood beside him, frowning as she tried to sort out questions from the deafening babble.

It seemed we were having a press conference. Peter would be enchanted, I thought bleakly as I edged toward the office. In an abrupt lull, I head Steve say, "The union organizers have vowed to stop any investigation into their pension records. I am appalled at this crude attempt to frighten me—or to silence me. I see this as a critical test of my candidacy, and I want to go on record right this minute to say I am not afraid. I will not be intimidated."

Cyndi put her hands on her hips and gave him a dazzling smile. "Senator Stevenson is overlooking the fact that the bullet was aimed at me. There has been a series of threats made against me this week, and one attempt to kill me. I have proof."

Despite her words, the majority of the cameras turned to Steve and the reporters surged forward. "When will the investigation take place, Senator?" "Have you or members of your family received any threatening calls?" "Will you demand the FBI investigate this incident?" "Have you spoken to your wife and children?" They continued forward, screeching questions at him.

Cyndi's smile faded, and her hands fell to her sides. Her eyes narrowed so angrily that I could almost see sparks shooting from them. After a moment, she spun around and marched through the door to the inner lobby. "I am going to my dressing room until the police come," she snapped at me, then went down the corridor without telling me how really, really pissed off she was. She didn't need to.

I was sitting behind the desk when Peter came into the office. I fluttered my fingers at him and said, "I called to speak to you, but the sergeant said you were out of the office. Did you have a nice lunch? I didn't, and I can't get these drawers open to see if there might be a bag of ancient corn chips left over from the days when Bogie was in bloom."

"What the hell is going on?"

"It depends on one's perspective, I suppose. If one is a state senator, one assumes teamsters are attempting to silence one. If one is the reigning Miss Thurberfest, one assumes a maniac is trying to drop a weight on one's head or put a bullet hole in the same general vicinity."

He made an exasperated noise as he sat down on the couch. "Is there any possibility you'll tell me what's going on?"

I told him the entire story, from Luanne's initial appearance on crutches to our graceless exit from the parade. "And it's not funny," I concluded with a frown.

"But it is. You are the last person in the entire town to be associated with a beauty pageant," he said, barely able to restrain his glee. "I can see you in the middle of all those giggly girls, sharing your wisdom about mascara and strategic padding. Do you get to crown the queen and chaperone her for the next year while she opens supermarkets and rodeos?"

"No, and I'm doing this to help a friend, not to provide you with hours of merriment. Caron was in the room when Luanne asked me to help. I was being a good role model, although I now wish I'd let Caron see my selfish, egotistical, fair-weather side. What are you going to do about the shot?"

"My men are running off the reporters and the rubberneckers. Then, once we can breathe, we'll take a look at the bullet hole. You don't seem all that concerned, however, since you took a side trip here instead of going to the station."

"It was closer," I lied.

He gave me a smirky look as he went back to the lobby. I called Luanne's number again, but there was no answer. It occurred to me that I might look around for the missing weight, since Mac was clearly busy with more important things. I went down the corridor and through the auditorium to the stage. The opening bars of "The Impossible Dream" blared, then mercifully stopped, which meant we were either making progress or we weren't. I poked around under a stack of flats, then kicked at a dusty pile of costumes. After a discouraging sneeze, I gave up and started back across the stage. Someone moved in a row near the doorway.

I stopped and squinted into the gloom. "Who's there?"

The figure stood up and came down the aisle. He was a young-ish man with stylishly cut hair and glasses. His face was as round as a child's, and his smile as innocent. "I'm Warren Dansberry," he said. "I was looking for Senator Stevenson, and someone said he'd gone to make a telephone call to his family."

"In here? There's a telephone in the office off the lobby and some pay telephones in the west corridor, but I can't imagine why he'd be in the auditorium." I came down the steps. "Steve mentioned your name earlier. You're his aide, aren't you?"

"His gofer and his errand boy," Warren said, grinning. "I'm the one he yells at when the schedule snarls up or some local party chairman gets too close. I guess you could say I'm a Renaissance whipping boy."

"Are the reporters gone?" I asked as we walked toward the lobby.

"They've regrouped across the street, although I don't know why. According to the master plan, the Senator was supposed to go back to the hotel suite until the pageant begins tonight. He likes to take a short nap before a public appearance. I don't know how he does it with the twins making such a racket, but he manages."

"The twins?" I inquired politely, all the while wondering what Peter and his men had discovered about the bullet hole in the convertible.

"Cassie and Carrie are four years old. They're cute, but they are rather feral little things. Mrs. Stevenson has her hands full all the time. He likes to show them off, and of course the constituents absolutely drool all over the girls. It's a way to emphasize Senator Stevenson's family ties and commitment to future generations."

One of Peter's minions, a bulldoggish man named Jorgeson, nearly leaped on me as we came into the lobby. "I was about to send out a search party, Mrs. Malloy. Lieutenant Rosen wants to speak to you—now."

Warren murmured something and wandered toward the office. I frowned at Jorgeson. "I went to the auditorium for a moment. What's the big rush?"

"The lieutenant's hotter than a jalapeño pizza. Something about some cock-and-bull story about a convertible and a bullet hole."

I bit back an acerbic editorial and followed Jorgeson through the lobby to the sidewalk. The reporters and camera crew were milling around across the street, salivating loudly enough to be heard on our side. Peter and a trio of uniformed men stood in a tight circle, but as I came through the door, he looked up. "Where's the bullet hole?"

"It's in the backseat, about a foot from the top."

"Where's the backseat?" he continued, ominously calm.

"In the car. I realize I'm a mere civilian, but that's the first place I'd look." I gestured at the curb, then met Peter's eyes. "I parked the car right here, not more than fifteen minutes ago. I parked it in this precise spot."

"Oh," he said. "I realize I'm a mere policeman, but I can't seem to find the car you say you parked in this precise spot. Neither can any of my men, and they're very good at finding big things like cars. We may miss a microdot every now and then, but—"

"I parked the damn car right here!"

He shook his head. "We'll keep looking, then, but we haven't had any luck thus far."

"Ask them," I said, pointing at the reporters, who in turn leaned forward as if they were magnetized. "Or ask Cyndi and Senator Stevenson. They were with me when I parked the car— right here!"

"There has been enough publicity already," Peter growled. He told one of his men to locate the Senator, then came over to me. "Will you swear this isn't some kind of publicity stunt, Claire? I trust you, and I can't imagine why you'd allow yourself to get involved in some crazy scheme, but I want the truth."

This—from the man who shared my bed and my benevolence. Oh, he was showing me his even white teeth and baby brown eyes, and he was oozing sympathy like an oil slick. He was offering me the golden opportunity to admit I was a liar and a publicity puppet for the Senator. Now, wasn't that really, really nice of him?

"The convertible was here fifteen minutes ago," I said calmly.

"Okay, okay. What about the car keys?"

I unclenched my teeth while I tried to remember my actions. "I drove back here and pulled to the curb in front of the door. My purse was on the floor; I leaned over to get it while Steve and Cyndi started inside. We were all worried that the sniper might be in the vicinity and ready to take another shot. I was relieved that the door was unlocked, since I don't have a key, and I told myself I needed to get one before tonight just in case Mac was late. Then I directly went to the office and called you." I didn't see the need to mention I hadn't called him first. The call to Luanne had taken no more than half a minute.

"Did you take the keys out of the ignition?"

"No," I admitted with a shrug.

"So you left the keys in the car, which happens to be our only proof that a shot was fired at the passengers in the backseat."

"A shot was fired. I heard the noise and I saw the bullet hole. Steve and Cyndi were there; why don't you ask them about the incident? You may think I'm a feebleminded dupe, but you ought to listen to a senator."

He gave me an unfathomable look, then told one of his men to put out an APB on the missing convertible. He wasn't especially pleased when I explained that I hadn't noticed the license plate, was vague about the model, and didn't know which dealer had loaned the car for the parade. I did, however, swear that one Sally Fromberger knew every bit of it, and would be delighted to find out the details for him.

"Or you might find Arnie," I added.

He gazed at the crowds swarming up and down Thurber Street, clustering around street performers and food booths, fingering bargains on tables, and simply ambling along in the sunlit street. Wails from a rock band in the beer garden competed with the mellower music from strolling minstrels. The junior-high band members had been released at the conclusion of the parade, and some of them tootled on their instruments as they jostled each other. The pom-pom girls gathered to squeal out a cheer and jiggle their stuff.

"Do you have any idea where we might find Arnie?" Peter said.

"I'd try the alleys and the dumpsters first," I said, tiring of the whole thing and in dire need of food and tranquility. "The animal control officer might have taken him to the pound, or he may be snoozing in the grass behind the Book Depot. Those of you with trained noses ought to be able to sniff him out wherever he is."

One of the uniformed men was sent to find Sally. As we trooped back into the theater, Warren approached us. "The Senator apologizes, but his wife had hysterics when she heard what happened and he felt he needed to go to her. He said to tell you that he'll be happy to talk to you at the hotel or tonight before the pageant, and he wants to do everything he can to cooperate with the authorities."

Peter ran his hand through his hair, then scowled at Jorgeson. "That's dandy, just dandy. What about the girl? Did she feel some need to vanish for a few hours, too?"

"I haven't seen her, Lieutenant."

"She said she would be in her dressing room," I said. Before I could offer to draw a map or even escort him, Eunice burst into the theater.

"Where is my gal? I heard something on the television about a shot being fired during the parade. I threw down the nail polish bottle and rushed over here as quickly as possible."

I caught Eunice's shoulders before she could burst onward. "Cyndi was not hurt. She's fine, as are the Senator and the driver. She was upset, naturally, and went to rest for a few minutes."

"Oh, thank God," Eunice said, putting her hand on her bosom. Her fingernails fluttered like rose petals in a breeze. "I realize I'm just a fat old woman riding on her coattails, but I care very much about her. Her mother and father are both dead; I've done everything I could to take care of her and see that she achieves her potential. All I've ever wanted to do was to help her."

I introduced her to Peter, who was mildly perplexed, then suggested the three of us go down to the dressing room. I heard the sound of a hammer and a muttered curse as we went through the auditorium, and I hoped Mac was not venting rage on the audio system—or its operator. Peter blinked at the damp, dreary basement wall, but said nothing.

I tapped on the construction-paper star. "Cyndi, Eunice is here, and the police would like to have a word with you."

It seemed to be my week for lack of response. I tried the door, which was locked, then tapped again. Once I had pounded loud enough to rattle the dentures of the dead, I turned around and gave Peter a timid smile. "I guess she wandered away, too. I should have insisted she stay in the office, right?"

He ignored the rhetorical question, although I suspected I would hear a lengthy exposition later. "What time will she come back tonight?" he said in a noticeably grim voice.

"I always have her arrive two hours before the pageant," Eunice cut in. "Some of the girls who arrive at the last minute look harried on stage, and the judges don't care for that. It simply isn't poised, and poise is everything, especially in the Big One."

"You could go talk to the Senator," I said. "Or get Cyndi's address from Eunice and run by there to talk to her."

"I don't want her to be any more upset before the pageant," Eunice declared firmly. "The judges can see that, too. Even though Cyndi's not a contestant, she's liable to encounter the same judges at other pageants. Concentration is everything. You may talk to her after the preliminary tonight, Lieutenant." She hurried down the hallway and went up the stairs.

Peter managed not to sputter, but his voice was strained as he said, "This is all very new to me, and I don't seem to have a feel for proper pageant procedure. It would be very helpful, Mrs. Malloy, if you were to sit down with me and explain it."

"Over food?" I said.

"A good idea, indeed. What time do you need to be back at the theater in order to oversee the preliminary round?"

"By six," I said, although the words turned to acid in my mouth. I thought up several incredibly wicked things to do to Luanne Bradshaw as we went upstairs and out into the real world.

"S"I"X"

Peter agreed to pick up Chinese and meet me at my apartment. I drove over to Luanne's house, parked in the driveway, and hurried to the front door. I knocked, rang the doorbell, and was peering through the window when she at last came across the living room and opened the door.

"My goodness," she murmured, "are we gripped with pageant fever?"

"Not exactly. I've been trying to call you for an hour to tell you what happened during the parade, but there was no answer. As usual, I assumed you were comatose on the floor and rushed over here to perform last rites and choose clothes for the mortician to dress you in. I was debating between the blue silk and the off-white linen, although the latter is a bit frivolous."

"I unplugged the telephone so that I wouldn't be disturbed by calls from siding salesmen and incoherent assistant pageant directors. Come have a cup of tea and tell me your big news."

I noticed her cheeks were flushed and her eyes bright. As she turned away and limped toward the kitchen, I could see how thin she looked, almost gaunt and bony. It was not the result of a sprained ankle, I told myself as I trailed after her.

"Do you have a fever?" I asked while she fiddled with the teapot.

"No, I left the electric blanket on the highest setting when I napped. I'm out of food except for a box of crackers and a can of tuna fish. And zero-calorie celery, of course."

"Are you on a diet? You look like an inmate from a prisoner-of-war camp, you know. Is there something you're not telling me?"

"Of course, there are things I'm not telling you. If you knew all the despicable details of my life, you'd never take me to lunch. It's an ephemeral response to all those svelte, petite girls with their skin-tight leotards and flabless thighs. It brings back memories of sleeker days, and I've always had a terror of turning into a lard pot. I promise I'll be ready for nachos the day after the pageant. Tell me what happened at the parade."

I gave her a brief synopsis, delayed only by her laughter when I repeated the confrontation with dearly departed Arnie and my subsequent humiliation on Thurber Street. She sobered when I told her about the shot that had been fired as we started up the hill, but was again convulsed with laughter when I related the awkwardness that resulted from leaving the keys in the evidence.

"Oh, my God," she said. "This is incredible, just incredible. Who do you think fired the shot?"

I took a sip of tea while I considered the possibilities, which immediately became limitless. "It depends on who the intended victim was. Steve is convinced it was initiated by the union, in which case the police will never find a clue to the sniper's identity. The media were enchanted with that theory, naturally—it's political intrigue, and in a dull election year."

"But what about the mishaps that have happened to Cyndi the last few days . . . the nail, the weight, and the nasty message written on her mirror?" Luanne said, frowning. "Do you think those were attempts on her life?"

"To her chagrin, Steve dismissed all that with the undeniable truth that she is a small-town beauty queen and therefore unworthy of such attentions. She may have bested other girls in the pageant circle, but she's a medium frog in a very small puddle. If the Senator were not so newsworthy, the local media might pick up the story, although it's pretty weak." I stuffed a cracker in my mouth. "Peter's meeting me at home, so I'd better run. I'll pick you up at five forty-five, unless you decide to stay home and sauté your svelte body under an electric blanket."

"I'll be ready. I arranged to meet the florist, the coach with the escorts, and the concession workers at six. The girls ought to be drifting in to get ready about then. Are the technical crewmembers planning to appear?"

I shrugged, then went to my car and drove to my apartment, the top floor of an older house across from the campus. The rooms were small and the plumbing whimsical, but it had a nice view of the lawn stretching down from revered Farber Hall, an official landmark that had been condemned years ago for obvious reasons. Carlton, my deceased husband, had been assigned a fourth-floor office and worried for years about being killed by a chunk of plaster. A chicken truck got him first, but he probably had a valid cause for concern.

I left my coat on a chair and went into the kitchen, where I found Peter, Caron, and Inez engaged in an epicurean frenzy. White cardboard cartons cluttered the table, along with cellophane packages of soy sauce and plastic tubs of hot mustard.

"Having fun?" I asked while I made myself a stiff drink.

"I must speak to you, Mother," Caron said through a mouthful of bamboo shoots. "Inez and I have decided that Mac is overbearing, rude, abusive, and not the least bit grateful for our assistance. There was no reason for him to call me all sorts of tacky names simply because I tried to familiarize myself with the equipment."

Inez nodded. "He wasn't very nice, Mrs. Malloy."

"We were both Shattered, absolutely Shattered," Caron said. "We are thinking about spending the evening at the college library. After all, we are volunteers—not slaves to be screamed at by your heavy-handed slave driver."

Peter gave me an amused look, but had enough sense to stay out of the situation. As I've mentioned before, he does have a rational side. I, on the other hand, was close enough to the edge to rush in where angels wouldn't even tiptoe.

"You and Inez are not going to the library tonight. You are going to the theater because we cannot stage this nonsense without you. This nonsense happens to be very important to Luanne, who has already agreed to give you an inappropriate black dress and a beaded purse. She bought your soul, my dear, and you will deliver it to the theater."

Inez blinked at Caron. "A black dress?"

"I was going to let you wear it," Caron said, dismissing the treachery with a wave of her chopsticks. "We'll go to the theater—if you promise to have a word with that man. You look awfully haggard, Mother. If I had my learner's permit, I could drive so that you could rest."

I dumped the contents of a carton on a plate and picked up a fork. "I have a hard time imagining myself dozing serenely with you at the wheel."

"Moo Shu pork?" Peter said, trying not to smile.

"Won ton very much," I said. I had no difficulty not smiling.

When we were done, Peter said he was going to Senator Stevenson's hotel to discuss the incident during the parade. He agreed to personally deliver the senator/judge/emcee to the theater at six-thirty, thus ensuring the continued well-being of a vital element of the pageant. I allowed Caron to sputter and Inez to whimper about the treatment they'd received from That Man, then ordered them to the car. We picked up Luanne and drove to the theater, all of us subdued by personal demons.

The door was locked. I tapped with my car key until Mac came through the adjoining lobbies and unlocked the door for us. Caron nudged me forward and hissed that I'd promised to have a word. Inez hid behind her. As Luanne hobbled away to the office, I smiled at Mac and said, "The girls are truly sorry if they damaged the equipment. They wanted me to offer their apologies."

"Mother!" gasped a voice behind me.

"What's more," I continued blithely, "they are willing to listen very carefully to your instructions and touch nothing except that which you indicate."

"That's a comfort," he said. His blue eyes swept coldly across the two cowerers, then alit on their protectress. "Now what was all this crap with the reporters and the police this afternoon? I didn't agree to spontaneous press conferences in my theater, nor to policemen crawling all over the stage like a bunch of damn cockroaches. Some fool wasted a good half-hour of my time wanting to know where I was during the parade."

"And where were you?"

"On the roof of a building, trying to put a bullet hole through Miss Thurberfest's forehead. My only regret is that I missed her— and that pompous excuse for a politician." He stalked off, muttering under his breath like a pouty locomotive.

Caron and Inez began squawking at me. A man laden with flower arrangements came through the door and asked for Mrs. Bradshaw. A bulky man in a baseball cap and two dozen young brutes swarmed the lobby. Caron and Inez stopped squawking, but made no move to follow Mac in order to be lectured on the equipment. Cases of popcorn appeared mysteriously. A man with a dolly of sodas asked me where they went, lady. A sextet of beauty contestants came giggling through the door, then halted to giggle some more at the horde of escorts. The team made several crude remarks. A second group of contestants giggled in.

It was showtime. Or almost, anyway.

People were dispatched here and there. The would-be queens retreated to the basement to ready themselves; the escorts were escorted to the greenroom to receive instructions from their leader, along with sharp comments about fast hands and virgin territory. Caron and Inez stared longingly as Julianna breezed through the lobby, but stumbled away with much grousing to find Mac. The smell of popcorn competed with the redolence from an increasing number of flower arrangements. Music began to waft out of lobby walls. It seemed to be going so well that I was actually smiling as I went into the office.

Luanne was on the telephone. I sank down on the couch and opened the notebook to make all sorts of checks, feeling optimistic that somehow we might survive the preliminary round without any devastating developments. Ho, ho.

There I was, smiling and checking and relaxed and pretty damn pleased with myself, when Julianna and Chou-Chou's trainer came into the office.

"Mrs. Malloy," Julianna said, her face pale under patches of blusher, "I think there's something really, really wrong downstairs."

"That's right," Heidi breathed. "We didn't want to upset the other girls, so we thought we'd better tell you."

"Low-wattage bulbs in the dressing room?" I said brightly, still firmly entrenched in my own little Wonderland.

Julianna shook her head. "You'd better come, Mrs. Malloy. Maybe I was just imagining it, but I thought I smelled gas."

"And Chou-Chou wouldn't stop barking until I put him in his traveling box," the other girl said. "He just hates his box, but he was like driving everyone absolutely crazy. Dixie said she would drown him in the toilet if I didn't make him be quiet."

Luanne covered the mouthpiece of the receiver. "I don't like the sound of this, Claire. You'd better go with the girls and make sure everything's okay."

I wasn't especially pleased with Julianna's premise that she might have smelled gas. I shooed them out the door and we hurried to the basement hallway. "Where did you think you smelled gas?" I demanded grimly. Julianna pointed at Cyndi Jay's dressing room door. I continued to the end of the hallway and knocked. "Cyndi? Are you in there?" No one answered and the door was locked. I sent Julianna to get a key from Mac, then bent down and sniffed the keyhole. It was impossible to miss the smell of gas drifting through the round, black opening.

I spun around and grabbed Heidi's arm. "Run to the office and tell Mrs. Bradshaw there's a natural gas leak in the dressing room. Have her call the emergency number for the gas company. Now!"

Several of the contestants came out into the hallway. I told them to evacuate the basement until the leak was stopped and the cramped rooms were aired. Despite their protests about hair to be curled, makeup to be redone, and costumes to be secured with safety pins, they trooped up the stairs to wait in the auditorium.

I tried the metal doors that led to the alley, but they were held closed by a chain and a padlock. Mac surely had a key, I thought in an increasingly panicky voice. We could cut off the gas, which was most likely leaking from the space heater, open the metal doors, and rig fans to blow out the gas. The girls could reassemble in time to do whatever they needed to do and be finished in time for the grand opening number.

I was about to go to the stage and yell for Mac when same loped down the stairs, the key ring jangling harshly in his hand. He brushed me aside and bent down to jab a key at the lock. "What the hell's going on?" he growled as he struggled with the key. "Did that airhead go off and leave the heater on?"

The lock clicked and he shoved open the door. We both recoiled at the wave of gas that washed over us and filled the hallway. I managed to croak something about the metal doors, then stumbled backward, my eyes watering and my throat afire. I started to back up the stairs, then stopped as a horrible idea flashed across my mind. Mac was fumbling with the padlock as I dashed back down the hall and into the dressing room. Cyndi was slumped in the chair in front of the table, her head lolling against her chest. I slipped my hands under her arms and tried to lift her. She may have been petite, but she was damn hefty, I thought as I fought to hold the breath in my lungs.

Just as my lungs threatened to explode, Mac came into the room, slung the body over his shoulder, and grabbed my wrist. I allowed myself to be dragged into the hallway and shoved through the open metal doors into the cool night air. I stumbled and fell, but stayed contentedly on the gravel as I fought nausea and hysterics. I succumbed to the first. Once I'd lost the lovely Chinese food, I sat back and stared at Mac. He was bent over a supine figure that was very still.

"Call an ambulance," he said.

"Is she . . . is she okay?"

"She's alive, but she won't be for long if you sit there and bat your eyelashes. Call an ambulance. Tell them to haul ass."

I ran around the building to the front door and through the lobby to the office. Luanne held the telephone receiver in her hand, but I snatched it from her, hit the disconnect button, and dialed 911. Once I was assured help would arrive within minutes, I told Luanne to send the paramedics to the alley behind the building and dashed back through the front door. As I reached the sidewalk, Peter's car pulled to a stop in front of me. Senator Stevenson sat in the passenger's seat; Warren and a woman were in the back.

I went around to Peter's side and managed to croak out an abbreviated version of what had happened. Then, ignoring his spurt of questions, I ran around the corner and along the sidewalk to the back of the building. Mac was still bent over Cyndi's body, his mouth covering hers as he administered resuscitation. I told him the ambulance was on its way, and was standing there helplessly as Peter came into the alley.

"How is she?" he demanded.

"Mac said she was alive. I ought to do something—but I don't know what to do. I—I didn't know she was in her dressing room. We should have unlocked her door earlier this afternoon. None of this should have happened. I feel—I feel responsible." The hysteria I'd resisted earlier caught up with me. My voice collapsed into gulping sobs and my knees buckled. Peter caught me and held me tightly against his chest as blue lights flashed in the alley. A siren deafened us momentarily, then faded in a whining spiral. Men scrambled from the ambulance, barking questions. Equipment materialized. A radio from inside the ambulance crackled with static fury. A police car added to the confusion. A curious crowd gathered at the top of the alley, babbling and pointing at the body surrounded by kneeling paramedics.

Mac, relieved of his job, moved away from the circle of paramedics. I forced myself to find some vestige of control, and fumbled in Peter's pocket for his handkerchief. Once I'd wiped my face, I let Peter join the fracas and walked over to the edge of the alley where Mac stood, his hands in his pockets and his expression flat.

"Thanks for dragging both of us out of there," I said. "I couldn't get a good grip on Cyndi, and I was about to pass out from the fumes."

Ignoring my expression of gratitude, he took a crumpled pack of cigarettes from his pocket and lit one. He took a long drag as he studied the paramedics clustered around Cyndi. In a bemused voice, he said, "I don't know how this happened. It wasn't supposed to happen. Damndest thing that it did."

"The heater was from antiquity. Either it had a rusted pipe or the pilot blew out. You shouldn't feel responsible for what happened," I said soothingly.

He gave me a surprised look. "Oh, I don't feel any responsibility for this, Claire. None at all." Whistling under his breath, he flipped the cigarette into the weeds, then strolled to the top of the alley and disappeared through the crowd of tourists.

Cyndi was loaded into the ambulance and taken away. A policeman dispatched the crowd, while another approached me with a scowl. "I need the girl's name and address, and that of her next-of-kin. Then you can explain your relationship and exactly what happened."

"Her information ought to be in a file in the office," I said, wishing Peter would rescue me from the grim-faced inquisitor. He and several other officers had vanished, however. I related what I knew, which didn't take more than a minute. I graciously added that Mac was the person who owned the theater and was most familiar with the heaters, and that he might be found on the stage or in the light-control booth.

The policeman snorted and went toward the front of the theater. I hesitated at the metal doors, still somewhat queasy as gas drifted past me. Peter and his minions were in the basement; I could hear low voices and the sound of doors being opened and furniture scraping on the concrete floor. I finally accepted the fact I could not force myself to go inside and walked back along the sidewalk to the front door.

Luanne was propped on her crutches in the office doorway. "What is going on? First Heidi came in here shrieking about a gas leak, then you barreled through to call the ambulance. Now there's a policeman hunting through the files . . . Is Cyndi——?"

"She was alive when they took her in the ambulance." Since the office was occupied, I leaned against the wall and tried to focus on a particularly odoriferous basket of flowers. "I don't know much more than that. I smelled gas and sent Julianna to get a key from Mac. He unlocked the door, and the room was thick with the stuff. He carried Cyndi outside and gave her artificial respiration while I called the emergency number. Peter and his men are examining the dressing room now. I suppose they'll find a rusty pipe or something."

"How long had Cyndi been in there?"

I let my shoulders sag. "I have no idea. Long enough to lose consciousness, obviously."

"Why wouldn't she have smelled the gas when it first began to leak? It has a very distinctive odor."

"Why would someone fire a shot at a convertible in the middle of a local parade? I'm an assistant pageant director, not an oracle." I looked at Luanne, who had much the same horrified expression I suspected I had. "What about the pageant? Are we going to cancel it?"

"I don't see how we can. Over two hundred tickets were sold in advance, and the girls have been preparing for this for weeks. Some of them have spent a fortune on clothes and accessories. I feel dreadful about Cyndi, but I have an obligation to those eighteen girls."

"Who are in the auditorium, and can't return to their dressing rooms until the basement is aired out. What's more, the reigning queen will not be available to perform in the opening number or crown her successor." I held up my hands and shook my head. "Don't even think about it. Personally, I suggest we tell everyone the pageant's been postponed for a month or two. Your ankle will be well. Cyndi will be back in bloom. The girls might have learned another step or two of the opening number, although I have reservations about that."

Steve came up the corridor from the auditorium. "What happened in the basement? The girls are dithering and crying, but none of them seems to know exactly why. A gas leak?"

I told him about Cyndi. He seemed deeply shocked, and suggested we go to the hospital to check on her. I mentioned the proximity of the pageant, and Luanne added quite firmly that the show would go on.

"I think your brain is sprained," I said. "However, I'll tell the girls to grab their things and use the greenroom to dress. Steve can explain that the opening number has been canceled because of the accident. He can read the names of the finalists, and tomorrow night he can crown the winner. We can then wipe our tears and go away from this place, which is beginning to have the allure of Bleak House."

A woman in a print dress and jacket came up the corridor. She eyed the three of us curiously, then slipped her arm through Steve's. Her hair was fashionably cut and colored, her clothes expensive yet conservative, her eyes a cool, appraising shade of gray. She would have been equally at ease in front of a country club fashion show committee or astride a thoroughbred horse. I was not surprised when Steve introduced her as his wife, Patti.

"I've been trying to calm down the girls, but they're frantic to know what's going to happen," she said in a soft voice that had a Southern lilt. "They were already excited about the pageant before this terrible accident occurred. Now they're buzzing so wildly I'm afraid they'll explode."

I spotted Eunice coming through the front door. "I'll go talk to them," I said hurriedly. "Someone needs to tell Eunice about Cyndi." I went down the corridor, aware of Luanne's black look burning into my back, and went into the auditorium. The girls crowded around me and demanded to know how Cyndi was. I told them the truth, which was I didn't know but that she was alive when taken to the hospital. Then I told them the latest plans.

Julianna regarded me mistrustfully. "There are policemen in the basement. Does that mean someone tried to murder Cyndi?"

"The police always investigate accidents," I said with more assurance than I felt. "I'm sure the gas company has found the leak and corrected it by now, and the police are simply there to assist. You all know this is an old building and therefore likely to have faulty plumbing, rotting ropes, and bent nails."

"What about the shot fired during the parade?" another girl said, moving forward. "My mom saw something on the news. Senator Stevenson said it was fired at him, but Cyndi was in the car, too."

"There could be a crazed rapist stalking Cyndi!" Heidi bleated helpfully.

"He could be in this theater right now," suggested a reedy voice from the back.

They inched forward, closing me in. Julianna said, "But the theater's been locked for rehearsals. No one could have walked in from the street."

"He must have been here all along," said a nasal voice.

"He? Why do you assume this horrible maniac is a man?"

Julianna's voice fell to a melodramatic whisper. "It could be one of us."

The girls glanced at each other and edged backward, thus allowing me to catch a breath of air that was not laden with perfume. "Now, let's not get any wild ideas," I said sternly. "We have a pageant to produce in less than an hour. It's going to be crowded in the greenroom, but we have no option. You'll have to make the best of it. Go get your things."

"I'm not going down to the basement," said a snub-nosed baton twirler.

The others nodded and repeated the avowal that they indeed were not going down there. I wasn't sure if they were afraid of a madman, the police, the stench of gas, or each other, but I was quite sure I was facing a mutiny of epic proportions.

"I can't carry up all your dresses, swimsuits, props, makeup bags, hair dryers, and whatever else is down there," I said.

"We're not going down there," said a mulish voice from the crowd.

We were in a wonderful stalemate when Eunice came into the auditorium. She clapped her hands and said, "Girls, I know that Cyndi wants you to put on the best pageant there's ever been. Now stop gawking and go fetch your things at once! Most of you look disheveled, and the judges simply will not look kindly upon a gal with inferior grooming. We must think poise, poise, poise!"

They obediently scuttled down the steps, no doubt panicked by the nightmare of being deemed inferior groomers. I thanked Eunice for her inspirational talk and asked her if she'd called the hospital.

"I spoke to a nurse in the emergency room. Cyndi is already much improved, although she is still unconscious. Her complexion is gradually turning pink, and she's breathing without artificial aid. They'll move her to a private room shortly."

I sank down in the front row. "Then she must be recovering. That's wonderful news, Eunice. I was terrified that she . . ."

"Cyndi's a tough cookie," Eunice said, sitting down beside me. "I'm usually around to rescue her, but this time it seems she owes you a debt of gratitude. Gratitude is hardly one of her strong points, so please allow me to express my thanks for your act of courage. I seem to have misjudged you, Claire; it must have taken great strength of character to go back into her dressing room."

"Mac carried her out," I said, wincing as the scene replayed itself in my mind. "And I wasn't courageous; I was too frightened for that."

"Why did you think she might be in there?"

I rubbed my face as I tried to remember what had gone through my mind. "I don't really know. I suppose it was because I never saw her leave the theater."

The contestants came up the stairs, their arms piled with pageant paraphernalia. They trooped across the stage and went behind the curtain. Abruptly the auditorium echoed with squeals and brays of manly laughter.

"The football team is in the greenroom," I said to Eunice. "I believe I suggested it in a previous life."

"The gals can hardly dress under that condition. Concentration is everything." She stood up and stalked across the stage, clearly concentrating on how best to squelch any malingering.

I felt a twinge of fear for the well-being of the football team, but sat and gazed blankly at the stage. Caron danced onto the stage and gave me a glittery smile. "Shall I take Cyndi Jay's place in the opening number? I know practically all of it."

"Where were you during all the excitement? I thought you'd be out front directing traffic by now, or holding a press conference to explain your perspective on the events."

"The television crews were busy," she said with a pirouette. "Are you absolutely positive I can't take Cyndi's place? That Horrid Man insists that I sit in this incredibly dumpy little closet and read some idiotic manual about lights. Inez is having oodles more fun than I am."

"No, I'm not," said a small voice from between the folds of the curtain.

"But you can see everybody," Caron said, still spinning about and flapping her wings. "All I see are mouse droppings and little squiggles that are supposed to clarify the entire premise of electronics since the day Franklin flew a kite."

"It's very dusty back here," Inez said.

"It's very, very dreary in the closet," Tinkerbell retorted sweetly.

I left them to debate the issue of dust versus drear, and went up the corridor to the office, thinking how exhausted I already was and how dearly I would prefer to be in my bedroom with a cup of tea and a mystery novel.

Luanne gave me a bleak wave. "Is everything under control?"

"The girls are forced to dress under the benevolent supervision of the football team, and my daughter has lost her mind," I said. "Other than that, the reigning Miss Thurberfest is at the hospital, someone fired a shot at someone, and I allowed a new car to be stolen from under my nose. This must be Friday the thirteenth and a dozen of its sequels."

"But we may survive. The police will eventually find both the sniper and the car. The rehearsals are over and done with, and it's too late to worry about some baton twirler blinding a judge or that icky little dog piddling in front of three hundred people. Cyndi's recovering from that horrible accident, and—"

Peter appeared in the doorway. "It wasn't an accident," he said in a mild tone.

"What?" I snapped, not the least bit mild.

He held up a plastic evidence bag. "In here is a tiny square of cellophane tape, not longer than a half-inch. May I use the tele-phone?"

Luanne pushed it across the desk. "Help yourself. But I don't understand why a piece of tape proves . . . anything."

"It was taped over the keyhole of the dressing room door."

He began to dial a number while Luanne and I gaped at each other like a pair of groupers.

"S" "E" "V" "E" "N"

"Suicide?" Luanne murmured bleakly.

Peter put down the receiver and ran his fingers through his hair. "It could be, although we'll have to discuss that with Miss Jay. She's recovering quickly, and has been moved to a private room for the night. We can talk to her in the morning. It's difficult to imagine someone accidentally taping the keyhole to contain the gas until the room was saturated."

"But what about all the strange things that happened?" I asked. "I'm having a hard time categorizing them as coincidences after this last incident. There really was a shot fired at us during the parade. When you find the car, you can dig the bullet out of the upholstery."

He had the decency to look a little abashed, if not as thoroughly embarrassed as I might have wished. "I believe you, Claire. Senator Stevenson backed your story most vehemently. He's convinced the shot was fired in order to intimidate him. I've notified the FBI, and they're going to snoop around quietly. They weren't too pleased with the delay between the incident and the call to the police station, but they finally agreed that a professional sniper wouldn't linger to wave at the coroner's convertible."

Luanne had been nodding like a dormouse in a teapot, but she shook herself and said, "You're convinced this revolves around Steve? What about the nail and the weight?"

"The nail was pounded back into its proper level two days ago, although I doubt we could have done anything with it. The weight has vanished. The other end of the rope has been sent to the lab." He gave me a narrow look. "I understand you went up to the catwalk to investigate?"

"Part of my job description," I said, wondering who'd snitched on me. "Then, basically, you can't do anything until you either find the car or talk to Cyndi?"

"I'm going to talk to"—he consulted the notebook—"Eunice Allingham about Cyndi's state of mind. I can't imagine anyone being so depressed at the idea of turning in a pageant crown that she would do something drastic, but I truly don't understand the ritual. Why would some girl care so desperately about an inane title like Miss Thurberfest?"

Luanne sighed and leaned back in her chair. "The ones who get involved in the pageant business do care. They may enter the first time for fun, or for the opportunity to perform in front of an audience. Some of them are pushed into it at a tender age by overbearing parents. I've seen three-year-olds in tiny tuxedos wink at the judges like seasoned gigolos. The publicity, no matter how meager, begins to infatuate them, as does the perceived glory. It becomes an obsession after a few pageants."

"I suppose," Peter said doubtfully.

Something was disturbing me, gnawing at me like a theoretical rat on a theatrical rope, but I couldn't force it into focus. "Did you find the source of the leak?" I asked Peter.

"There wasn't a crack in a pipe; the gas was on and the pilot was off. If we hadn't found the bit of tape, we might have assumed the pilot had been blown out by a draft. But someone put the tape over the keyhole to prevent the hallway from filling up with gas until it was nearly too late. Cyndi's darn lucky it finally seeped through the hole."

For some obscure reason, his response failed to answer my question. I covered my face with my hands and tried to decide

what I'd expected to hear. All that came to mind was the realiza-
tion I was nurturing a ferocious headache. "Do you want me to go
with you when you interrogate Eunice?"

"No. I don't want you to do anything except supervise the
pageant, Claire. Thus far we don't know what we're investigating—practical jokes, hit men from out of state, attempted suicide,
a maniac in an evening gown, or none of the above. But whatever
it may be, we will run the investigation without any volunteers."
He smiled at me, but I could see it wasn't all that easy for him. In
fact, I suspected it was all he could do not to shake a finger at me
like a stern, stubbly grandfather. After a moment of silence, he
said, "I know it will be a challenge to a meddler of your vast
experience and expertise, and I know it'll take a lot of willpower
and self-restraint, but this time I want you to stay out of it."

"I'll stay out of it. I simply don't like the idea of someone
lurking around my pageant stirring up mischief. It offends my
sense of decorum. If I have to endure this with a modicum of
grace, everyone else should have to do the same." I shrank back as
his eyes bored into me. My angelic smile faltered briefly, but did
not fail me. "Now, don't get all excited, Peter. I shall utilize all my
energy running the preliminary round of the pageant tonight."

He wasn't especially convinced, but he stood up and put his
notebook in his pocket. I suggested that he come by my apartment
later—not to tell me about the investigation, mind you, but to
have a companionable beer. Even less convinced, he nodded and
left to be officious elsewhere. Steve, Patti, and Warren must have
been hovering outside the door, for they came into the office before the smoke cleared.

"What's going on?" Steve demanded.

"Cyndi's out of danger and has been moved to a private room,"
Luanne said. She glanced at me, then added, "The police don't
know if it was an accident or attempted suicide."

Or attempted murder, I amended silently.

"Oh, my God," Warren said. He sat down next to me and

wiped his forehead with a handkerchief. "That poor girl. I can't believe she'd try to kill herself. She didn't have any reason to do something crazy like that. The last time I talked to her she was filled with all sorts of schemes about a career in Hollywood."

Patti's voice was soft but it held a hint of anger. "That girl was a schemer, all right. A cheap, little, two-bit schemer."

"She was just trying to do something with her life," Steve protested. "She had dreams of fame and riches, but she wasn't any more ambitious than a lot of girls her age. And she sure had a lot of them beat for looks."

Patti silenced him with a look that was hardly the sort to which he'd been referring. "That is not the topic of conversation," she added coldly.

"When was the last time you talked to Cyndi?" I asked Warren.

"Right after the trip to Hollywood," he said. His cheeks turned red and he looked down at his impeccably polished shoes. "Cyndi was scheduled for some pageant in a podunk town, and decided at the last minute not to compete. Eunice was so upset that she literally kept Cyndi sequestered in her bedroom until she agreed to break off the affair. It was probably best for everyone involved."

"The girl was a leech," Patti said. Steve started to protest, then closed his lips and turned away to scratch his head. Warren glanced up at his boss's wife, his expression enigmatic rather than outraged. He, too, turned away.

"So Cyndi wanted to run away to Hollywood to be a movie star," I said conversationally, hoping one of the three would hop back in the fray. No one seemed inclined to hop, and Luanne was frowning at her watch. I gave up on my devious ploy and said, "She may still have the opportunity, since she's already recovering from the ill effects of the gas. However, it's almost time for the preliminary, so I guess I'd better check with everyone."

Everyone seemed to know what to do without my admonitions or advice. The ticket booth was manned, as was the concession stand. The flowers had been arranged on the stage, and a table had been placed in front of the first row for the judges. Mayor Avery and Ms. Maugahyder were in place, legal pads positioned and pitchers of water within reach. Squeals and shrieks drifted from the greenroom; the escorts, visibly disappointed, waited in the west corridor. Eunice stood in the middle of the stage, arguing into the auditorium about the placement of the spotlights.

"If I put in another pink gel, they'll look like a flock of flamingos," muttered a voice from the dark.

"Complexion is everything," Eunice shot back. "We must enhance the rose tones of their complexions. The faint blush of a dewy rose, my dear man—not pink."

I wandered onward and found the audio booth, which was as dreary as Caron had avowed. Said avower was perched on a stool in front of an intimidating display of switches and glowing lights. To my surprise, she was not sulking. To my greater surprise, she was wearing a Viking helmet with two horns.

"That will look dandy with the black dress," I said from the doorway. "You'll look like a black angus out for a night on the town. Did Luanne slip it to you as an added inducement?"

"The door in the corner leads to the prop room. I found a key in a shoebox in that pile of junk, and decided to explore it instead of studying the really, really fascinating manual on electrons in the dark ages. Anyway, the room's covered with a zillion inches of dust and packed with all sorts of awesome stuff, like mooseheads and spears."

"Oh," I murmured.

"I've been thinking," Brunhilda continued, tilting her head until the helmet slipped over one eye, "that I have somewhat of an innate talent for the theater. I could really get into serious drama, like Shakespeare and old plays, or one of those avante-garde thingies where everybody gets naked and nobody knows why."

"Oh," I murmured.

"I can see myself on stage, in the big climactic scene. The object of all my love and devotion says he's my brother or my father or broke or already married, thus ripping my fragile psyche to tatters. Since life is no longer worth living, I take the dagger from my bodice"—she took a rubber dagger from her T-shirt—"and plunge it into my breast." She plunged it as threatened, rolled her eyes upward, and thoughtfully toppled off the stool with a series of strangled yelps meant to convey the shredding of her psyche.

"Oh," I murmured.

She made a few more noises as she wallowed in her version of death throes, then got up and brushed off her fanny. "I think I'll join the drama club, Mother. I'll get the lead in the next performance, and you can watch me die every night."

"Oh," I murmured, this time in farewell. I cruised back through the greenroom, across the stage where Eunice was still arguing dewy roses versus flamingos, ascertained that the judges were comfortable and equipped with necessities, and went up the corridor.

As I reached the top, I heard voices around the corner in the lobby. Although I had sworn not to involve myself in the investigation, I was curious enough to stop and listen. It was, I felt certain, my duty as assistant pageant director to keep an ear on things.

"Let me hear it one more time," Patti said in a voice devoid of any Southern warmth.

"The affair's been over for months," Warren said wearily. "I was madly infatuated with her, and she's a hot little number. I was sorry when she broke it off, but not devastated. It was just one of those steamy affairs, intense but short-lived."

"Very good, Warren. The twins might believe you. No one any older will, of course."

Intrigued, I crept forward. They moved away, however, and their voices were lost in the babble as the doors opened and the crowd began to drift in for the pageant. Showtime.

Several hours later I parked my car in the vicinity of the curb and went upstairs. Caron trailed after me, wailing steadily about Mac's assessment of her fine motor skills and her lineage. I should have been offended, in that I was hardly a matriarch of any of the species that he felt had produced such an inept offspring, but I was too damn tired.

I was sipping scotch and groaning over the next day's schedule when I heard Peter come up the stairs. I let him in, fetched him a beer, and settled down next to him on the sofa.

He studied my admittedly wan face. "A disaster, right?"

"It wasn't on par with the *Hindenburg* or the seventy-two election. It limped along without any major glitches, although we had an incessant run of minor ones. The girls were pinker than petunias onstage—complexion being everything—and the audio was spotty. The curtain closed on approximately half of the talent numbers, which wasn't all that tragic. We knew the damned dog would piddle in the middle of the stage, and piddle he did. In the interviews, eleven of the girls were majoring in communications but hoped to work with retarded children and do a bit of modeling. The remaining seven really, really admired Mother Teresa and the First Lady. They wanted to be surgeons, pediatricians, or just like Betty Crocker."

"Titillating and provocative answers to tough questions."

"No one was maimed, however, and we did achieve seven finalists for the production tomorrow night. We wiped away our tears, let the lucky finalists speak briefly into the cameras about how incredibly, totally thrilled they were, and sent everyone home. Luanne could barely hobble when I dropped her at her house; I'm worried she won't be able to show tomorrow night. Want to come?"

He put his arm around me. "No. Want to elope to Brazil?"

"No. Want another beer?"

"No. Want to hear about the investigation?"

I gave him a startled look. "What a peculiar thing for you to say, Lieutenant Rosen. One would almost suspect you'd listened to three renditions of 'The Impossible Dream' and gone berserk. In that I did indeed listen to them, perhaps I'm hallucinating."

"I am not suggesting you throw yourself into it, Claire. This beauty pageant thing escapes me, and I thought we might discuss it. You've had a chance to observe these people. What do you think has been going on?"

I tried to hide a tidal wave of smugness behind a pensive frown. "For one thing, Cyndi Jay seems to be somewhat different than the façade she presents to her fawning fans. Warren described her as a hot number who aspired to be a Hollywood starlet rather than a modest Miss America. When Steve attempted to defend her, Patti referred to her as, and I quote, 'a cheap, little, two-bit schemer.' All this about our sweet, cooperative, perky Miss Thurberfest. And Eunice said something about the girl lacking gratitude. Cyndi doesn't seem terribly popular with those who know her best, but I don't think she's a likely candidate for suicide."

"Then she's either terribly accident-prone or she was correct when she swore someone has been trying to hurt her—or kill her."

"There was the message on the mirror," I said, gnawing on my lip. "It could have been written by one of the contestants, although I can't imagine why. Luanne looked through their applications, and none of them was in a pageant before and therefore might have held a grudge. Once the judges choose the successor, Cyndi will become a nonentity, one of hundreds of thousands of small-town dethroned beauty queens, unless she wins the Big One, of course." I hummed a few bars to clue him in on the jargon.

"Or goes to Hollywood and becomes a big star," Peter said. "I haven't even seen her. Is that remotely possible?"

"She's pretty, although not breathtakingly so. I had a brief glimpse of her dancing, and it was adequate but uninspired. And I've been wondering all along if she was quite as sweet and sincere as she seemed, which means she's not Oscar material. I imagine she'll be one of the great horde of nameless, faceless girls who troop to Hollywood every year and end up as waitresses and, with luck, mute extras in crowd scenes."

"The producers won't drool over the opportunity to cast an ex–Miss Thurberfest?" Peter put down his beer and put his other arm around me. "I would be delighted to drool over the assistant beauty pageant director, however. I'm just a small-town cop who's easily impressed."

I evaded his mouth and said, "All this publicity might help her, though. If the national press picked up the story of a maniac stalking a beauty queen, they might decide to play it up for the human interest element. Even a story in a tabloid would give her an advantage over the horde."

Sighing, he picked up his beer and leaned back without a drop of drool. "But the press is much more enchanted with hit men and political figures. We've already had a call or two from the syndicated press boys, wanting to know if we can confirm the Senator's story about the shot. We can't, of course, because we don't have the convertible."

If he was alluding to some individual's lack of care in leaving car keys in an inviting location, I saw no reason to delve into it. "It's a great big convertible, all white and shiny. It has posters taped on the door and a bullet hole in the backseat. I'm surprised you and all the king's men can't find it, but I'm not trained in that sort of thing. I'm sure it will turn up sooner or later."

"We can't find the driver, either. He was supposed to return the car at four o'clock and occupy himself hosing down pickup trucks at the back of the lot, but he didn't appear. His boss says this is not remarkable, since Arnie has a fondness for sunny afternoons and booze. There were several comments made about the missing car and its value, and even a few mutters about the Thurberfest and a possible lawsuit."

"Do you think Arnie hopped in the car and went for a spin?"

"I don't know; we can't find him. I'm sure he'll turn up sooner or later," he said, flashing his teeth at me.

I politely overlooked his transparent attempt to needle me. "Did

Eunice have any enlightening opinions about Cyndi's frame of mind?"

"Once I convinced her to stop bellowing insults at the light booth, I asked her what she thought. She said Cyndi was perturbed that Senator Stevenson was to participate in the pageant, because that meant the aide would be there. The affair has been over for several months, but Eunice was concerned that her gal would have limp hair from the memories. On the contrary, she didn't seem especially concerned that her gal had almost died from asphyxiation a few hours earlier. She said Cyndi was upset about the pranks in the theater and the shot during the parade, but definitely not suicidal. On that note, she returned to insulting the ceiling of the auditorium. It was most peculiar."

"Did you question McWethy about the incidents in the theater?"

"Jorgeson did, and learned nothing useful. The nail wasn't sticking up earlier in the week, and the ropes were replaced last year. McWethy didn't see any unauthorized people in the theater, didn't write on the mirror, didn't fire a lethal weapon at the Senator, and didn't have any idea why the gas was on when the pilot wasn't."

"The mirror!" I yelped.

"As in looking glass. They apply a metallic silver substance to the back of glass, although I'm unclear on the details. I could look it up at the library if you really want to know, but—"

"Was the message on the mirror when you examined Cyndi's dressing room?"

"Had it been there, someone would have mentioned it," he said drily. "I didn't hear about it until you stirred yourself to report the shot. Cyndi's door was locked at that time, and we didn't go inside. Did it occur to you to mention the threat to us when it first was discovered?"

"Of course it did. But on the way to call you, I stopped to ask Mac about the weight, and then Luanne and I were sidetracked by Steve's arrival."

"An attractive variety of politician—if you like the blow-dry look."

"I suppose so," I said agreeably. "Then he and Eunice got into a shouting match, and Cyndi was overcome with the vapors. Rehearsal ran late. I was going to ask your advice over lunch, but I ended up running Luanne home to settle her in bed for the afternoon." I stopped rather abruptly and looked down at the ice cube bobbing in my glass. "Then I had to drive the car in the parade, and you know everything that happened after that point."

"So the message was wiped off between the rehearsal and your return to the theater at six. Who has a key to the dressing room?"

"Mac and Cyndi, I would guess. Mac was in the theater when Luanne and I left shortly after one. He's difficult to spot in the shadows, but he does seem to lurk about to keep an eye on things. I doubt anyone could sneak all the way down to the basement and back without being challenged."

"And keys to the front door of the theater?"

"Mac, again, and Luanne—but she was in bed with her ankle propped on pillows, and she gave it to me tonight so we can be sure of getting in the theater to rehearse tomorrow. I don't know who else might have a key. Most likely, Cyndi or Eunice decided to wipe off the lipstick with a tissue so that Cyndi wouldn't have to look at it and indulge in further bouts of hysteria." I didn't mention that I'd ordered the two to leave the message intact for the police, nor did I mention that Cyndi was slyly proud of her crude threat.

And I saw absolutely no reason to add that Luanne was elevating her ankle with the telephone unplugged. It was neither here nor there. She was my friend, and I was fairly certain something was wrong with her. It was connected in some opaque way with the beauty pageant. Luanne was not a petty, jealous woman, and I didn't believe for an instant that she had anything to do with the malicious pranks or the more malevolent turn of events.

I realized Peter was regarding me curiously, and pushed my

worries to a corner of my mind for later consideration. To distract him, I obligingly offered to accompany him to the hospital the following morning to question Cyndi Jay. My altruistic gesture resulted in a tedious lecture about civilian status, official investigations, meddling, and previous promises that had been made under duress and therefore not kept as well as some would have preferred. Pretty standard stuff.

I meekly acquiesced to everything he said, then announced through a yawn that it was midnight. I promised to keep my charming nose out of the official machinations, gave him a lingering kiss in the doorway, and went to my bedroom to decide how next to proceed. A gossipy chat with Patti Stevenson about Cyndi and Warren's torrid-turned-tepid affair? A candid chat with Mac about keys and weights? A booming chat with Eunice about the lipstick on the mirror? A really, really sincere chat with Julianna and Heidi about the mood in the communal dressing rooms?

The possibilities were delicious, but the proximity of the finals drove me to an uneasy sleep.

When I went into the kitchen the next morning, Caron was at the table, telephone glued to her ear. "She can't wear that orange dress," she said into the receiver. "And the green doesn't make her skin look sallow. It enhances her eyes. Well, it would if she'd use more eye shadow. That Emerald Reflections with the glitter, I should think, or Mystic Sea."

"Talking to Mary Kaye?" I asked as I put on the teakettle.

"Julianna's in the finals, Mother," Caron hissed at me. "She has some absolutely crazy idea about her orange dress. It makes me shudder just to imagine it, but Inez simply can't dissuade her. Will you talk to her?"

"I think I'll pass." I looked through the cabinets for anything at all to eat, but they were very much in the same sad state at Luanne's. I settled for the bottom of a vaguely blue hamburger bun and hid out in the living room until Caron stopped shrieking and hung up.

"What do the girls think about Cyndi's accident?" I called.

Caron came into the room with the top of the vaguely blue bun and a glass of milk. "They don't think it was An Accident, Mother. They think some horrid man tried deliberately to murder Cyndi. Dixie heard a male voice in the dressing room."

I almost dumped my tea in my lap. "When was that?"

"How should I know? All the finalists were really relieved to know that it wasn't one of them, because that would be too creepy for words. You can't exactly share your blusher with a schizo, or let her zip up your dress. She might strangle you!" Caron grasped her neck and stuck out her tongue at an oblique angle. Her eyelashes fluttered wildly, although she managed to watch me all the while.

"Very good. You're ready to graduate to poisoning and suffocation. I think I'll have a word with Dixie before the rehearsal this morning."

"Peter won't like it," she said, picking up her half-eaten bread and sprawling across a wing chair. "I heard him yelling at you last night. He'll have an absolute fit if you interfere in his investigation."

"Thank you, dear Abby. I have no intention of interfering in anything; I just thought the girl might feel more comfortable talking with a woman rather than a policeman."

"And you promised him you wouldn't ask one little question of anyone," she continued solemnly. "You promised, Mother, and you're always going on and on about keeping one's word and being honest. Don't you care about not lying to him?"

Ah, the perspicacity of youth. I thought of several justifications, all shaky, and a couple of self-righteous explanations, both weak. I selected the best of the lot and said, "I have no intentions of lying to him. The whole thing is a messy, ill-defined jumble of pranks, and no one's been seriously harmed."

"Luanne's on crutches, Cyndi's in the hospital, and the Senator barely missed a bullet between his eyes," she began, unimpressed by my sophistry. "Unless the bullet was meant for you, of course."

"Me? That's absurd, Caron. Senator Stevenson and Cyndi are deities of varying stature; I'm a mere pedestrian in the human race. I was coerced into chauffeuring them at the last moment. No one had any reason to think I'd be in the parade—or to shoot at me."

"Whatever, Mother." The coldblooded wretch popped the last of the moldy bread in her mouth. "I have to go to Inez's now. Julianna needs all the help she can get. Orange. I mean, really . . ." With a snort, she went into her room, and a few minutes later gave me a wave and left.

I hadn't moved. My tea was cold, my breakfast discarded. No one wanted to shoot booksellers, I assured myself—except for illiterati and television executives during sweeps month. No one had a motive. Not that I could think of a motive someone might have for trying to kill Miss Thurberfest, charming or not. A sweet girl or an ambitious schemer.

In the tradition of fictional amateur sleuths, I fetched a piece of paper and a much-gnawed pencil, then settled down to list everybody who had the least connection to the pageant. The contestants, initially eighteen but now the chosen seven, had no motive beyond jealousy, and the shot and the gas seemed a tad extreme. Mac had no motive. Eunice certainly wanted her gal healthy and curly for the Big One. Steve Stevenson and his wife had no reason to wish Cyndi harm. Warren might have been bitter and heartbroken, but if that was the case, he was hiding it well. Very well. I wrote down Sally's name, then crossed it out with a sigh. Mayor Avery and Ms. Maugahyder seemed a little remote from the events, although anyone who agreed to judge a beauty pageant was suspect on general principles.

The notion of hired thugs from New Jersey (or wherever they resided in the off-season) appealed, but it only made sense in relation to the incident during the parade. Surely we would have noticed men in black shirts and sunglasses if they had wandered in to watch a rehearsal.

I wadded up the paper and threw it in the direction of the wastebasket. I made another cup of tea and was considering a visit to my place of business to assess the effects of the Gala Sidewalk Sale on my next quarterly payment when the telephone rang. Hoping it wasn't Caron with a demand that I rush over to beat some sense into misguided Julianna, I cautiously picked up the receiver.

"Claire," Peter said, "I need you."

"I know you do, but I'm not ready for that kind of a commitment. Although I'm not the most self-sufficient woman of the eighties, I—"

"At the hospital. Cyndi Jay refuses to speak to anyone unless you're present. She says you're the only person she can trust."

"She said that?"

His voice was not happy. "That's what she said. I pointed out that this was a police investigation and that she had an obligation to answer my questions, but she refuses. We've had one round of hysterical tears thus far, and another is simmering."

What an intriguing quandry for him, I thought with a small smile. "Gee, Peter, I wish I could help you, but I don't want to meddle in official police business. I'd better go to the theater and see what's happening over there. But thanks for asking."

"I need you to come here so that I can get some answers from the girl. The Feds are here, and they are increasingly impatient to hear Cyndi's version of the shot. Will you come over here now?"

"Wowsy, the Feds and everything. It sounds too official for the likes of meddlesome me." I held the receiver away from my ear as he produced a string of testy words, then interrupted, saying, "If you're absolutely positive you want me to assist in the investigation, and you aren't going to mind that I—"

"Please come to the hospital."

I listened to his teeth grinding for a moment. "If you insist, I suppose I'll help this one time." I told him I'd be there before too long, and waltzed into my bedroom much like Caron Malloy on centerstage.

"E" I "G" H "T"

As I went through the hospital lobby, I saw a man with a television camera and the interviewer who'd caught me in front of Sally's cafe. I gave her a smile, received a blank look in return, and continued on to the elevators, pondering the ephemerality of fame. The nurse at the desk raised an eyebrow when I asked for Cyndi's room, but gestured down the hallway.

Peter met me at the door. "Thanks for coming, Claire. The girl still refuses to say a word to anyone, and the boys from the FBI are ready to indict her—or throttle her. Others of us might assist."

"I have no idea why she chose me as her confidante, but I'll do my best." I went to the bed and gazed down at Cyndi, whose eyes were closed. Her hair was neatly curled over one shoulder and she'd found the strength to apply makeup, but her face seemed pale. "Hi, Cyndi," I said softly.

Her eyes opened in a mascaraed flutter. "Mrs. Malloy, how kind of you to come. I just didn't know where to turn, and you've been so great." She clutched my hand with strong, white fingers neatly capped with pink nails. "I'm frightened. There's a madman out there who's trying to kill me, but no one will listen to me. They all say it's some political feud or something. It's not, though. Make them believe me, Mrs. Malloy!"

"I'll try. I would have thought you'd prefer to have Eunice with you, since you've known her so much longer."

A conservative man in a conservative suit stepped out of a corner. "How long have you know Eunice Allingham?" he asked. A second man hovered discreetly behind him.

Cyndi blinked at me, then said, "Three years, I guess. She owns a discount beauty-supply house, and I shopped there so much we became friends. My parents died when I was twelve, and I lived with my great-aunt until I got my apartment last year. My great-aunt does her best, but Eunice has been like a mother to me. She shops with me and helps me try new hair styles. She makes sure I eat a healthy diet, so that my ends won't split." She delicately lifted up her hair so that we could confirm the durability of her ends.

I blinked at Cyndi. "Then why don't you want her to hold your hand and offer moral support now?" The two FBI agents were blinking, as was Peter, but I ignored them all. "It does seem more logical," I persisted.

"She doesn't believe me," Cyndi said through a sniffle. "I need someone who believes me, Mrs. Malloy, and you're the only person in the whole, entire world that I can trust."

Peter came to the side of the bed. "Will you tell us what happened during the parade?"

As trustee, I allowed the girl to continue clutching my hand while she recited the story of the nail, the weight, the mirror, and the shot (fired directly at her, close enough that she felt heat on her thigh, and missing her only because of a tiny bump in the street). We waited for her to continue, but her eyes welled with tears and she began to fumble for another tissue.

Once she'd blotted her cheeks, Peter said, "What happened in your dressing room yesterday afternoon?"

"I don't know."

One of the Feds let out a little explosion of breath. "You went to your dressing room to wait for the police, Miss Jay. Did anyone accompany you at that time?"

"No, everyone was too busy listening to Senator Stevenson describe his so-called brush with death. Nobody seemed to care that I was the one who was almost killed, that I was the target of this madman on the roof. It may have been dangerous for me to go to the basement by myself, but I just had to be alone so I could figure out how to protect myself."

"Was anyone in the basement at that time?" the second Fed asked.

"I didn't see anyone. I was sitting at the table, looking at that nasty message on the mirror and trying to think who could be that horrid. All of a sudden, the lights went out. Mrs. Malloy can tell you that it's like a cave down there—no windows or cracks or anything. Well, I almost had a heart attack right then. It was awful."

The Feds moved forward, enthralled by the narrative. "And then what happened, Miss Jay?" one of them said.

"My head just exploded; it was like a light show at a rock concert. I woke up this morning in the hospital with a sore throat and the worst headache of my life. A nice young orderly had to tell me where I was—and why."

Peter glanced across the bed at the two agents. "The doctor had no reason to examine the area until she woke up this morning and complained of the pain. There's a contusion an inch above her right ear. The blow was enough to make her unconscious, although it wouldn't have done any permanent damage beyond a bump and some bruising afterward."

I sank down on the end of the bed and stared up at Peter. "Someone really did try to kill her. He knocked her out, taped the keyhole, turned on the gas, and locked the door on his way out. There is a maniac stalking this girl."

"I knew I could count on you, Mrs. Malloy," the victim said with a teary smile of gratitude.

"I'll do everything I can," I said as I patted her foot through the blanket. I turned to gaze at the Feds. "What have you found out about this sniper? Did anyone see anything or hear the gun when it was fired? How about the people along the sidewalk?"

One sucked on his lip. The other looked across the bed and said, "Does this woman ride with your posse, sheriff? Is she packing a six-shooter and a shiny tin badge?"

"I am here by invitation," I reminded them with a cool smile. "It's rather obvious to those who were awake for the last five minutes that someone is attempting to kill Cyndi during the pageant. She's been trying to tell us, but we haven't taken her seriously." I patted her foot again. "Do you have any idea who this person might be?"

"It has to be a pitiful sex maniac," she whispered. "I get along just great with everyone, and everyone seems to like me."

Peter and the Feds asked her numerous questions, but she continued to swear she had no clues to the identity of anyone who might try to hurt her. She listed the pageants she'd been in over a three-year span. No, she assured us, the girls were all too nice to nurse a grudge. She was a communications major but had no problems in the department. No time for friends or outside activities, since the pageants required all her free moments. Warren had been her first and only boyfriend. She'd been really, really sad when she broke up with him, but the relationship was distracting her and concentration was, well, it was like everything in the pageants. No, she hadn't laid eyes on him for six months, although she understood he was still the Senator's aide and likely to be around during the Miss Thurberfest events.

She broke off the monologue and looked at me. "How did it go last night, Mrs. Malloy?"

"It went just fine," I said mendaciously. "We canceled the opening number, since you weren't there, and the other parts of the program went fairly smoothly. We'll miss you tonight."

Her face crumpled and she sank back into the pillow. "I'm truly disappointed that I won't be there. I mean, it's such a special moment when a reigning queen has a chance to tell everyone what a special year she's had, and how much it's meant to her. When she crowns her successor, I use up a whole box of tissues; I honestly do." She fluttered at the three men. "I'd like to rest now. My head is still throbbing from that horrible gas, and I can't think of a single thing I haven't told you."

Peter and his friends left the room, murmuring among themselves. As I got up, Cyndi said, "I can't thank you enough for believing me, Mrs. Malloy. You've been wonderful. Could I ask one tiny favor before you leave?"

"Certainly," I said.

"Would you bring me my cosmetic bag? One of those nurses put it away in the closet, and I hate to think what those silly old tears did to my mascara. I told Eunice to bring the waterproof kind, but she brought this cheap stuff instead."

I found a lumpy pouch on a shelf in the closet and gave it to her. "Shall I ask a nurse to bring you something for your headache?"

"No, you've been too kind already. If I lie here quietly, I'll feel better. Perhaps if you closed the blinds just a tad. . . ?"

I closed the blinds just a tad and tiptoed out of the room. All sorts of medical persons busily strode past, dressed in pastels. A lady in a gray dress pushed a cart piled with magazines and candybars. An orderly mopped a swath down the middle of the hall. A teenaged girl in a pink pinafore gave me an incurious look as she carried a vase of flowers to some deserving soul. Peter was nowhere to be seen.

Frowning, I went to the elevators and jabbed the button. He might have had the decency to wait for me. He might have wanted to ask my opinion. He might have introduced me to his friends, although I would have been somewhat reserved after the wisecracks in Cyndi's room.

The elevator arrived. When the doors opened, I found myself

face to face with the woman interviewer. I smiled, she looked blank, and I decided to use the stairs. Once in the lobby, I went to the pay telephone and called my clerk at the Book Depot. She reported that business was better than usual, and that a short, rosy woman who'd come by to pick up a report was very disappointed not to find one. We discussed what books might be put on the table under the portico in honor of the unreported sidewalk sale, then I hung up and walked slowly across the parking lot.

The television van was parked a few rows back. I stopped to stare at it. At some earlier time, Peter had said there'd been enough publicity already. Eunice was worried that bad publicity would mar the innocence of the pageant. Luanne had said the only scheduled press conference was the one immediately after the preliminary round.

I got into my battered car and drove to Luanne's, my forehead still creased as I thought of all the publicity there'd been in the last two days. Steve Stevenson had held an impromptu interview in front of Sally's cafe at the time of the luncheon. The press had converged on the theater less than ten minutes after Steve, Cyndi, and I had arrived in the convertible. I suspected Cyndi Jay was currently answering questions in her hospital room.

Luanne was sitting on her porch, a glass of tea in one hand and a stalk of celery in the other. With a sniff of disdain for the celery, I joined her and said, "Don't you have any Twinkies?"

"No, and I don't have any cellulite, either. Why are you scowling so fiercely?"

"There has been entirely too much publicity."

"That may depend on your point of view. If you're a candidate for political office, there's no such thing as too much publicity. Some of those people have been known to pay good money for it, you know. They like it."

"Every time I turn around someone's holding a press conference," I continued. "Before the luncheon, after the parade, after the pageant, and now in Cyndi's hospital room."

"I fear you may have cellulite of the brain. Here, have some celery. Did you know it takes more calories to eat celery than celery has, which means it's a negative caloric situation?"

I told her about the interview in Cyndi's hospital room. She was as appalled as I had been that someone had made a serious attempt on Cyndi's life. I listed everyone I could think of with any involvement in the pageant, and we both agreed we could spot no motives.

"So what's the deal about publicity?" she asked, once we'd abandoned the futile discussion. I told her about meeting the television interviewer and cameraman in the lobby and again in the elevator. She was not exactly dumbstruck, although she managed a faint frown for my benefit.

"Then you suspect the media are conspiring to murder Miss Thurberfest?"

"No," I said irritably, "I was simply wondering why they've appeared at the critical moments."

"Steve's interview before the luncheon was hardly critical."

I took a stalk of celery and bit into it with unnecessary vigor. After a minute of loud mastication, I had it. "Maybe not for him. But Cyndi found the message on her mirror that morning. She might have wanted to offer her astounding discovery to the viewing public, and then lost her chance when Steve turned on the dimples. She was watching him through the window, and she looked perturbed."

"She may have felt she deserved some of the attention, but that doesn't mean . . . whatever it doesn't mean. She was a little bit jealous."

"Or extremely irritated—if she'd called the press and arranged for them to show up at the cafe. They did as suggested, but found a real live political candidate and jumped him. And that afternoon when we returned to the theater, I left her alone in the office while I went to find Mac. When I came back to the lobby less than ten minutes later, there were television cameras and reporters again, all screaming questions. Cyndi must have called them; otherwise, how would they have known something newsworthy had happened?"

Luanne jabbed me with a piece of celery. "And of course she was furious when they ignored her and went for the hit-man theory. She stomped down to her dressing room to sulk, and that's when someone bopped her."

"One of the girls heard a male voice in the dressing room," I added excitedly, then deflated. "But I don't know when Dixie heard the voice. It couldn't have been at that point, anyway, because the contestants weren't in the theater. They were home napping or padding or gluing together split ends. I wonder whose voice she heard?"

"For some mysterious reason, there aren't all that many men in a beauty pageant. We've got the two male judges: Steve and Mayor Avery. Steve's aide appeared for the first time yesterday afternoon. McWethy is always skulking around the theater."

"I think we can eliminate Mayor Avery; he's followed his schedule religiously, which means he hasn't been bothering us, and his major concern seems to be keeping his eyeballs in their sockets when confronted by a svelte thing in a leotard. He had to struggle last night not to howl like Chou-Chou. It has to be one of those three, and Warren's the most likely candidate to go to Cyndi's dressing room for a chat about the good old steamy days."

Luanne chewed pensively on the celery. "But he didn't appear at the theater until late yesterday afternoon. The girls were gone. We agreed a few minutes ago that he doesn't have a motive. No one has a motive."

"Someone must have a motive to murder Miss Thurberfest. Otherwise, we'll have to fall back on the maniac-off-the-street business, and you know how I hate that in mystery novels."

"We're not in a mystery novel. Maybe it's a sloppy muddle without a stringer of red herrings, a cast of characters with highly suspicious motives, and a divinely dramatic denouement in the last chapter. We don't have a parlor in which to stage the denouement; we have a stage populated by girls who twirl batons and interpret feelings. For that matter, we don't have a corpse, one of the more essential elements."

"And we can't have a murderer without a corpse."

"You're blotching, Claire. I'd prefer to think you're not disappointed that Miss Thurberfest wasn't fatally asphyxiated."

I gave her a cool look as I stood up. "Don't be absurd. I certainly don't want someone to murder Cyndi so that I can exercise my little gray cells—which have no cellulite deposits on them. I am deeply relieved that the girl has recovered, especially since I now seem to be her best friend and advisor. It's not a murder mystery; ergo, we don't have an official police investigation for me to interfere in. I'm going to the theater to see if I can have a word with Dixie before the rehearsal. I can catch Mac afterward, and then run by the hotel for a word with Warren and Steve."

"Aren't you a little bit worried about that policeman of yours?"

"He's not the least bit worried about me. Are you coming to the theater for the rehearsal so that you can waggle your finger at me?"

"If you can bear more blotches, I think I'd better hobble inside and elevate this damn ankle until tonight. I'll make the vital calls from here. All you need to do is arrange the talent schedule and let the girls run through tonight's opening number. Then you may play Miss Marple to your heart's content—as long as Peter doesn't catch you in midclue."

"I have no idea where he is at the moment," I said. "He and his friends from the FBI are probably fingerprinting rooftops or scraping tire tread off Thurber Street. No one suggested I tag along."

"Is someone's hypotenuse bent just a degree or two?"

"Perhaps."

I drove to the theater and curled up with the notebook in the office. Luanne had made several pages of terribly cryptic scribbles that I assumed had something to do with the production number.

A choreographer I was not. A cryptologist I was not. A qualified assistant pageant director I was not, nor was I a brilliant logician who could put her finger on the villain in the plot. If there was a plot.

I dismissed the heresy and called Luanne. I let the telephone ring twenty times before replacing the receiver, telling myself that she had unplugged it as before. It was an irritating habit, I decided, but nothing more. I made a mental note to mention as much to her, then picked up the notebook and walked down the corridor to the auditorium.

The seven finalists were on the stage. Julianna had breezed through the preliminary round with interpretive ease. Heidi and Chou-Chou had survived, no doubt partly because the judges and audiences anticipated further canine catastrophes. Bambi McQueen, a dedicated twirler, was whispering with Lisa R., who'd realized an impossible dream, and Lisa K., who had stopped the show with her recitation of an original poem, "America: My Country 'Tis for Me." The sixth finalist, a hefty girl named Bobbi Jo, was also a twirler, although she spiced up her act by blindfolding herself and torching the tips of her baton. The seventh finalist was the clarinet-playing, eavesdropping, loquacious Dixie.

"How's Cyndi?" Julianna asked as I joined them.

"She's doing fine. She looks a little pale, but she doesn't seem to have suffered any permanent effects from the accident. You might want to stop by the hospital for a short visit, or call her. At the moment, however, we have a serious dilemma. Mrs. Bradshaw can't come in today to help with the opening number, and I can't figure out what her scribbles mean. Does anyone have any brilliant ideas?"

Heidi belied my opinion of her by suggesting a variation of the number they'd worked on for the preliminary round. We discussed the schedule for the talent presentations and the various elements of the spectacle, then I left them to argue over who would dazzle the judges from Cyndi's mark on the center of the stage.

As I went up the corridor, I considered the wisdom (or lack thereof) of calling Peter to relate my significant insight into the "leaks" to the press. He might be grateful. Then again, he might sigh mournfully and reiterate his sermon on amateurs and professionals. He might stoop to personal remarks. Steeling myself, I took the civic-minded approach and called him. Once I'd dutifully related my hot theory, I leaned back in the chair behind the desk and waited for a blast of hot air from the receiver.

It was more of a mild breeze. "You just can't keep your nose out of it, can you?" he said, chuckling.

Chuckling? I wrinkled my meddlesome nose and said, "Sorry to disturb you, Lieutenant. Perhaps the pageant has destroyed my mind. I assumed you might be interested in knowing how Cyndi manipulated the press."

"Thus proving. . . ?"

"I don't happen to know what is thus proven. Something very vital, I'm sure." I tugged on the drawers while I tried to find something very vital in the theory that Cyndi Jay was determined to get all the publicity she could before her voluntary abdication.

"I've got an interesting tidbit for you," he said, still sounding amused. "The State Police found the convertible in front of a tavern in Starley City. They found its driver inside the Dew Drop Inn, and according to the report, Arnie was thrilled to have someone with whom to share a beer."

"Then Arnie simply wandered up the street, saw the car, and felt an obligation to repossess it?"

"He said those were his instructions, although he wasn't at all sure who issued them, and the officer who took the statement said the alleged car thief was not noticeably articulate after an eighteen-hour marathon at the Dew Drop Inn. Arnie then claimed it was his duty because of a certain politician's driving skills. I thought you drove the car in the parade."

I explained Arnie's confusion, then said, "What about the caliber of the bullet? Can you determine from the angle where the sniper might have stood?"

"The car is at the lab, and I expect a report fairly soon. The FBI agents are hovering over the lab boys, who are not delighted by the supervision. Arnie is asleep in a cell, although we'll probably just boot him out when he sobers up. His boss has declined to press charges. Hold on for a minute, Claire."

He put me on hold and I fumed to a saccharin version of a sixties rock tune for nearly five minutes. I was about to hang up and redial when he came back on the line.

"The report from ballistics just came in," he said, "accompanied by two irate Feds. The bullet was a blank."

"A blank?" I echoed (yes, blankly). "What does that mean?"

"Well, it means no one made a serious attempt on Senator Stevenson's life, or on Cyndi Jay's, if she's your candidate. The bullet would have stung like hell, but it wouldn't have killed either of them. The Feds are now growling about false pretenses, obstruction of governmental operations, and the consumption of their time and the taxpayers' money. We're going to the Senator's hotel for a chat."

I hung up the receiver and leaned back in the chair. The bullet was a blank, not intended to hurt anyone. The only danger we'd been in was from the reporters and television crews afterward. More publicity, leaked to the press by Miss Thurberfest and reaped by Steve. Could everything that had happened in the last three days have been mischievous pranks? No, I thought morosely, the attempted asphyxiation hardly fell into that category.

But if I put it aside, I could envision the others as publicity stunts. Steve liked the free publicity, but he had rather lucked into it. Cyndi, on the other hand, would have profited greatly from it. She had lucked out of it, but not from any lack of effort on her part. Steve had upstaged her due to his position.

The nail was on her mark. Cyndi couldn't have anticipated that

Luanne would come onstage and essay a middle-aged kick on that very spot. Had Cyndi been the victim, perhaps she would have stumbled but caught herself. The weight had missed her. So had the bullet, which wasn't life-threatening anyway. And the message on the mirror—had the unsuccessful murderer wiped it off, or had Cyndi? When she went to her dressing room, she was aware the police would join her. Could she have felt it prudent to clean off the lipstick before the police could take photographs and send a sample to the lab?

I almost tipped over backward as I remembered a small incident when Eunice and I first saw the message. Cyndi had wiped her cheeks with a tissue, and the tissue had left red streaks on her cheeks. Sanguine red streaks, as if the tissue had been used to clean off her fingers or erase a sloppy letter from the mirror.

My hand trembled as I evinced my civic duty and called the number of the Farberville police station. I subsequently learned that Peter and the Feds had left the building. I called Luanne and determined her telephone was still unplugged. I could think of only one other person with whom I wished to speak, but decided the conversation would be best conducted in person. Over sanitized sheets in the hospital room.

I went down to the auditorium to check on my charges. My daughter the budding dramatist was standing on the judges' table, while her less flamboyant friend cowered in a seat in the front row. The seven finalists were scattered around the stage, their expressions rebellious.

"We need to see some vitality," Caron said imperiously. "You're not going to win over the audience if you flop like a bunch of rag dolls. Now this time, let's have vitality." She cued Inez with a penetrating glance, and Inez obediently pushed the button of a cassette player. "One, two, three—kick! Move it, girls, move it!"

The girls, who were all three or four years older than their dictatorial director, moved it. The results were not appalling. We wouldn't open on Broadway any time soon, but we wouldn't have to fish anyone out of the orchestra pit, either. Contemplating how badly my standards had slipped in the last few days, I went onto the stage and congratulated the finalists on the dexterity of the production.

"Can we leave now?" one of the Lisas sniveled. "This place gives me the creeps."

"You look a little creepy," Bambi murmured.

"Do I detect a hint of jealousy in your voice? Or is it more obvious in the quivering of your thighs?"

"That's enough," Caron said from the table. "I don't think we need to run through it again, and all of you need to go home and rest for the performance tonight. Let's have everyone back at six sharp, refreshed and brimming with vitality."

Julianna gave Caron a lethal look, but managed to rally a sweet smile as she turned to me. "Can we use the dressing rooms in the basement, Mrs. Malloy? The greenroom's awfully crowded."

"It smells like dog piss," a Lisa added.

Heidi bristled like a pit terrier. "If it does, it's not Chou-Chou's fault. I won't name names, but someone has a week's worth of dirty underwear in her bag. It reeks worse than the boys' locker room."

"You ought to know. After all, you've certainly visited it upon occasion, haven't you? That's what the guys say."

I told myself that they were simply gripped with prefinals terrors. I gave Caron a look as lethal as Julianna's, then said, "Yes, you may use the two side dressing rooms tonight, although Cyndi's is sealed. The number looks great, as do all of you. Would you please come to the theater at six so you'll have time to arrange your swimsuits, evening gowns, and talent costumes?"

"And try to be refreshed," Caron muttered sullenly. She climbed off the table and flopped down next to Inez, since no canvas directors' chairs were available.

As the girls started off the stage, I caught Dixie's arm. "Could I have a word with you?"

"I swear I'll get the steps down tonight. I do just fine until I think about the people watching and then I forget which count we're on. But I know I can do it, Mrs. Malloy; I took three hours of freshman dance appreciation and got a B plus."

"She should have taken basic arithmetic," Caron said in an aside to Inez. It carried to the back row of the auditorium.

I dragged Dixie to the area behind the curtain. "No, that's not what I wanted to discuss. Someone mentioned that you heard a male voice in Cyndi's dressing room yesterday. I need to know what time you heard it."

She stepped back. "I don't know. I mean, it was like yesterday and I was a wreck because of the competition. My mother made me eat an early supper, and I just about barfed I was so nervous. Taco salad, too."

"Dixie, this is important. Please try to estimate the time that you heard the male voice."

"I'm too nervous to think," she said, shaking her head at me. "Last night I was so ecstatic that I couldn't even sleep. Right now I can't think of anything except my clarinet piece and what I'll do if I get runs in all my panty hose. I brought six pairs, but maybe I'll stop and buy another one or two. Can you see the judges selecting someone that has a railroad track down her calf? It'd be ludicrous, Mrs. Malloy."

I wished I had a railroad tie in my hand. I took a deep breath and said, "I understand how nervous you are, dear. Why don't you buy the extra pairs of panty hose, then go home and lie down? Perhaps then you'll remember what time you heard the voice in Cyndi's dressing room, and you can call me."

"I have to practice my clarinet sonata. There's this one section that's like really high-pitched, and if my reed is too wet I get this awful screech."

I knew she wasn't bluffing; I'd heard the results of a wet reed the night before. "Yes, you go home and practice for a bit—and then think about my question. Will you do that?"

"Yeah," she said over her shoulder as she fled toward the greenroom.

Sherlock Holmes never had to deal with witnesses terrified by the vision of a panty hose crisis. I went down to the floor of the auditorium and suggested that the director and her assistant vacate the premises.

"You know, Mother," Caron said, "if we had the girls move counterclockwise while doing the touch-kick-touch step, we could—"

"Take five dollars from my purse and squander it on the sidewalk sale and the street festival," I said with great restraint. "Hot dogs, nachos, cotton candy, popcorn. Bargains galore. Bed races. Jugglers. You'll love it. Sally Fromberger promises."

Caron gave me a pitying smile. "We don't eat that sort of thing anymore. The camera adds at least ten pounds, and we don't want to look pudgy. Isn't that right, Inez? I mean, if we have even one inch of fat, we won't get the best roles."

Although Inez had brightened momentarily when I listed the potential goodies, she nodded. "Actresses have to work out every day, and they keep on a very strict diet of caviar and champagne."

"We'll have that for dinner," I said. "In the meantime, leave this building and don't come back until six thirty. The finalists resembled a lynch mob, and I can't say I blamed them."

"Some people simply can't accept constructive criticism," Caron sniffed. She poked Inez, who dutifully sniffed, then the two of them stalked out of the auditorium and up the corridor, one of them propounding loudly on rag dolls and ingrates and the other murmuring in the same vein.

The door to the greenroom opened and the seven finalists went up the west corridor, every one of them an ingrate if their discussion was a valid indication. After a minute, the door in the lobby banged closed. I glanced at my watch. It was one o'clock, which meant we were right on schedule. It also meant I could run by the hospital and tell Cyndi that I knew she was responsible for the series of pranks that had supposedly befallen her.

Then, if I could find a free minute, I might run by the police station and explain to Peter and his friends that they had been on the wrong track. Barking up the wrong tree. Making snooty remarks about the wrong person. Not, of course, that I'd allow any superiority to creep into my voice, or let my mouth curl up in a smug fashion. I'd just sit back and wait for them to acknowledge that, while they were pestering Senator Stevenson, I'd simply analyzed the situation and arrived at the truth.

I was having a wonderful time imagining all this when I heard the lobby door slam. I waited for footsteps to come down the corridor. The theater remained silent. Reminding myself that Mac was somewhere, I went up the corridor and looked around the lobby. Perhaps Mac had come in and retreated to the light booth, I thought as I stopped in the office to get my purse and the ubiquitous notebook. In any case, I wanted to talk to Cyndi as soon as possible.

I drove to the hospital, and rode the elevator to Cyndi's floor, still caught in my reverie of Peter's congratulations and the Feds' abashed expressions. My smile faded as I opened the door to Cyndi's room and saw an obscenely obese man on the hospital bed.

"Hiya, honey," he said. "You got the bedpan?"

"Where's Cyndi Jay?"

"I don't reckon I know. What I do reckon is you'd better get the bedpan over here right quick."

I hurried down the hall to the nurses' station. "Where did you move Cyndi Jay?" I asked a nurse with stern black hair and a harried frown.

"I didn't move her anywhere, nor did anyone on the staff. The patient decided to leave without her physician's permission. Outside of utilizing physical restraints, there was no way to stop her."

"When did she leave?"

"More than an hour ago. If you require further information, you'll have to speak to her attending physician. He makes rounds at six o'clock tonight."

"But she did leave voluntarily?" I said, perplexed.

"She made several extremely rude remarks and stomped out like a pouty child. For some reason, she seems to feel the hospital is more of a television studio than a place to care for the sick. Once I shooed that cameraman and interviewer out of her room, the patient became most abusive and said she was leaving." The nurse shot me an unprofessional look. "I hope she collapsed in the lobby for the camera's benefit—without her mascara."

"And you have no idea where she went?"

"I was not at all interested in her destination." The nurse picked up a clipboard and strode down the hall to administer TLC to a more worthy patient, whether he desired it or not.

It seemed we'd lost Miss Thurberfest.

"N" "I" "N" "E"

The elevator door opened. Eunice Allingham gave me a vaguely surprised look, then started down the hallway toward Cyndi's room, a small canvas bag swishing briskly at her side.

"She's not there," I said. "She left an hour ago."

Eunice halted and, after a pause, came back to join me. "Oh, that's good news. The doctor must think she's completely recovered if he's already sent her home."

"The doctor hasn't seen her lately. It seems the floor nurse was not willing to allow the camerman and the interviewer to linger in Cyndi's room for a little press conference. Cyndi was so miffed that she packed her bags and walked out. I suppose she went to her apartment."

Eunice shook her head. "She wasn't there fifteen minutes ago. I stopped by to fetch her a pretty nightgown and a few things, and the apartment was vacant." Her eyes narrowed. She crossed her arms and leaned forward to peer at me. "That aide, Warren Dansberry—did he come to the hospital to visit the gal?"

"I have no idea," I admitted. "He certainly could have been here."

"That young man cannot be trusted, any more than his boss. The Senator promised he'd keep Warren away from Cyndi, but I didn't believe him at the time. If he weren't a capable liar, then he couldn't be a politician. I can see it all as clearly as I can spot a potential winner in a pageant well before the talent presentations. Warren either came here or called Cyndi to suggest she meet him at some sleazy motel for a continuation of that tasteless affair. Poor Cyndi was so dizzy from the gas that she probably didn't know what she was saying when she agreed to meet him. This is vile, vile, vile. We must take steps immediately."

I resisted the urge to click my heels and salute. "We don't know that the two are in a sleazy motel. Cyndi might have gone to a friend's house. She might be at her great-aunt's house, or shopping, or . . ." I shrugged, out of ideas where Miss Thurberfest might be at the moment.

"There is no time to lose," Eunice continued. "This town is riddled with sleazy motels, and that man is devious enough to register under an alias. Not that he would do so to protect Cyndi's reputation, of course. He undoubtedly aspires to follow in his boss's path. Warren Dansberry is a very dangerous young man. I've said it before, and I do not hesitate to say it again."

She said it with such volume that a nurse carrying a tray stopped to stare, and patients along the hallway peeped out of their rooms. I took Eunice's arm and led her toward the elevator.

As we waited, I said, "We can't raid every motel in town. Heaven knows how many city directors, lawyers, doctors, and judges we might find *in flagrante delicto* on a sunny Saturday afternoon. We could go by the Senator's hotel, however, and see if he has any theories."

She muttered in agreement and followed me to my car. We drove down the street in relative silence, she huffing like an over-aged jogger and I frantically praying Peter would be gone by the time we appeared at the Senator's doorstep. Wincing at the possibility, I suggested we swing by Cyndi's apartment, the great-aunt's house, Eunice's house, and even my apartment next to the campus.

"Why would she be there?" Eunice said, eyeing me intently.

"She wanted me to be at the hospital this morning while she

was questioned by the police and the FBI. She seemed to think I was the only person who would believe she was being stalked by a madman."

"Is that what she said?" Eunice turned her head to stare out the window. "And did you believe her, Claire?"

"I did at the time," I said with a grimace. "Now I'm not so sure. I'm beginning to suspect Cyndi arranged those little pranks in order to get publicity. She could easily have staged the incidents with the nail, the weight, and the message on her mirror." Love of humanity required me to pay attention to the driving, although I wished I could see Eunice's face. "The bullet fired during the parade was a blank. I suppose the shot could have been fired to frighten the Senator, but it's equally likely that Cyndi arranged it in hopes the media would think it was fired at her. If that is indeed the case, then she had to have an accomplice."

"An accomplice? I suppose she would have needed one, wouldn't she?" Eunice said slowly. She shifted the overnight bag in her lap, arranged the sun visor above the windshield to her satisfaction, then turned to study my profile. "Do you think I crouched on the the rooftop of a bar in order to fire a gun at the convertible? I'm a fifty-one-year-old woman who's overweight, out of shape, and hardly a member of the National Rifle Association. Don't you find it hard to imagine me in the role of a calculating sniper?"

I had been thinking that precise thing, but she had a point. "It had to be someone who was willing to take a risk for the perceived betterment of Cyndi's career," I said at last.

"Beauty pageant queens do not desire that sort of publicity. The gals represent a fragile fairyland where poise, charm, and beauty are everything. They've won a piece of the dream and they cherish it as they would a delicate butterfly. Negative publicity might give the public the idea that the gal is involved with undesirable people—like Warren Dansberry or Senator Stevenson. Yes, there are some things I could tell you about the golden boy with the dimples."

"Oh?" I said encouragingly.

"But I shall not say a word. I never allow my gals to gossip, and I refuse to set a bad example. Now I shall give you directions to those various places, although I am certain we won't find Cyndi. Once we've wasted our time, we will go to the hotel and confront the Senator."

Eunice's porch was unoccupied, and Cyndi's great-aunt was sure that she had seen neither hide nor hair of her niece. My porch was cluttered only with leaves. Cyndi's apartment, one of dozens in a pseudogarden setting, was messy but empty. On the way to the hotel we stopped by the theater, but the doors were locked and the interior dark.

We took a circuitous route to avoid the Thurberfest, and eventually found a parking place in front of the hotel. As we entered, I crossed my fingers and mentally transported Peter and the Feds to a distant locale, but once Eunice had pounded on the door and we were ushered into the hallowed suite, I discovered that my telepathic powers were, as usual, inadequate.

Patti Stevenson brightly introduced everyone. The Feds were disgruntled to see me, and Peter managed nothing more than a grim smile. I mumbled something about needing to discuss the evening schedule with Senator Stevenson, but it was such a feeble ploy that everyone graciously ignored it. I opted for a corner chair, feeling as if I'd been caught shoplifting in a bargain basement.

In contrast, Eunice was unswayed by the invisible currents in the room. "Where is Warren Dansberry?" she asked the Senator's wife. "I demand to see him at once."

"He and Steve took the twins to the street festival," Patti said, remarkably composed for someone caught in the eye of the storm. "I needed a break, and it requires at least two people to chase after Cassie and Carrie. They ought to be back soon."

"Why are you looking for Dansberry?" a Fed asked.

Eunice turned on him. "Because he is responsible for Cyndi's abrupt departure from the hospital. Although it was voluntary, I can sense his insidious presence. He may be with this woman's children at this time, but I am more than confident he has planned a tryst with the gal."

"She left the hospital?" the Fed said. He and his cohort had a whispered conversation. I could see Peter was itching to join them, but civil service has its privileges. He passed the time shooting dark glances at me, which I excused on the premise he was offended by his exclusion. One of the Feds went into another room and closed the door. The other said, "Once we've confirmed this, I think we can terminate the investigation, Rosen. The girl got wind of the results of the lab report. She knows we're aware the bullet was a blank and therefore part of some crazy scheme of hers to get free publicity. She obviously has fled to avoid further questions."

"She has not," Eunice snorted.

Patti went to Peter's side and put her hand on his arm. "Then you won't have to question Steve? He truly had nothing to do with the girl's misguided ideas. He may have leaped to an erroneous conclusion about the sniper, but I can assure you that he never intended to mislead you or the FBI agents. He's wanted all along to offer you his fullest cooperation."

Peter glanced at me, no doubt assessing my reaction to the hand resting on his arm. I smiled politely and said, "Then you aren't interested in where Cyndi Jay is at this time? What about the attempt to asphyxiate her in her dressing room?"

"We have reason to believe she was responsible for that, too," he said. "That aspect of the official police investigation is under local jurisdiction, and we'll need to question her concerning it. At the moment, however, her whereabouts are not pressing. Someone will go by her apartment later today or tomorrow to take her statement."

The Fed came out of the bedroom and nodded at his partner.

The nod must have been laden with implication, because the three men left before I could ask Peter what his remark meant. From her expression I could see that Eunice was as perplexed as I. Patti Stevenson, on the other hand, looked relieved. She asked if we wanted coffee, and we accepted. She called room service, then sat down on the sofa, neatly crossed her ankles, and folded her hands in her lap. Someone's cotillion had had a lasting effect.

"You mentioned that you wanted to speak to Warren?" she said to Eunice.

"I thought Cyndi might . . . be with him," she said. Her face was gray and her voice unsure. Her eyes, usually glittering with beady authority, were confused; they darted about the room as if seeking a haven. She sat down next to Patti and let out a sigh I could feel several feet away. "It's obvious that I don't know what's going on, though, and I must ask your forgiveness for barging into your hotel room like this. Something very odd has happened to Cyndi. She's not the gal I nurtured through the early pageants. I had hopes for her, you know, the highest of hopes. Her talent presentation is strong, and her dedication admirable. Before she began that tawdry affair with Warren, she talked of nothing but Atlantic City. Now she makes disparaging remarks about the Big One and reads movie magazines rather than hair-styling manuals and makeup guides."

"I know, I know," Patti said soothingly. "I did everything I could to stop the affair, as did Steve. Both of us pleaded with Warren to leave Cyndi alone so that he could concentrate on his job. I know you won't believe me, but Steve spent hours and hours at Warren's apartment trying to reason with him. He did everything he could short of firing Warren."

"But it's definitely over now?" I asked.

Patti smiled grimly at me. "It is definitely over; I can assure you of that. Warren was upset at first, but he's settled down and has his eye on a more suitable girl who works at the state capital. She's from a family very much like my own, with a strong tradition of political involvement and dedication to serve the public." She gave a little laugh. "It must run in the blood. My great-grandfather and grandfather were both judges, one circuit and the other on the state supreme court. My father is serving his fifth term in Washington," she added, mentioning a powerful figure from a Southern state. "And I married Steve, who's always dreamed of rising through the system to serve his country. I'll be at his side, as willing as he to make whatever sacrifices are necessary."

I decided she would make an elegant First Lady, at whatever level she and her husband were aiming for, including the Big One. Rather than delve into it, however, I nodded and said, "Then Warren's not likely to want to stir up an old affair?"

"Heavens, no. It was all over and done six months ago, and he hasn't even mentioned her name. She's a"—she glanced at Eunice and reconsidered—"an ambitious girl who was willing to use Warren for her own purposes. Her dalliance with him opened the door to the state film commission and resulted in the Hollywood trip."

"But I had the highest hopes," Eunice said in a wavery voice. Her eyes filled with tears, and one spilled over to dribble down her cheek, leaving a wet zigzag over the webbing of wrinkles. Patti hurried into another room and returned with a box of tissues. Eunice wiped her cheek, then looked up with a hint of her more typical beadiness.

"Yes, I see now that Cyndi did use Warren," she said. "By using him, she also used your husband's political office for her own dark purposes. She used me, too. I devoted a great deal of time and energy, not to mention giving her a substantial discount at my store. I had thought I could dissuade her from her plan to give up the pageants for a seedy existence in some Hollywood apartment, working at a menial job while offering sexual favors for bit parts. But I must force myself to swallow a bitter, bitter pill and admit that she is still determined, despite my warnings. All these endeavors to get publicity . . . the wrong sort of publicity. A faked murder attempt, vulgar, simply vulgar. We cannot have that sort of gal in our pageants."

I was startled at the transition from mourning to condemnation. Before I could consider it, the door flew open and two children came into the room in a flood of screams, laughter, accusations, and tears. Warren followed more sedately, holding a limp cone of cotton candy in one hand and several balloons in the other.

"Mrs. Allingham, Mrs. Malloy," he murmured as he sat down and loosened his tie. "You'll have to forgive me; we rode the ponies eleven times." He glanced at Patti, who was picking whisps of pink off the girls' chins as they shrieked about a clown. "Is it too early for a stiff drink?"

"Where's Steve?" she said.

"Daddy has to shake every single person's hand on the whole street so every single person will vote for him," one of the twins explained shrilly.

"But when he shaked the clown's hand, it fell off!" the other added. She proceeded to fall off her mother's lap in a paroxysm of giggles.

Warren's smile was forced and he sent a hungry look toward the bottles on the wet bar. "The Senator is working the street, but he ought to be here soon. I was there when he did a spot for a roving local news team, and he did a fairly good job. We got in at least a minute and a half. Not a lot of substance; just the standard bit about how much he enjoyed spending time in his district and that sort of thing. Thank God, the reporter didn't mention the industrial tax incentive."

Patti smiled tightly. "I'll review it with him first thing tomorrow morning. Anything else?"

"When the terrorist threat issue came up, he squared his shoulders and declared himself above intimidation and willing to fight for the American way. All he needed was a blue leotard and a red cape. He was going to hold the twins while he spoke to the camera, but they decided to stick out their dear little tongues."

Patti frowned at the girls who were flopping merrily on the floor. "I am very disappointed in you," she said icily. "We all want Daddy to win the election, don't we? We've talked about how we behave when Daddy takes you out to meet his constituents."

I stood up and started for the door. As Eunice joined me, I asked her in a low voice if she still wanted to speak to Warren. She shook her head. We made appropriate noises and left Patti to discuss campaign demeanor with her girls.

I drove Eunice back to the hospital so that she could fetch her car. She remained pensive and quiet, but as she climbed out of my car, she said, "What about that gal named Julianna? Has she had any pageant experience in the past?"

"I don't think so, but I've been told she intends to go to medical school to become a neurosurgeon."

"They do have their dreams, don't they?" Eunice strolled away, looking very much brightened. Her pink Cadillac roared out of the parking lot in a rosy haze of dust.

I consulted my watch. It was three-thirty, which meant I had two and a half hours to idle away before going to the theater for the glorious finale of the Miss Thurberfest pageant. The street festival and sidewalk sale were perilous options, since I was likely to bump into Sally Fromberger. Peter was busy with his officious Feds, and I had no desire to be subjected to a lecture. I had no reason to go to the theater; we would go on at eight o'clock no matter how hot the hell or high the water. Cyndi Jay was loose on the town, but I had no idea how to find her. According to Peter, she was not in any danger from anyone but herself. She would be found eventually, and would dutifully confess to her manipulative scheme. Her accomplice would be named. What the police would do to the pair was beyond my meager grasp of the law, but I supposed the police would not be especially gracious about the expenditure of time and energy.

The pageant would be history within eight hours, I thought. There was a light at the end of the tunnel, and its batteries were working. On that note, I went home and took a sinfully hot bath and a lovely nap.

Late in the afternoon Caron and Inez stomped up the stairs and into the apartment, sounding somewhat like the Stevenson twins. I was informed that Julianna had blown her chances via the orange dress and was beyond reason. I pointed out that the girls would not receive an agenting fee in any case. I was informed at great length that it was a matter of principle rather than monetary concerns. Aesthetic, Mother. Color-coordinated aesthetics.

It was all so amusing that I was actually delighted to see Peter park out front, come up the sidewalk, and disappear beneath the porch. His footsteps on the stairs sounded leaden, but I figured I was safe from all but a terse lecture. After all, we had no investigation beyond the tidying of a poorly faked murder attempt. Cyndi would be found for questioning, unless she was on the road to Hollywood, chatting with a truck driver about how awesome it was to be, like, actually going, you know.

He greeted me with a brush of his lips and a plea for a beer. Once Caron and Inez had consented to discuss Julianna's wardrobe elsewhere, I sat down next to Peter.

"Have the FBI agents stalked into the sunset?" I asked.

"Yep. Would you like to stalk into another sunset with me? I was thinking we could try Jamaica or some tiny town in Mexico."

"I thought you'd be perturbed with me. I realize I promised to stay out of this one, but Eunice insisted on going to the hotel. She presumed that Cyndi was up to something with Warren." I wound my finger around one of his black curls, which had a gray hair or two. "Why did you say Cyndi was responsible for the episode with the space heater?"

"How about Tahiti? The two of us in a little grass shack, the stars shining like diamonds, the breeze redolent of orchids and whatever else grows in your basic paradise setting."

"Mosquitoes, most likely. Why did you say Cyndi was responsible?"

"Then we'll have to take mosquito netting with us," he said, draping his arm over my shoulder. His head fell back on the top of the sofa and he closed his eyes. "I have this incredibly romantic vision, right down to the aroma of the breeze and the salty taste of your skin. There we are on the deserted beach, shaded by palm trees, our bodies glistening from the sun, our arms locked around each other. Then you sit up, push me away, and demand to know the results of an official police investigation seven years ago." He opened one eye and gave me a narrow look. "I don't think I meant that in a metaphorical sense—the pushing-away part."

"I like my life the way it is. I don't want to be the Betty Crocker of the bookselling industry. I'm very territorial these days, and I want control, not obligations. I've been married. Now I prefer to be a self-centered single person."

"So do I. Why can't we do it together?"

I wiggled out from under his arm, intensely uncomfortable. I went into the kitchen, put some crackers and cheese on a plate, stared out the window at a weedy yard that was not a beach, and went back into the living room with a bland smile.

"Shall we watch the news?" I said. "Senator Stevenson's two beastly children may be sticking out their tongues."

After an opening story about a barroom brawl, a follow-up concerning the antics of a city director and his busted bookie, and the promise of a cheery weather forecast at the end of the thirty-minute show, the children did indeed display little pink tongues. Their father dropped them and got in a few words about the deep pleasure he took from meeting the people, several of whom were standing in the background making faces at the camera.

Peter and I were behaving in an equally undecorous manner when I heard Cyndi Jay's voice. We jerked apart to stare at the television set.

"I just couldn't bear to miss the pageant tonight," she said from her hospital bed. "I realize how incredibly dangerous it is for me to go to the theater when a ruthless maniac has tried four times to murder me, but I owe it to the lucky girl who wins the title of Miss Thurberfest for the upcoming year. I feel in my heart that I have to be there, not for myself but for her—whoever she is." Cyndi blinked back her tears and smiled into the camera. "And I want to wish all seven of the finalists the best of luck. No matter who wins, they're all really, really cute girls."

"What can you tell us about this alleged maniac, Miss Jay?" the interviewer demanded on the viewers' behalf.

"The police haven't made any progress in unmasking him. I guess they're too busy to worry about me, what with all the politicians in town and crowd control at the Thurberfest and everything."

"Then you have not been offered police protection? They've done nothing to find this alleged person and restrain him?"

"They say they haven't made any progress. I have a pretty good idea who it is, though. I can't say anything now, but I intend to speak to a certain person this afternoon. If we can't arrive at a satisfactory agreement, I'm afraid I'm going to have to say the name. It's the only way I have to protect myself."

"When will you expose this alleged murderer?"

She paused long enough for the camera to zoom in for a close-up of her wan, brave, discreetly made-up face. "Tonight at the pageant. I'll be there, and—" A blurry white figure moved in front of the camera, cutting off our view of Cyndi's trembling lips. Inaudible dialogue drowned out any further comments.

The interviewer gave us a recap of who she was, where she was, why she was where she was, and what she'd learned in this startling interview with Miss Thurberfest. She assured us that she would be at the theater to stay on top of the unfolding story of the beauty queen and the maniac who stalks her, then deftly moved on to a story about cattle mutilations in another county.

"What on earth did that mean?" I murmured, thoroughly be-

wildered. "I thought you said she was behind the so-called asphyxiation attempt. If she's behind the entire plot, who the hell is she
going to name?"

"We found her fingerprint on the tape and on the knob of the
heater. The blow to her head could have been self-administered."
He let out an irritable sigh. "I'd better call and have her picked up
for questioning before the pageant. Maybe I'd better warn the state
psychiatric facility to make up an extra bed. The girl is so deluded
that she might get herself in real trouble."

He went into the kitchen to call the department. I listened to
him with a fraction of my mind while I tried to make sense out of
Cyndi's latest ploy for publicity. She'd finally had her minute of
glory in front of the camera, only because Steve Stevenson had no
excuse to be in her hospital room. But what would she say tonight
at the pageant—gee, guys, I forgot to mention that I'm stalking
myself for the publicity?

"Have you figured out who her accomplice is?" I asked Peter
when he returned. "She does have one. Being shot at requires a
second party to shoot at you."

"It had occurred to us, but as soon as we received the ballistics
report, the FBI agents were hot to talk to Senator Stevenson. Their
only involvement was if someone attempted to affect the outcome
of the election through the threat of violence, which is federally
frowned upon. When Cyndi disappeared of her own volition, it
confirmed our suspicion that she was behind the sniping. The
agents murmured something about a case in Las Vegas and evapo-
rated before my eyes. They'll be back in a few days, poorer but
wiser, to finalize the paperwork."

"You're all being rather casual about this."

"About a bunch of practical jokes and two murder attempts
staged in hopes of a press conference?"

"You might have put a policeman outside Cyndi's hospital
room."

He gave me a wry look. "We have every available man on duty

because of the Thurberfest. Several thousand citizens roamed the streets yesterday in a drunken stupor, and many of them are doing so again today. Pickpockets from three states are in town, as are a handful of muggers and rapists. We've issued more moving-violation tickets in the last two days than we normally do in a week. The girl was safe in the hospital; the security people there were keeping an eye on the entrances and the hallway."

"But they didn't prevent her from leaving."

"No one could have prevented her from leaving." He gave me a long, enigmatic look, then ran his fingers through his hair, sighed, and told me he was leaving.

I told him I would not attempt to prevent such a thing, and was in fact going to the theater. He said an undercover officer or two would be there to watch for the errant Miss Thurberfest, should she carry out her threat to appear and expose her pet maniac, and we agreed to meet later to celebrate the conclusion of the pageant. After another strange look, he left.

I called Luanne, who sounded drowsy as she said she'd be ready to be picked up shortly. Caron and Inez had not returned. Hoping they were already at the theater, I drove to Luanne's house and helped her hobble down the sidewalk to my car.

"You certainly unplug your telephone a lot," I said as we started for the theater.

"Do I? I assumed nobody ever bothered to call me."

"I've bothered to call you a dozen times in the last three days," I said mildly. "Is there something I don't know?"

"I would imagine there are quite a few things you don't know. For instance, do you know the capital of New Zealand? The name of Hoover's Secretary of State? How to make tofu lasagna? Where have all the flowers gone? Why do fools fall in love?"

"Could you be serious for one minute?"

"I don't want to be serious for one parsec," she said, laughing coldheartedly at my frustrated tone. "I want to survive the pageant with a smile, then go home and nurse my ankle so that I can again waltz with Mr. Haling, the widower next door who grows fantastic tomatoes and peeps through my window when I undress at night."

I considered the wisdom of taking my hands off the steering wheel long enough to wrap them around her throat and choke some sense from her. I told her as much, then said, "I care about you and I want to know what's wrong. If necessary, I'll deputize Mr. Haling and we'll cram tomatoes down you until you barf seeds and agree to confess."

She made an odd noise and looked down at her lap. "I'll tell you in a day or two, Claire. There is a certain complication in my life, and I can't discuss it until the pageant is over and the girls are gone. You'll have to settle for that. Mr. Haling only likes dark-haired, sultry women. He wouldn't give you a vine-ripened tomato if your life depended on it."

I let it go and told her everything that had happened since I'd visited that morning. "At ten o'clock Cyndi was a victim. By one she was a perpetrator. By two she had moved into *absentia,* and by five into delusional megalomania," I concluded. "I once thought she was a sweet, harmless, vacuous girl."

"We must hope she doesn't float down from the catwalk in the middle of the pageant, her well-manicured finger pointing in accusation. If Mayor Avery saw the news, he's probably trembling in his boxer shorts."

"Peter has all the available uniformed officers out looking for her. I'm sure they'll find her and stash her away in a nice, safe place until she says something coherent."

We parked in the alley and went around to the front door of the theater. Luanne went to the office, and I wandered down the corridor to make sure the stage was lit and the flowers still in place. The stage was lit, but in the spotlight I saw Caron and Inez.

"Try to put a little feeling into it this time," Caron snapped.

"But I don't feel anything," Inez said. "I mean, why should I scream at you when you haven't actually done anything?"

"Pretend I ran over your cat. Pretend we're on a desert island

and I ate the last cookie. This is acting. You're supposed to fake it."

"You don't drive, so you couldn't have run over my cat. And if we're on a desert island, why do we have cookies? Wouldn't it make more sense if you ate the last coconut?"

I slithered into the auditorium and perched on the arm of a seat.

"Then I ate the last coconut!" Caron said, flapping her hands and scowling like a vulture that had chanced on a chicken.

The seven finalists entered the auditorium. They were subdued, I supposed from prepageant jitters. I pointed at the stairs that led to the basement. Julianna snorted when she saw the two thespians and marched down the stairs. Dixie shot me a frightened look, then allowed herself to be swept away with the group.

"You ate the last coconut," Inez said as loudly as she dared.

"Yeah, I did." Caron put her hands on her hips and sauntered away, then looked back over her shoulder with a sneer and said, "And I don't care. What are you going to do about it, bitch?"

Trembling, Inez raised her arm and pointed a gun at Caron. "I'll kill you, you slut."

Caron made a face at the low-key avowal, but regained her sneer and took a step toward the back of the stage. "I have no fear of you. You haven't got the nerve to pull the trigger." She froze for several seconds, then in an aggrieved voice said, "That's the cue, Inez. You're supposed to shoot me now."

Abruptly the lights around the two went out, leaving them in stark white puddles. "Go on, shoot her," yelled a voice from the control booth above my head.

Inez's hand shook so wildly I was afraid she'd drop the weapon. She glanced at me for reassurance that it was both appropriate and acceptable to shoot her best friend in the back while being observed by the mother of same.

"Sure, go ahead," I called amiably.

"Well, okay." Inez pointed the gun at Caron's back and closed her eyes. She took a breath, then curled her finger around the trigger. The result was a most satisfactory flashing bang. A tendril of smoke curled from the end of the barrel. Caron lurched forward with a screech, staggered around so that she was facing the audience, and fell to her knees with an agonized groan.

It was not bad for an amateur. The voice from the ceiling made a comment to that effect, and we were both waiting for the death rattle when Julianna came up from the basement.

She grabbed my hand. "Mrs. Malloy, you've got to do something. I smell gas down there. We all do," she said loudly enough to cut off a particularly gut-wrenching groan from centerstage.

Mine, I think, was just as loud.

"T"E"N"

I bellowed at Mac, who bellowed back as I dashed down the stairs
to the basement. The remaining finalists were huddled in the
dressing room doorway; I hoarsely ordered them upstairs and continued to the star-studded door at the end of the hall. With each
step the odor of gas grew stronger. The door was locked. I was
pounding on it as Mac loped up behind me.

"There's no one in there," he said, fumbling with his key ring.
"The police sealed it yesterday. Maybe they forgot to turn off the
goddamn space heater."

"The seals are broken. Would you hurry?"

I went back to the foot of the stairs and yelled for someone to
call for an ambulance. Mac unlocked the door, shoved it open,
then stepped back and turned to look at me.

"It's too late for an ambulance," he said flatly. "Have them call
the police."

He went around the corner and threw open the metal doors
that led to the alley. I amended my message to the group in the
auditorium, then crept down the hallway, choking on gas acrid
enough to have physical shape and color, and looked in the room.
Cyndi was once again limp in the chair in front of the table, her
head bowed so that her chin rested on her chest. But this time her
eyes bulged in surprise and her tongue protruded through purplish
lips. A cord of some sort cut tightly into her neck. I approached

until I was close enough to determine it was the cord of her hair dryer, and that she was dead.

I took a tissue and gingerly turned off the gas, hoping I wasn't obliterating fingerprints. Then, my head threatening to explode and my eyes burning like embedded embers, I stumbled out to the alley and kneeled on the gravel. And, yes, lost another meal.

"At least we know how to go through the motions," Mac said from a shadow. He lit a cigarette and drew deeply on it. "Rather déjà vu-ish, isn't it?"

"A girl is dead—murdered," I croaked.

"I have to agree this one's not a suicide," he said in the same conversational tone. "A logistic impossibility. How the hell did she get into the theater?"

I sat back on the gravel and watched the red tip of the cigarette fly through the air. "She left the hospital around noon, or perhaps twelve-thirty. I would guess she came in a minute or two before I left this afternoon, right after the rehearsal ended. I heard the door bang, but I thought you were either coming or going, and I didn't bother to investigate."

"You didn't hear me. I was in the prop room. Someone's been snooping around in there, and I was trying to determine what's missing."

"A rubber knife, a gun, and a Viking helmet," I said numbly, trying to grasp what had happened in the last minute or so. Gas, the dressing room door locked, the body in the chair, the alley. The admittedly unnerving sensation of déjà vu, which was getting déjà vieux. I was still sitting on the gravel when the alley filled with flashing blue lights, sirens, scratchy radios, and stern men in white coats. Stern men in blue coats followed, and at last Peter crouched beside me and rubbed my shoulder.

"Can you tell me what happened, Claire?"

I told him what I could, which was little beyond the premise that Cyndi had returned to the theater to hide out until the pageant began at eight o'clock. He went through the doors to the basement. I stood up and coerced my knees into behaving well enough to get me around to the front of the building and to the office.

The seven finalists, in various emotional states ranging from mute shock to copious tears, were there. Caron and Inez hovered in a corner, their expressions leery. As I entered, Luanne pushed herself out of the chair and put her fists on the desktop. "What the hell is going on?"

"Cyndi's dead," I told them. "And it wasn't an accident or a pseudosuicide attempt that backfired. She was murdered."

"When?" Luanne demanded. "How?"

"This afternoon. Someone tied a hair-dryer cord around her neck before turning on the gas."

A uniformed police officer came into the office. "The Lieutenant would prefer that no one discuss the incident until he's had the opportunity to question each of you individually. He wants you to wait in the auditorium."

"I'm not going back in there," Heidi said. The others nodded. The policeman studied them for a moment, no doubt better trained to deal with school children at crosswalks and jaywalkers. "No way," Heidi added with a sniff. Six more noses sniffed disdainfully. Caron and Inez merely blinked.

While he contemplated how best to handle the impasse, I sat down on the corner of Luanne's desk. "In half an hour the pageant crew will arrive, and not too long afterward an audience of three to four hundred friends and doting relatives will storm the doors."

"We'll have to cancel as quickly as we can." Luanne picked up the telephone receiver, but the policeman came across the room and took it from her hand.

"Lieutenant Rosen says not to let anyone do anything until he gets here, ma'am."

"But that's absurd. There's been a murder here, today, in this building. A girl is dead. We can't simply go about our business as if nothing unusual has occurred."

"Lieutenant's orders are not to let anyone do anything until he gets here," the policeman repeated.

"I'm not going through with this," Julianna squeaked. "I can't go up on the stage and wink at the judges knowing that Cyndi's . . ."

"Me, neither," Heidi said. "Chou-Chou has a terribly delicate constitution."

Bambi shook her head. "I'm trembling too hard to twirl anything. I probably can't even zip my zipper or put on earrings. I want to go home."

"So do I," Lisa said. The second Lisa began to cry. The girls crowded around her, sending dark looks at the policeman.

The impasse was escalating into open warfare. I cleared my throat and said, "We have more than an hour before the pageant begins. I'm sure Lieutenant Rosen will allow us time to cancel before everyone arrives. Now all of you—sit!"

They sat. I slumped on one end of the couch and tried to think. I had gotten nowhere when I heard Peter's voice in the lobby. The policeman was not keen to allow me out of the office, but Peter opened the door and crooked a finger at me.

"Mrs. Malloy, I'd like to speak to you," he said.

I fluttered my fingers at Cerberus and went through the door. Peter and Jorgeson stood near the concession stand. Neither smiled as I joined them.

I was asked to repeat my story, which I did. "I don't know if I heard Cyndi enter the theater at one," I added, "but it seems logical. McWethy said he was in the prop room, and the finalists had already left."

"But you didn't see anyone?" Peter said.

"No, but it's not all that odd. I've been using the east corridor since the office is on that side. All Cyndi—or whoever it was— had to do was slip down the west corridor and cut across the front of the auditorium to the basement stairs. I left within minutes of hearing the door, and at that point Mac was the only one in the theater."

Jorgeson flipped open a notebook. "According to his initial statement, McWethy came in at eight-thirty and left for lunch at one-fifteen or so. He came back at five forty-five to unlock the doors for the finalists and the production people. He then went to the lighting booth to adjust some gels so that he wouldn't have a bunch of flamingos flapping around the stage." He stopped and reread the last few words, his lips moving silently. "I don't know why he'd have any birds, Lieutenant. There's a yappy little dog swimming in piss in a box in the greenroom, but no birds that I found."

"Can anybody confirm McWethy's alleged movements?"

"Not really. He said he wandered down the street to check out the festival. He saw a few thousand people, but he doubts anyone could swear he was in any particular place at one time. It's pretty crazy out there, what with the noise, confusion, crowds, and free-flowing beer. It'll be damn hard to confirm an alibi unless he asked somebody the time."

"How long had Cyndi been dead?" I asked.

Peter flashed his teeth, but the gesture lacked warmth. "Ah, our Miss Marple of Thurber Street is at it again, Jorgeson. If she says one more word, no matter how innocent, I want you to take her to the station and hold her as a material witness in a murder investigation."

"You want I should call around for a warrant?" Jorgeson murmured. "I can think of two or three judges that would sign one, as a personal favor."

I was formulating a response to their adolescent remarks when Luanne hobbled across the lobby. "What am I supposed to do about the pageant, Peter? I've got seven semihysterical girls moaning in the office, and not one of them is the least bit interested in becoming the new Miss Thurberfest. We've got to get the word out immediately that the pageant is canceled."

"That'll take the heat off someone's burner," I said. "Cyndi announced on the news that she was going to expose the maniac who's been trying to kill her. I still think she and an accomplice staged some of those pranks for the publicity. She didn't stage the final one. No one, not even a delusional beauty queen, can strangle herself with an electrical cord."

Luanne poked me with the tip of her crutch. "So the murderer had to silence her before the pageant. Isn't that rather obvious?"

"What about her accomplice? Wouldn't he be equally panicked when Cyndi announced she was going to make startling revelations at the pageant?"

"It's the same person," Luanne said. She stopped for a moment to think it over, then said, "Are you saying Cyndi had both an accomplice and someone trying to kill her?"

Peter glowered. "How many people do you have in the cast of this fantastical conspiracy? What about the eighteen girls in the preliminary? Do you want us to bring in the thousands of people on the street for questioning? What about those who stayed home and therefore have no alibi?"

I was denying mental malfeasance when Steve Stevenson, his wife, and the twins entered the lobby. Patti held the twins' hands in a tight grip, and they looked properly subdued after the earlier scolding. Little blue eyes were alertly casing the joint, but little pink tongues were restrained by angelic smiles.

Steve held out his hand to Peter. "I'm sorry I missed you this afternoon, Lieutenant Rosen. The primary's less than a month away and personal contact makes a world of difference in the final tally."

Peter shook the proffered hand. "We came by to discuss the shooting incident during the parade, but you've no doubt already heard that the bullet was a blank."

"Patti told me what you said. I'm shocked that Cyndi would

take that kind of crazy risk simply to get publicity," he said with a sad smile. "I feel in some way responsible for her actions; I suggested her name to the film commission, which led to the trip and her grandiose scheme of becoming a Hollywood starlet. I hope you won't deal too harshly with her, Lieutenant."

"She must be stopped, however," Patti said. "Even though the bullet was a blank, it could have done some damage had it hit someone. And this nonsense with the gas heater in the dressing room—that could have resulted in a serious tragedy."

"Ah, well, it has," Peter murmured.

While he told them what had transpired in the last forty-five minutes, I went back to Luanne and said, "So do we postpone the pageant?"

"We have no choice, Claire. Even if the police allowed us to use the facility, the girls certainly aren't going to participate. If you and I were the only contestants, we'd both end up as runner-ups." She rubbed at the black shadows beneath her eyes. "I feel dreadful about Cyndi. She shouldn't have returned to the theater, but that doesn't mean she deserved what happened to her. She was young and pretty, and now she's dead."

"Which is why we can't let the murderer get away with it," I said in a low, cold voice. Jorgeson's shoulders twitched as he moved away with great nonchalance to study the popcorn machine.

Luanne gave me a piercing look. "We? Why don't you say that a little louder so that Peter can hear you? You know how delighted he is when he thinks you're meddling in a police investigation."

"Who's meddling? I simply think we ought to assist the police, who have no idea of the identity of the murderer. It's not necessarily a maniac off the street. It could be someone in this building."

"Someone in this building?" she echoed incredulously.

"It's a better theory than the maniac one. Every one of us had some free time this afternoon, you know. Warren and Steve took the twins to the street festival, and Steve has admitted he was wandering around shaking hands. Warren could have slipped the pony man a few bucks to keep the girls occupied. Patti was alone in the hotel room. Mac says he left the theater for lunch and didn't return until time for the pageant, but he doesn't have a solid alibi. Eunice drove away in her Cadillac three hours ago; maybe she deduced the location of Cyndi's hideout and came here to plead the case for the Big One. One of the finalists could have gotten hold of a key. I went home and took a nap." I took a deep breath and forged ahead. "You had your telephone unplugged. You could have come back to the theater and bumped into Cyndi."

"Curiouser and curiouser," she said. Her voice hinted at anger as she added, "Why would I have wanted to bump into and subsequently bump off Cyndi Jay?"

"I don't know. I don't know why anyone wanted to murder her, but someone did."

"Oh, go home and unplug your brain." Luanne hobbled as furiously as possible toward the office, her crutches leaving a trail of crescent-shaped indentations in the carpet.

When I rejoined Peter, I saw that Warren had arrived in time to hear the news. He looked ill, his face mottled and his lips trembling. Patti clung to her husband's arm. She looked somewhat composed, but a nerve twitched along her jawline and her white fingers dug into Steve's sleeve. Steve had a hand on his forehead, and his voice cracked as he said, "I can't believe this. She was such a vivacious thing, so full of energy and dreams."

"I wish I hadn't spoken so sharply," Patti said with a small choking noise. Her fingernails bit into her husband's arm so deeply I feared for the Italian silk. She locked eyes with him for a moment, then shuddered and said, "Warren, take the girls down to the auditorium and let them play on the stage. I don't think I can handle them at the moment. I need to—I need to sit down." Her knees buckled, and Steve caught her arm before she crumpled.

Peter took her other arm, and the three moved slowly toward the office.

Warren glanced at the twins, who were occupied trying to find ingress to the concession stand and several shelves of candybars. "This is so terrible, Mrs. Malloy," he said. "Who could do such a thing?"

"The police are as eager as you to find that out. I suppose this is hardest on you, since you and Cyndi were so close."

"That's right." He gave me a fleeting look before turning back to watch his charges. "We had an intimate relationship for several months."

"Did she have her apartment then? Is that where you . . . spent time together?"

"She moved into it a month or so after we began dating. When I was in town, we stayed there. She occasionally visited for a weekend at my apartment. Does any of this matter—now that she's dead?"

"Perhaps not," I admitted with a sigh. I envisioned the messy apartment and the arthritic great-aunt moving painfully through the rooms, trying to decide how best to dispose of Cyndi's possessions. Of which there were a lot, along with an expensive wardrobe of evening gowns, stiletto heels, and swimsuits that would most likely disintegrate in water. "Did Cyndi's parents leave enough money to support her through college?" I asked abruptly.

"I don't think they left much of anything. Her father was a construction worker and her mother a clerk. Typical blue-collar, struggling to pay the bills and save a few bucks for a fishing trip once or twice a year, she told me once. The great-aunt has a small annuity and Social Security, but nothing beyond that."

"Then how did Cyndi afford the college tuition and the apartment?"

"From the pageants, I assumed. They give away scholarships and prizes, don't they?"

"The local ones don't give away much of anything," I said, shaking my head. "Maybe a small scholarship or gift certificates, but no cash prizes of any consequence. How did she pay for the necessities?"

"Cassie! Get down from there, you little piglet!" He shrugged at me, then went across the lobby to save the concession stand from destruction. Once he had a child under ea arm, he told them they were going to experience theater and carried them down the corridor toward the auditorium.

"Well, what did she live on?" I repeated to the empty lobby, Jorgeson having followed his superior into the office (to tattle, most likely). "She didn't have an inheritance; she didn't have a job. She did have an apartment, a car, a wardrobe that spoke of bank-rolls, and sufficient funds to eat, buy gas, and stay overnight at pageants in other towns."

To my relief, no one answered.

I went into the office, which resembled a can of sardines—although sardines hardly ever snivel, cry, moan, argue, or glower at each other. After a good fifteen minutes of the above behavior, we agreed to postpone the pageant for a week. Mac, who'd been fetched (and most unwillingly, from the intensity of his scowl), grudingly admitted that the theater would be available. Steve murmured that he, too, would be available. Luanne thought she might be off crutches in a few days. The seven finalists opined they would be recovered by then and be able to sing, interpret, twirl, twirl fire, recite, tootle a clarinet, and otherwise rise to the demands of the tradition. The two members of the production crew nodded without enthusiasm, no doubt having planned to be off-Broadway bound within a week.

Peter then announced that, if everyone was now agreeable, he might conduct an investigation of the crime. We all agreed that such a thing seemed more than appropriate.

Luanne, Caron, Inez, and I dragged out of the theater several hours later, having been the last four worthy of interrogation in the auditorium. The other three had been grilled like shish-kebabs. I had been asked to sign my statement, then had received yet another interminable lecture from Super Cop. Had he paused long enough to allow me to insert a word or two, I would have suggested he inquire into Cyndi Jay's personal financial affairs. As it was, I decided to wait until I had some information to present. On a silver platter, tied in a pink ribbon.

I dropped Luanne and Inez off at their respective houses. As I drove home, I told Caron what Mac had said about the prop room. "I hope you replaced the toys once you finished playing with them," I concluded.

"We were rehearsing, Mother. If we can work out some mathematical connection, we're going to do a skit at the Math Club banquet. Inez has an idea for a script about Pythagoras. He's Greek, so there has to be tragedy in there somewhere. None of those guys expired peacefully in their togas."

"I don't think Greek tragedies involved guns. They tended to stab each other or drink poison," I said dubiously. "And the Romans were the ones who ran around in the short sheets."

"Inez and I do not intend to get bogged down in the details. It's terribly important to see the overall picture, like who's madly in love with whom and who's been dropping notes from the balcony."

"I think you're mixing your melodramas." I stopped at the curb in front of the duplex. "You go on inside and occupy yourself with an encyclopedia. I want to make a quick condolence call."

"It's almost ten, Mother. Don't you think it's a little bit late to drop in on people? You won't let me make telephone calls this late. You go on and on about being considerate and not disturbing people who might want to go to bed early, although I don't know a single person who goes—"

"Go call Inez," I said, vowing never again to offer any maternal insights into ethics, consideration, friendship, loyalty, courtesy, or anything else that might be flung back in my teeth. The child's arsenal was already formidably stocked.

I drove to Eunice's street and cruised slowly past her house, watching for police cars, marked and unmarked. The lights were on inside the house, but the coast seemed clear enough to risk a visit. I parked and went up the sidewalk. She came to the door, dressed in a tattered terrycloth bathrobe and floppy bedroom slippers. Her hair was wound around fat pink rollers, and her face was coated with a glistening white cream, which emphasized her red-rimmed eyes.

"I thought you might appreciate some company," I said through the screen.

"The police came by to tell me—that Lieutenant Rosen fellow and another man. Having already given up on the girl, I myself was surprised by the intensity of emotions that swept over me when I heard what had happened. Cyndi and I were very close until that man seduced her and put all those absurd ideas into her head. Many a time we shared a motel room, drinking diet sodas and pretending the boardwalk of Atlantic City was outside our room. We used to shop for evening gowns, have a nice salad for lunch, and then simply while away the afternoon trying new hairstyles. One must have the quintessential style for the Big One; the humidity there can frizz a gal in ten seconds flat." She wiped her eyes with a wadded tissue from her pocket, then opened the screen door. "You mustn't stand on the porch. Please come in and have a cup of tea with me."

I did as requested, although a short discussion led to an agreement that scotch was a more fitting refreshment. The living room was filled with ordinary furniture, but the walls were covered with photographs of smiling girls in swimsuits bisected by white ribbons to remind them who they were. A few rusty trophies gathered dust on the top of a bookshelf stacked with fashion magazines.

Eunice waved me to a brocade sofa, produced a bottle and two tumblers, then sat down across from me. "That policeman said poor Cyndi had been murdered. I was aghast, totally aghast. The class of gals in the pageants is usually quite good; the undesirables are screened out when the applications are first read, and often discreet inquiries are made concerning the family. I'm afraid I misjudged Cyndi Jay. Oh, her appearance was good and her poise a distinct advantage . . . but a girl who's lacked maternal guidance in the formative years sometimes is simply simmering below the surface. The wrong sort of man comes along, and the gal is easily led astray. Moral fiber is so vital these days, so very vital."

"She seemed ambitious," I said encouragingly.

"That is an understatement. To develop some unwholesome idea of going away to Hollywood, and then to stage a series of seemingly vicious practical jokes to garner publicity!" Eunice drank an inch of scotch, then leaned forward and jabbed the air. "I should have known she was nothing but a cheap hustler when she first took up with that man. They tried to pretend it was a typical dewy-eyed love affair, but I knew different. I've been around the track myself, and I saw what was going on."

I resisted the urge to dwell on an image of Eunice in gray sweats, puffing around the track with the wrong sort of man in hot pursuit. "What was going on?"

"I do not gossip and I do not speak ill of the dead," she said with the warmth of Queen Victoria squelching insubordination. "What's done is done. There's no reason to stir up old gossip, especially now that poor Cyndi has passed away. I shall visit the great-aunt in the morning to assist with the arrangements; the policeman agreed that would be appropriate. The old gal is not well, and has little money."

I dove through the opening. "Where did Cyndi find money to live on? The apartment, a car, the pageants—all that must have been expensive, and she didn't have a job. It doesn't sound as if her great-aunt supported her." I cocked my head and tried to look mildly curious, rather than salivating for gossip. I also poured several inches of scotch into Eunice's glass.

"Thank you. No, she had no time for a job. I believe she had some sort of scholarship at the college, a result of pooling various pageant stipends. I usually footed the pageant bills, from the application fee to the last-minute dash for a different shade of lipstick or a piece of ribbon. I aspired for her," she added mistily, "and, yes, for myself."

While she paused to compose herself witl ⌐he aid of her drink, I sat back and allowed my theory to evaporate before my eyes. Although I had not yet had time to seriously consider its implications, several unsavory aspects had hovered in the back of my mind. Blackmail had hovered the hardest.

I was on the verge of saying goodnight and going home to brood when she said, "As for the apartment rent, the car, the elaborate stereo equipment, clothing, and all that sort of thing, I have no idea where she found the money."

"She didn't win it at the pageants?"

"How much money do you think is available to the runner-ups at the Miss Drumstick pageant in Stump County?" she said with a nasty little laugh. "Millions—or even thousands? Hundreds? Hardly, I must say, hardly. The winner might receive gift certificates from the dry cleaner and the drugstore, and at most a few hundred dollars for education. The state levels are better, of course, and the winner of the Big One can expect to end the year in a very healthy position, but the local pageants are merely training grounds, an opportunity to practice the necessary skills and fine-tune the gals."

"Then how could she finance a move to Hollywood? A move like that costs money. She surely knew she'd need to make a deposit on an apartment, no matter how seedy, and survive until she found a job."

Eunice gazed at me slyly, or perhaps only drunkenly. "Yes, it would require a certain amount of money, wouldn't it?"

"Does she have a savings account?"

I expected a shrug, but received a firm negative. Eunice shook her head hard enough to send a pink roller across the room, and said, "No, the gal had less than fifty dollars when I spoke to her at the hospital this morning. I asked her how she intended to pay the bill, and she said she didn't intend to pay anyone anything. They could sue her, she said, but it was very much a blood-and-turnip situation, and she would be in Hollywood, in any case."

"So she was almost on the way out of town? I didn't realize she was quite so prepared to leave," I said, surprised.

"While I was at the hospital, Cyndi asked me to call the bus station and find out at what time tomorrow she might catch a bus for the West Coast. I was floored, absolutely floored. I was aware that she planned at some time in the future to leave Farberville, but I had supposed she was thinking in terms of months—not hours. Once I'd recovered from the shock, I demanded to know how she would pay for the bus ticket."

I put down my glass before it slipped out of my hand. "What did she say?"

"She said she'd have plenty of money by tomorrow morning, plenty of money. I decided she was giddy from the gas and did nothing to dispel her pitiful fantasy. Maybe she thought she'd receive some sort of monetary award for being present at the pageant to crown the new queen." Eunice finished off her drink and stared at me until I began to wiggle uncomfortably on the uncomfortable sofa. "Mrs. Malloy," she said with careful deliberation, "I must ask you what may prove to be a painful question. I do hope you won't take offense."

"No," I said, clutching a throw pillow.

"Have you ever considered using a more intense shade of eye shadow? That which you're using at present simply makes you look gaunt, and I do think you could be somewhat attractive if you'd enhance your eyes."

I was thrown off balance enough to agree to a free color consultation at her store. I thanked her for the refreshments and conversation, then said goodnight and drove home, chewing on my lip as I dodged potholes, trying to decide whom Cyndi Jay was black-mailing. And for what.

Once at home, I sat down at the kitchen table and made yet another list. The nail: Cyndi. The weight: Cyndi. The message on the mirror (both written and erased): Cyndi. The bullet fired at the convertible: Cyndi's doing, but an accomplice—unknown. The candidates for sniper of the day: everyone .. the town except Steve, Cyndi, Caron, Inez, and myself. That narrowed the possibilities to twenty thousand plus.

The first incident with the space heater.

I put down the pencil and made a cup of tea while I considered it. Cyndi had again lost her bid for press coverage that might lead to some sort of national attention and a foot through a casting director's door. She had been angry enough to do something wildly outrageous, I thought as I sat down and doodled on the paper. Such as stomp down to the dressing room, tape the keyhole, bop herself with her hair dryer, and then wait patiently for the police to find her. She could have reasonably expected them within five or ten minutes, and thus could have been confident she would be rescued before anything too dreadful happened. Perhaps she had been nodding off when someone had fortuitously chanced upon this golden opportunity. Said someone calmly locked the door and switched off the lights.

It required two elements: physical presence in the theater, and a key. Mac, Steve, and Warren had all been there, and in the confusion might have slipped away for a moment. Steve (motive unknown) had disappeared to call his wife, and Warren (bitterly brokenhearted) had been in the auditorium, claiming to be looking for the Senator. Mac (motive unknown) had come up the stairs from the basement. Eunice (shattered dreams) had arrived in the aftermath, but that in no way proved she hadn't been in the basement a few hours earlier. Patti (motive unknown) was at the hotel during the afternoon, presumably tending to her small terrors. And Luanne (no motive whatsoever and utterly absurd to suspect of having one) had been asleep, her telephone unplugged to avoid siding salesmen and assistant pageant directors.

I repeated the last conclusion several times, both aloud and mentally. I then moved on to the second element: the dressing room key. Cyndi had one, which was neither here nor there. A second key dangled from a thick steel ring clipped on the belt loop of a pair of overalls. It had jangled upon occasion, and had been produced twice when the dressing room had been locked.

I returned to the listed pranks. I imagined Cyndi both on her knees in the middle of the stage to pull up a nail and creeping along the catwalk with a knife to saw partway through a rope. Mac had been in the theater every moment, lurking in the dark corners of the stage or fiddling with controls in the light booth. As resident phantom, nothing escaped his notice. Surely such bizarre behavior by Miss Thurberfest would have merited comment.

He had to be in on her scheme. Could he have fired the shot at the convertible? He hadn't been at the theater thirty minutes before the parade, and might well have been on a rooftop positioning his weapon. And loading a blank bullet . . . since he had a roomful of stage weapons, many of which my daughter had joyfully stumbled across.

I tossed down my pencil and went to Caron's room. Unsurprisingly, she was sitting on her bed, the telephone receiver attached to her ear and a bag of pretzels within easy reach. She gave me a startled look, covered the mouthpiece, and said, "Yes, Mother? I'm in the middle of a terribly important call. Inez is describing this really dramatic scene in which Pythagoras learns Euclid has stolen his theorum. Pythagoras is furious, naturally, and says he'll hunt him down and kill him in the name of pure mathematics."

"I'm tingling, but you can tell me the outcome later. What sorts of things are in the prop room?"

"Props, Mother. They're what the actors use instead of real things. Well, some of them are real things, but they've been set aside for the plays." She uncovered the receiver long enough to warn Inez I was Still There, then waited with all the patience of a teenaged martyr for me to run out of idiotic questions.

"I know what props are," I said with all the patience of a teenaged martyr's mother. "I've seen the dagger and the revolver. What other mock weapons are in the prop room?"

She warned Inez it might be a very long while. "A crossbow made of styrofoam, although it may have something to do with Cupid. A bunch of spears with cardboard points. Dueling pistols carved out of soap." She broke off to suggest to Inez that Euclid and Pythagoras meet at dawn, then gave me an exasperated look. "This skit is awfully important to my career. If you'd tell me what you want, I'll try to remember what all's in there."

"A rifle," I admitted.

"I think I saw something with a long barrel way in the back corner under the Arc de Triomphe. It may have been a piece of pipe; I was hardly entranced by it. Now can I talk to Inez?"

A prop-room rifle would be just the thing to shoot a blank bullet in a make-believe murder attempt, I thought excitedly. It would prove Mac's involvement in Cyndi's scheme. Then again, it wouldn't prove any involvement in her murder—but it was a beginning.

"I think I'll go over to the theater and have a look," I told Caron. "If Peter calls, don't tell him where I am. Tell him I'm visiting a sick friend or shopping at the all-night grocery mart."

"You want me to lie to Peter?"

"Yep," I said, cutting her off before she could sputter how I was always going on and on, et cetera. "He probably won't call, anyway, and I'll be back in thirty minutes. If your deep commitment to the truth precludes a white lie, then just stay on the telephone until I get back."

I grabbed my purse and car keys, and hurried down to my car, honestly believing I'd be back in thirty minutes.

"E""L""E""V""E""N"

I couldn't help it. I was compelled, virtually propelled, by an inexplicable cosmic force. The key to the theater was screaming at me from the bottom of my purse. If ignored, it might burst into flame *à la* spontaneous combustion, and Caron and I would be transformed into crusty loaves of French bread in the ensuing incendiary catastrophe.

Besides, I told myself as I parked discreetly in the alley, it would take a mere five minutes to determine if there was a rifle in the prop room. If indeed it was there, I would go home and call Peter to tell him Caron had remembered seeing it. With a trace of diffident self-deprecation, I would hesitantly offer my gossamer little theory about Mac's involvement in Cyndi's scheme. If there was a length of pipe better suited to the dark purposes of plumbers than those of snipers, I would go home and call Peter to wish him pleasant dreams.

I stopped at the corner and studied the sidewalks for any undercover men lolling about. Several blocks down the hill the street festival raged relentlessly. Wholesome family entertainment was history; the children and the ponies were gone, and the street was now filled with jolly throngs of revelers. I could hear one rock band in the beer garden, and strains of another from one of the bars on the far side of the Book Depot. The insidious boxes known as ghetto blasters were carried on more affluent shoulders. Drunks yelled to each other, as did roving gangs of college boys with conflicting ideas of where next to go or what next to drink. The few policemen in sight were all watching the crowds. As well they should.

I unlocked the front door of the theater, and carefully locked it behind me after I slipped inside. Light from the street bathed the lobby in the eerie yellow glow of an aquarium; it was more than adequate to guide me around the potted plants and down the corridor. Once in the auditorium, I switched on my flashlight and went across the stage toward the audio booth. As I reached the door, I heard a small noise. I stopped to frown at the dark rows of seats. The noise was more a creak than a scuttle; I waited for it to be repeated, but heard nothing. I decided it came from the age of the building rather than a furry, red-eyed, bewhiskered inhabitant.

The door to the audio booth was not locked, thus saving a certain amount of face for those who hadn't entertained the possibility. I continued through the room to the second door and opened it with equal success. The room was minute, no bigger than Cyndi's dressing room, but bursting with decades of accumulation. Ionian columns leaned against a flat depicting a sylvan glade. Another flat, done in exacting perspective, seemed to lead to a road that disappeared into the horizon. The furniture covered all periods from Louis XVI through colonial America to modern teachers' lounge. Two styles of telephones were visible, along with a television and an ancient radio. The Viking helmet hung from a brass coatrack.

How Caron chanced upon her treasures was truly a mystery, I thought as the flashlight splayed across the mess. A thick layer of dust coated everything, softening silhouettes and hiding scars. I sneezed several times, both in response to the dust and in hopes of frightening away any of the furry things previously mentioned.

The Arc de Triomphe leaned against the back wall. I picked my way over boxes of clothes, an oar, spears, and rolled-up rugs, and reached said landmark without a skinned shin or a stubbed toe.

Behind the arch, in the very darkest shadow, was the object of my foray. I pulled the cylinder free and sighed in relief. A rifle. With no dust on its tip, and no dust on its trigger.

I allowed myself one quiet "Ah, hah" while I considered what to do. Earlier I'd promised myself to leave the rifle in place and merely suggest its existence to ol' Super Cop, thus saving myself a must-you-meddle lecture (recited by rote, but still nettlesome). But if I replaced it and it subsequently disappeared, we might lose a vital link between Cyndi and Mac. I told myself to stop using "we" in terms of the investigation. As Luanne had pointed out in an unnecessarily acerbic voice, there was no "we." The only "we" in the official investigation was going to get herself in deep trouble if she persisted. Then again, I couldn't leave the rifle to be carried away by an unseen hand—even if I knew whose face worked in conjunction with the unseen hand.

I almost wished Caron were with me to offer up some pertinent pearl of wisdom I'd instilled in her. The beam of light fell across the top of a coffee table. The patina of dust glittered like a moonlit beach, smooth and deceptively silky. Unwanted thoughts stole into my mind. Claire and Peter under a palm tree, K-I-S-S-I-N-G. First comes love, then comes marriage, then come bills and fights and obligations and lack of privacy and power struggles and acrimony and divorce. Which didn't rhyme, but had a certain inevitable ring to it.

Granted, this was a pretty goofy time and place to stand around creating perverse variations on old jump-rope rhymes, but the cosmic force had a sly sense of humor. Claire Malloy, dressed in corduroy (that one wasn't easy), went to the police station to kiss her fellow. How many lectures did he give her?

Could I cook dinner and share my bed on a nightly basis? Would he insist on an entire shelf in the bathroom? Could he possibly know what to do with a fifteen-year-old girl who lost her mind on a regular basis? Did he realize my electric blanket had only one control, and I preferred sizzle to freeze? And what was wrong with the status quo, for pete's sake?

It was the pageant, I told myself angrily. The pageant was amock with sweet young things aspiring to Barbie their hearts out for the nice young Kens. To play house and make babies. Peter and I were troupers, gray-haired veterans of the matrimonial wars. We had no business rejoining in this societal myth. I vowed to read no more fiction until my head cleared.

All this nonsense gave me enough courage to reach a decision about the rifle. The decision fell neatly between brash and prudent: I would take the rifle to the office and lock it in there for the moment. The second it was secured, I would go home and call Peter, who would sputter for a while, sigh, and agree to send a minion down to take it to the crime lab. I then would invite my policeman over for a glass of wine, and when the ambiance was proper, offer my case for the continuation of the status quo.

I shut the door of the prop room, went out of the audio booth and shut that door, and started across the stage with the rifle held delicately between my thumb and forefinger, my pinkie curled as if I were prepared to sip tea from the barrel. I was awash in smugness when I heard a noise from the rear of the auditorium. It was not a creak. It was not a scuttle. It was not a rat. Rats don't cough.

"Who's there?" I demanded in a remarkably steady voice. I shined the flashlight over the rows of seats, noticing uneasily that their backs curved like tombstones. "Who's there, damn it?"

A flashlight clicked on, blinded me for a brief second, then glinted off the rifle before returning to the carpet near the doorway to the west corridor. "I came by to pick up some notes I left here earlier," said Steve Stevenson as he came down the aisle and joined me in the middle of the stage. "What on earth are you doing here, Claire? Is that a gun you're carrying?"

I waited until my heart stopped pounding louder than a beatnik's bongo drum. "Good grief," I managed to say, steadiness having deserted me, "you almost gave me a heart attack. I had a vision of a giant rat with emphysema. This pageant has addled my brain."

"The entire thing has been a nightmare for all of us," he said, politely not commenting on my alleged deterioration. "I'm truly sorry if I startled you. I must admit you rather startled me; I never dreamed anyone was in the theater. Would you like to sit down for a moment?" He glanced at the rifle and gave me a faint smile. "Or, if you prefer, we could creep downstairs and shoot rats. When I was a kid, I used to go out to the dump at night and take potshots at them. In a small town, one settles for small amusements."

"No, I . . ." My powers of glib invention had eloped with my nerves. I shrugged ruefully and held up the rifle. "I found this in the prop room, and I think it links Mac to the blank fired at the convertible. Initially he and Luanne were the only people who had keys to the theater; I have Luanne's now, and—" I broke off to stare at him. "How'd you get in the theater, Steve?"

"Through the door," he said, dimpling at my silly question.

"It was locked when I arrived, and I locked it after I came inside. Do you have a key?"

"Why would I have a key?"

I reminded myself that he was a politician, and probably had a dominant gene that required him to respond to questions with questions. "Let me see if I can answer that," I said slowly. "Mac still has his key, unless he gave it to the police. I doubt he would loan it to you. I have Luanne's key in my purse. Therefore, there must be another key. Mac is the logical person to have made a copy and given it to someone, but again not to you."

"And why not?" Steve said, dimpling madly.

"I don't think he likes politicians. I don't think he liked Miss Thurberfest, either, but he did cooperate with her on several occasions. He might have given her a key so that she could work on the details of her scheme. Rehearsal is everything, you know."

"But that doesn't place the key in my possession. My opponent has accused me of all sorts of skullduggery, but he hasn't suggested I'm cursed with powers of mental teleportation. Surely you're not that addled?"

"Don't rush me," I said. I nibbled on my lip, wishing I had one of my innumerable lists in hand. "Let's assume Cyndi had a key to the front door, given to her willingly or unwillingly by the theater owner. Let's go further out on the hypothetical limb and assume she put it on a key ring with her dressing room key. Now, she had her keys earlier this afternoon, because she came to the theater and managed to get inside her dressing room. She couldn't have counted on the front door being unlocked; she knew the rehearsal schedule and most likely waited until she felt the theater would be empty."

"Astute analysis on her part."

"Oh, yes," I agreed. "She was a clever girl, our Miss Thurber-fest. She conceived of a plan to make the national tabloids, coerced an accomplice into aiding her, and almost pulled it off. When we overlooked a detail, she slyly drew attention to it. She even went so far as to insist the most gullible person in town come to the hospital and be persuaded that a maniac was stalking her with evil intent. The gullible person fell for it like a red-blooded, American chump. But let's not waste our precious time complimenting Cyndi on her astuteness."

"Yes, the key. We're up to early this afternoon when she came to the theater. Please continue, Claire."

"Cyndi said in the taped interview we saw on the five o'clock news that she was going to talk to someone before the pageant. It seems logical to presume she made an appointment to meet that person here in the theater, which would be empty from one until six."

"This is really impressive," he said. "I don't think I would have thought of that."

"Thank you," I said modestly. "She let the person in and locked the door. They went down to the dressing room for a conversation. At some point she realized she hadn't considered a vital detail of her scheme. Anyone who reads mystery novels knows it's potentially fatal to have secluded conversations with blackmail victims, especially in dark little basement rooms in unoccupied buildings. It never turns out well for the blackmailer."

"I tend to read memorandums and task force reports, but I do have time for a novel every now and then," he admitted with a round of particularly boyish dimples. "And you're right, of course. Blackmail victims are always unhappy with the situation, and willing to do almost anything. Who on earth do you think she was blackmailing?"

"The person who took her keys from the dressing room. That would be you, of course."

"Me? What damning evidence do you suppose she had on me?"

"I don't know, and for some reason, I don't think you're going to tell me." I nibbled on my lip for a long while. In the middle of the nibbling, I checked my watch and discovered we'd been engaged in the queer discussion for more than ten minutes. I considered the wisdom of a secluded conversation in a dark building with a man I'd just accused of murder, but he did not frighten me. All those dimples.

"Are you stuck?" he asked, interrupting my meanderings. "This is a large gap in your entertaining theory, Claire, and if I remember eighth-grade algebra, you have to progress through each and every step of the proof to arrive at an irrefutable conclusion. That's about all I remember, since Miss Heinbecker was the best-looking woman I'd ever seen in my fourteen years of life, and I spent most of the classtime staring at her like a love-struck calf, which I was."

I held up my hand to squelch further adolescent confessions. "I'll get it in a minute." I tapped the butt of the rifle on the stage while I tried to think of what Cyndi had on him. Maybe I was all wrong, I thought darkly. It seemed more likely that she knew some murky secret about her ex-lover, Warren. Warren could have done everything I'd accused Steve of, from visiting her dressing room after the parade to keeping the appointment that afternoon. Being an aide, he might have aided his boss by loaning him the key so he could return to pick up whatever notes he'd left.

"What notes did you leave here?" I asked abruptly.

"Nothing of any great value. Just a few papers that I intended to read tonight. Warren took the girls to see *Snow White,* and it's incredibly peaceful in the suite. It's difficult to concentrate when both ears are assailed."

"When did you leave them?" I persisted. "You weren't carrying anything when you arrived this evening."

"Then I must have put them down yesterday, I suppose. As I said before, they're not terribly important. I've been carrying them around for several days, hoping for an idle moment in which to glance over them. I wish I could remember exactly when I did take them out of my pocket; it would help me remember where I laid them."

I didn't buy a word of it, but I doubted I was going to win the skirmish. Senators did not prowl around dark theaters to find missing papers. Aides existed for that sort of thing. Aides ran errands, baby-sat, carried briefcases, and covered minor lapses from grace. Suddenly I had it.

"Warren and Cyndi had a torrid affair, right?" I said, hoping he hadn't noticed the flicker of enlightenment that had flashed across my face. "Eunice was against it from the start, and eventually you tried to wrest apart the ill-fated lovers, right?" He nodded at each of my rhetorical questions, clearly intrigued now that we had started up again. "You insisted they have separate rooms in Hollywood," I continued. "You even took the room between them. Did your room have an adjoining door to Cyndi's room, by the way? Kids can tiptoe down the hall on the way to steamy hotel-room trysts, but senators must be more discreet, especially those from conservative districts. In fact, a senator might use his aide to disguise the affair from the beginning. It would be so easy to allow everyone to think the two kids were carrying on like—like two kids. The aide could invite the girl to stay in his apartment for the weekend. Some people might cluck and mutter about today's youth, but no one would be scandalized. Then the aide moves out and the senator moves in."

"What a novel idea," he said wonderingly. "Is it from a novel?"

"Warren wasn't convincing," I said. "Those of us who have been around the track, so to speak, know when a young man is not adequately heartbroken after an affair is ended so coldly. His acting skills do not rival his political ambitions."

"Do you think you can prove any of this?"

"I think I might be able to. Warren may not have minded covering up for the affair, but he might balk at taking a murder rap for you. The police are awfully good at worming the truth out of people, and once they determine that you were the one having an affair with an eighteen-year-old girl, they'll realize you had a good reason to silence her, particularly after her ominous remarks in the taped interview."

"You're most likely right," he murmured, nodding. "It looks quite bad for a senator, especially a married one with small children, to have an affair with a young girl. It was a dreadful error on my part. Warren tried his best to talk me out of it, but I was in one of those midlife crisis periods. Turning forty, married to the perfect wife and helpmate, facing a brilliant future, and lying awake nights wondering if I'd missed something along the way. Something dangerous, exhilarating, irresponsible, absolutely crazy. I was the solid, reliable college student, and an uninspired but passable law student. I took a position with Patti's father the day after graduation from law school. He trained me so I could return to my district and win the senate seat. It was to be followed by four years as attorney general, the governorship, and then, of course, onward and upward." He shook his head and sighed. "It was a good game plan, and it might have worked. I had the financial backing and the right connections with powerful people. My family is incredibly photogenic, and I seem to have a certain appeal to both women and upscale neoconservatives. And I threw it all away for a shrewd girl who was a good deal more ambitious than I."

"You were supporting her all this time, weren't you?"

"At first it was a small loan every now and then, but after a few months she began asking for a little bit on a regular basis. I really didn't mind too much, but I did try to cut off the payments once I'd broken off the affair."

"Why'd you break it off?" I asked curiously.

"I'd filed for the primary that day, and it finally occurred to me that this was not appropriate behavior for a would-be attorney general. When I pointed this out to Cyndi, she readily agreed to call the whole thing off—as long as I sent money every month. Then, yesterday after the luncheon, as we walked back to the theater, she told me she intended to leave for California within a few days. She wanted fifty thousand dollars. Well, that was impossible."

"So once the press had been sent out of the theater, you went down to her dressing room to talk to her?"

He looked at me for a long time, his forehead creased as he considered what amounted to a full-fledged accusation. "Are you saying that she reiterated her demand and I tried to kill her? You must have an awfully low opinion of me, Claire."

Moi? Simply because I believed he was a coldblooded killer with a political conscience? I clucked sympathetically. "Yes, murder can certainly taint a reputation. But if you took her keys at that time, how did she plan to get into the theater this afternoon to hide?"

"I don't know," he said, scratching his chin as he frowned at me. Suddenly the dimples popped back into view. "Maybe I called her at the hospital and suggested it. I told her I'd meet her at one-fifteen with the money, or at least as much as I could put together on a weekend. When she refused my counteroffer, I had to stop her from exposing me. I probably thought I might get away with it."

I resisted an impulse to pat him on the arm and cluck some

more. "I doubt it, Steve. The police would have uncovered the truth about the affair by tomorrow, and then they would have come straight to you."

"But you're so much more clever than the police. From the moment I met you I thought you'd make a great political aide. Once all this is cleared up, we'll have a quiet dinner somewhere and I'll use all my wiles to persuade you. But first I have to tell you about the key—"

He stopped as spotlights came on with a loud snap. We were both blinded, caught in the glare as if we were deer on a dark country road. I tried to shield my eyes with the flashlight as I squinted into the auditorium, but I could see nothing. I heard a popping noise, and turned to see if Steve had heard it too. His hand was on his chest. As I stared, redness spread from beneath his fingers in a widening pool. He gave me a surprised look. Dimples appeared for a brief moment, then faded into smoothness. He crumpled to the floor of the stage.

I dove for the darkest corner, gulping back a scream as I thudded into the bottom of the staircase. A second pop was followed by a ping from the wall above my head. A third bullet struck the wall a tad lower and a tad closer. The next ruled out any hope of scrambling toward the protection of the greenroom. I realized I was clutching the flashlight and hurled it toward the orchestra pit. It rolled unevenly past Steve's body, with the arrhythmic noise of a faulty shopping cart, and fell into the orchestra pit.

A pink spotlight began to sweep across the stage in a chillingly methodical pattern. Sucking in a deep breath, I crawled up the spiral staircase, wincing at the faint rattle of the loose bolts. The catwalk was high enough to be protected by the short curtain across the top of the proscenium. I didn't have any really good ideas about what to do once I was thirty feet above the stage, but I could see that the stage offered no protection.

The light caught the tip of one shoe as I scampered like a squirrel. As I moved around the spiral, I could almost feel the sting

of a bullet in the back. The impact would throw me off the staircase. I probably wouldn't be around to feel myself hit the floor.

When I reached the top, I stayed on all fours and crawled down
the catwalk. Perhaps, I thought in an hysterical voice, there would
be a similar staircase at the end of the catwalk. I hadn't seen one,
of course. Then again, I couldn't go back down and present a
lovely target to the killer in the light booth. Who was . . . not
Steve Stevenson, boy wonder of state politics, who no longer suffered from a midlife crisis.

The spotlight moved up the staircase like a luminescent stalker.
I scuttled to the end of the catwalk, which simply ended in midair,
and lay down as flat as I could. While I waited to be picked off, I
closed my eyes and tried to guess who was on the business end of
the gun.

"Claire? Where are you?"

It was McWethy. I decided it would be less than wise to answer
his question. I burrowed deeper into the metal runway. McWethy,
the accomplice. McWethy, the possessor of the keys, the phantom
of the playhouse. McWethy, a homey sort who as likely had a gun
rack in his pickup and spent weeks every year attempting to kill
Rudolph and his antlered friends. A deer caught in a spotlight
freezes. Steve had frozen. Now he was dead.

Suddenly the spotlight went out. Red and yellow fireworks filled
my vision, then slowly shrank into nothingness. No longer feeling
like Bambi, I lifted my head to look down over the edge of the
catwalk. I might as well have peered into an ink bottle. Admittedly, it was preferable to being trapped by a spotlight, but it
wasn't exactly improving the situation in terms of getting out of
the theater in a tidy, intact fashion.

I was considering any potential advantage in creeping back to
the top of the staircase when the houselights came on. After a
moment wasted trying to figure out what the hell was going on
now, I eased forward until I could see the stage below me. Mac

stood next to Steve's sprawled, lifeless body. He held a rifle in his hand.

I must have let out a small noise, for he looked up at me with a scowl. "What are you doing up there, woman? You seem to find something irresistible about that place."

I ducked back so that he couldn't (easily, anyway) put a bullet between my lovely green eyes. "You won't get away with it," I said with amazing coolness, not one degree of it heartfelt. "The police are on their way at this moment."

"Did *you* call them?" He sounded perplexed rather than alarmed.

"No, I didn't call them. But someone on the sidewalk must have heard the shots and called them. They'll be here in less than a minute."

"You must have ridden the little yellow bus to school. How could anyone have heard a shot fired all the way in the back of the theater?"

I was tired of logic games. "I told several people where I was going tonight, and I also told them that you were Cyndi's accomplice. I don't know why you killed Steve—maybe you were in love with the girl and lost your control when you heard him discussing the affair—but in any case, you won't get away with it."

"I won't get away with it? *You* won't get away with it. I don't even know what it is, but I damn well know I haven't done anything. Now are you going to stay up there like a turkey buzzard in a dead tree, or shall I come up there and drag you down here?"

"Don't consider it, buddy. I have a gun."

"Is this rusty thing your so-called gun? This is from the prop room, and it isn't capable of firing anything but blanks of wadded paper. I don't know what you used to shoot the politico, but it wasn't this."

I risked my future to look down at him. He was holding the rifle, which I'd dropped in panic—bullets always unnerve me. "I'll tell you what," I called, "I'll stay right here while you call the ambulance and the police. I promise not to move. Okay?"

"You are the oddest damn woman I've ever met," he growled. "Yeah, you stay up there in your roost, and I'll call the police from the office. Any messages for them?"

"Ask for Lieutenant Rosen," I said in a small voice. "And please ask him to hurry."

"T"W"E"L"V"E"

Jorgeson had to come up to the catwalk and coax me down as if I were a terrified kitten on a branch. My fingers were raw from having dug into the metal surface, and my knees were scratched and sore. Jorgeson held my elbow until we reached the lovely security of the stage, which was swarming with policemen, paramedics, plainclothed men with cameras and black cases, and one disgruntled medical examiner whose turquoise pajamas showed beneath his trouser cuffs. All of them stopped to stare as Jorgeson escorted me across the stage to a still figure with crossed arms and an exceedingly stony expression.

I opted to take the initiative. "Arrest that man," I said, pointing at Mac.

Mac shrugged his bony shoulders. "You might prefer to arrest this woman."

"I might," Peter said levelly. "However, I suppose we ought to explore the issue before I call the paddy wagon. In that the team would like to begin the homicide investigation, I suggest we continue this in the office." He instructed Jorgeson in a low voice, conferred with the medical examiner, barked at an unseen person in the light booth, and then brusquely gestured for McWethy and me to follow him off the stage.

Mac unlocked the office door. Peter sat down in the chair behind the desk, thus leaving me no choice but to sit next to a purported murderer on the couch. Oblivious to my frown, Peter took out a notebook. He arranged a pencil beside it, studied both for a moment, then looked at us and soberly recited the Miranda warning.

Once Mac and I agreed we understood our rights, he said, "This is preliminary, just to give me an idea of what the hell is going on. Both of you will be taken to the station shortly to give formal statements. With luck, some of you may be home by dawn. Others of you may be less fortunate. Mrs. Malloy, why were you in the theater?"

I explained about the rifle and the inexplicable cosmic force. It did little to ease the cold anger in Peter's eyes, but it was the best I could do. I then repeated the crazy conversation with Steve and the subsequent events that resulted in my hiatus on the catwalk.

Peter wrote down several pages of notes, then regarded me for a long while, his mouth almost twitching. He looked at my companion. "And why were you in the theater, Mr. McWethy?"

"Pretty much the same reason," he said as he lit a cigarette and leaned back. "I thought the prop room was an ideal place to hide a weapon, but when I came back to the theater and saw the girls with the revolver, I realized they'd been prowling around in there. I should have buried the rifle in the pasture out behind my house, but I hate to discard anything that might be useful in the future. Except ex-wives, of course. That's not to say I've buried any of them in the pasture. I'll admit I've considered it."

"Then you did assist Cyndi in some of her pranks?" Peter continued, ignoring the diversion with a pinched smile.

"Not with any enthusiasm, Lieutenant. It seems Eunice Allingham knows some loudmouthed chippy down at city hall. The chippy told Cyndi about a small exchange of favors with the wiring inspector, the exchange involving cash on my part and a passing report on the inspector's. Hell, this building is ancient; it would have cost a fortune to bring it up to current standards. The inspector was cheaper than at least one of my ex-wives."

I held back a smile of triumph. "Then Cyndi used that information to coerce you into giving her a key and helping her with her dirty deeds in your theater?"

"Mrs. Malloy," Peter inserted rather rudely, "if it isn't too much of a bother, I'd like to conduct the inquiry. I am not only a trained detective, but also the head of the Criminal Investigation Department. Unless you've received a mail-order badge, you are a civilian. A civilian who is up to her neck in very hot water, I might add."

"I arrived at the conclusion before you did."

"Could that be because you operate without restraint or reason? Without concern for your well-being? Without regard for previous promises to mind your own business and stay out of this?"

I nodded politely. "That seems accurate, Lieutenant Rosen, if not especially conducive to further cooperation from a concerned citizen who was merely assisting the police."

Mac cackled at this temperate exchange of words. "You two know each other, right?"

Peter slapped down the notebook. "Yes, Mr. McWethy, in one sense, I suppose we do. Let's return to the immediate problem of a dead body on the stage, wild accusations, and the rest of this muddle. You came down to the theater to pick up the rifle, which you'd left in the prop room. Would you please continue?"

He crossed his legs and looked at me through a cloud of smoke. "I heard voices, and being an inquisitive sort myself, I tiptoed down the corridor to see who all was trespassing in my theater. About halfway to the auditorium, I heard a series of shots. I will admit I stopped for a moment to consider my options, then went on to the doorway in time to see Claire creeping along the catwalk, her fanny swishing like a widemouth bass in an eddy. The lights went out, which again led me to consider various options. After a couple of minutes of nothing happening, I turned on the house lights and went up to the stage to see if I could do anything for the Senator. It was a damn sight too late to do anything except compose a eulogy."

"He's lying," I said. "He shot Steve. He tried to lure me down so he could shoot me, but I refused to cooperate."

"Why would I do that?" Mac gave Peter a manly, aren't-women-something smile. "I figured you boys would realize my involvement with the pranks sooner or later, although it didn't seem as if you were going to find the missing weight. There was something about 'The Purloined Letter' that caught my fancy when I was but a mere lad drinking RC Cola and munching Moon Pies back in Carroll County, USA. An idyllic youth . . . me and Poe and a dog named Blue."

"Then you stole the sandbag?" I said, scowling at him.

"In that it belonged to me, I think a more appropriate term might be 'recycled,' don't you? For the record, that was strictly wacko Miss Thurberfest's idea. She's the one who climbed up to the catwalk, sawed the rope, pranced around on the stage at a prudent distance from her mark, and ultimately entertained us with the bout of vapors. I told her it was harebrained. I told her that the bit with the nail was overly melodramatic and that I'd be delighted to push her into the orchestra pit whenever she wished. I don't know why the silly girl declined my heart-felt offer." His eyes narrowed and his voice turned grim. "I also told her not to fool with the space heater, but it was clear she was driving with one headlight by that point. I didn't think to tell her that locking the dressing room door and turning off the light were not condu-cive to being rescued by the gallant men in blue."

One of the gallant men gazed stonily across the room. "Did it not occur to you that we were investigating a homicide and you might want to share that significant tidbit with us?"

"Well, now that you mention it, it did occur to me. I was thinking I might wander by the station tomorrow and spill the whole crockpot of beans on your desk. But what I did isn't Al Capone stuff. The girl was weird and her head was crammed with grandiose ideas, but I just did what I was told to do. I didn't hurt anyone or break any laws. I had no reason to kill her—or that politician with the slick lips and manicured fingernails. I wouldn't waste the energy on either of them."

"The police dislike being called in on false pretenses, and firing at the convertible is worthy of attempted assault, reckless disregard, and whatever else we can find in the books," Peter said.

Mac blew a stream of smoke toward the desk. "You may get to slap my wrists, Lieutenant, but I don't see myself chopping any cotton at the state penitentiary."

"You deserve worse," I said. "You participated in a prank that might have led to a car wreck—at best. Your role in the incidents in the theater may have been passive, but firing a rifle at a car in the middle of several thousand people is both active and totally idiotic. How did Cyndi persuade you to do it?"

"Now that the girl's dead, we'll allow that to rest in peace."

Peter picked up the pencil and rolled it between his fingers. "Let me see if I've got this," he at last said, flashing his teeth at me. "Senator Stevenson had an affair with Cyndi Jay, and used his aide to cover it up. It ended by mutual consent and a monthly payment. When she upped her demand, the Senator murdered her. He felt such minimal remorse that he amiably admitted it all to Mrs. Malloy, blaming it on a pesky midlife crisis. Someone in the light booth also heard the confession, and turned on the spotlights in order to shoot the two of you. Mrs. Malloy has explained her presence with her usual candor and charm. Mr. McWethy has explained his participation in the conspiracy and his presence in the theater. I have an accomplice, who will face a plethora of minor charges, if not some time in a restrictive environment. I also have a trespassing meddler. The question is: Do I have a murderer?"

"He did it," I said.

"I still think you did it," Mac murmured. He sent a haze of smoke into my face and gave me a crooked smile. "Maybe Cyndi wasn't the only broad who was willing to do anything to attract attention."

"Jorgeson would have noticed a weapon on the catwalk," I said, trying not to cough.

"What do you think I did with the weapon—swallow it? You do overestimate my talents."

Peter's pencil broke with a loud snap. "Quiet, both of you. One of the uniforms will take you to the police station so that you may each give a formal statement concerning every single thing you've done in the last three days. I want to know everything you've had to eat or drink, I want to know when you brushed your teeth, and I want to know the precise color of the pajamas you wore to bed each night. It will occupy you for many, many hours. The investigation of the scene will occupy me for a similar time, so perhaps we will meet again at dawn." He started for the door.

"I need to do something about Caron," I said meekly.

He told me I could use the telephone and stalked out of the office. While Mac watched me with an amused look, I dialed my house and listened to the busy signal. Without maternal control, Caron would talk until she heard my footstep outside her bedroom door. Which might occur in twelve hours. I called Luanne's house and allowed the telephone to ring until it became obvious she wasn't hobbling across the room to answer it.

Peter would have to send someone to my apartment, I decided as a nasty tendril of pain shot across my temples. Still under Mac's smirky scrutiny, I went into the bathroom and checked the medicine cabinet behind the mirror. Someone in the theater's illustrious past had experienced a headache, but the label on the bottle was spotted and brown. The lone tablet in the bottle was equally spotted and brown.

Wondering if Luanne had stashed a bottle of aspirin in the desk, I sat down in the chair and tugged at the drawers. They did not budge.

"Do you have a key for these?" I asked Mac.

"I did, but I gave it to the Bradshaw woman last week. She wanted a place to keep the files and things, although I doubt anyone would be really desperate to get the invoice from the florist or the girls' dossiers."

"Oh," I said brightly. "It's not important. My head'll explode at some time in the next few hours, but we can hope it happens with my usual candor and charm."

A shiny-faced policeman who should have been at a high school prom came into the office and told us we were going to the station. As we went across the lobby, Peter came up the corridor. I told him about the small problem of reaching Caron, and he agreed to send someone over to transport her to Inez's house for the duration. Although his voice was mild, I could tell he was still angry.

"I'm sorry," I said. "I shouldn't have come here tonight, but I wanted to make sure my theory was right before I told you about it. I was going to call you the second I got home."

"Is there anything else you've forgotten to mention?"

I toyed with the idea of mentioning Luanne's behavior, even though it had nothing to do with the crimes. I glanced at his face and decided he did not want to hear any jump-rope rhymes, no matter how quaint and winsome they were. "No, nothing. Has someone gone to the hotel to tell Patti what happened?"

"I'm going now. You and I can discuss certain things later, but I need to wake Mrs. Stevenson to inform her that her children no longer have a father and she no longer has a husband. This is not an intriguing game, Claire; it's ugly and painful and real. A nineteen-year-old girl was murdered this afternoon, and a promising young politician tonight. You're damn lucky to be alive."

On that cheery note he left the lobby. Our pimply policeman ordered us to follow him to his car. It would have been impressive had his voice not cracked, but I nodded and did as I was told. As we drove down Thurber Street, now deserted and lined with litter, I rehashed the noticeably peculiar conversation with Steve. He had, as Peter put it, amiably admitted everything. The covert affair. The blackmail demand. The first attempt to kill Cyndi by simply locking the door and hoping for the worst. When the worst didn't happen, a call to the hospital with an invitation for a quiet little conversation. Murder. Remorse, but accompanied by dimples and a shrug. Had he actually admitted anything, or had he enjoyed my theory because he knew it was wrong? All wrong. Politicians and stagnant pond water were equally transparent.

Beside me, Mac lit a cigarette and gazed out the window, as serene as an elderly passenger on the deck of an ocean liner. He was hardly the type to express remorse, I thought with a frown. A century earlier he would have worn black and leased his six-shooter skills to the highest bidder. I wished I could come up with a motive that explained why he'd killed Cyndi and Steve, but I couldn't.

I worked on Warren for three blocks, but I couldn't come up with much of a motive for him, either. If he hadn't had an affair (and it seemed he hadn't), then he would hardly fly into a rage and strangle Cyndi with the hair-dryer cord or shoot the Senator from the light booth. I considered the possibility that he nurtured a secret passion for Cyndi, and had been forced to watch helplessly as the Senator took advantage of her youthful innocence. How many nights had he driven around town while his boss and his beloved frolicked in his very own bed?

It wasn't great, but it might play and Warren did have opportunity. He had been in the theater at the time of the first attempt on Cyndi's life. During the festival, he could have slipped away from his charges to meet Cyndi at the theater. He could have abandoned them to Disney's enthralling clutches for a few minutes this evening.

Eunice? She had a motive, although a feeble one. Cyndi had betrayed her, had laughed at her affections, had cast aside her financial investment and her dreams of the Big One. Eunice had spoken to Cyndi in the hospital, and could have arranged a meeting at the theater. As I replayed the conversation at Eunice's house that evening, I realized that she knew the truth about the affair, or at least had a healthy suspicion. Her acrimonious attack of Steve indicated as much. She might not have murdered Cyndi (it sounded extreme, even to me), but she might have listened to Steve's "confession" and gone berserk with rage. Really extreme.

Before I could rationalize away the extremities, we arrived at the brick building that housed Farberville's finest. The teenaged policeman parked, ordered us out of the car, and with a jaunty step guided us into Dante's Inferno.

As Peter predicted, the early birds were hopping around as I came out the glass door to the sidewalk. The sky was metallic gray, the air oppressive with humidity. The infant officer had disappeared, as had my fellow grillee. The whiskery deskman had informed me that no one was available to drive me back to my car, which I'd left behind the theater about a decade ago. He hadn't sounded overly apologetic about it, either.

I trudged along the sidewalk, muttering to myself and kicking an occasional beer can. Now Peter could determine, should the mood strike him, where I'd been every blasted second for the last seventy-two hours. The final six had been spent in a grubby little room, done in contemporary dungeon. The scarred table was now covered with cups of cold coffee. Ashtrays brimmed with acrid cigarette butts. Somewhere within the hallowed walls, a clerk was facing the inspirational job of typing a two-pound manuscript of my mundane movements. I had been ordered to return within twenty-four hours to sign it. I doubted it was of publishable quality.

"Hey, Senator," called a jovial voice.

I halted and looked back at a battered pickup truck, the predominant color of which was rust. Arnie waved enthusiastically from the driver's side. His eyes were red, his smile effusive. I recognized the symptoms. "Hey, Arnie," I said, edging back to the far side of the sidewalk in case he decided to jump the curb.

"Did they arrest you for reckless driving?" Arnie continued. "Don't you have political amnesty? No, wait a minute—they call it something else. Diplomatic immobility. Don't you have any diplomatic immobility, Senator?"

"Only in the sense I'm without transportation." As soon as the words came out, I regretted them. I prayed he'd missed the message, but Arnie was too sensitive for that.

"Hop in, then. We'll just have ourselves a little spin around town. This is a great time to tour, since everybody's asleep. No traffic, no kiddies in the street, no cause to slow down for anything—except a stray dog or a suicidal squirrel. We can do every single street in town before most folks read their Sunday newspapers over bran flakes and instant coffee."

"It sounds like a grand idea, Arnie, but I'm tired and I need to get home. It's been a hard day's night, and then some."

"No problem, Senator. I'll run you home." He disappeared for a moment as he leaned across the seat and opened the passenger's door. "Aw, come on. I'll drive real careful; I swear it on my brother-in-law's bass boat. It's got a hundred-and-fifty-horsepower outboard you wouldn't believe. Wowsy, can that baby take off like a bat outta hell!"

Which is what I was afraid he might do, the very minute I was beside him. I shook my head. "Thanks, anyway, but I think I'll walk."

"Suit yourself, Senator," he said, sprawling across the seat once again to claw at the elusive door handle.

I risked it all to cross the sidewalk and push the door closed for him. He gave me a grin, touched the visor of his cap, and glanced in the rearview mirror to see if any police cars were going in or out of the station parking lot. As he started to pull away, a flicker of an earlier statement came back to me.

"Arnie! Stop, please," I called, trotting a few steps in pursuit. He stopped and leaned out the window. "Change your mind,

Senator? You ole Washingtonians never seem to know what all you want to do."

"I'd appreciate a ride to the theater. Is it possible that we can drive very slowly so that we can talk?"

"Whatever makes you happy." He waited until I was settled beside him, then slammed the truck into first gear. We peeled away from the police station in a haze of burning oil and a shower of gravel.

I waited to hear a siren come to life behind us, but apparently all the good little cops were home asleep and the big bad ones inside the station bullying innocent witnesses. Once I could pry my cold white lips apart, I said, "I wanted to ask you about the parade, Arnie. Did you tell the state policeman who found you that you'd been given instructions?"

"Lordy, lordy, I get instructions all the time. My brother-in-law sez don't drive the boat so gosh darn fast or you'll rip off the bottom on a stump. My boss sez hose down the trucks until they glitter like Christmas balls. My counselor at AA sez all sorts of things, but you may be able to tell I don't pay a whole lot of attention to him."

"I'm curious about the parade. What were the instructions concerning the convertible?"

He took both hands off the steering wheel and began to count on his fingers. "First, be there at two-thirty or else. Go to the parking lot and do whatever they say through those megaphones. Don't drive too fast, and don't drive too slow. Don't say anything nasty in front of the passengers. Don't discuss politics with the Senator."

I grabbed the wheel and jerked it to the side, thus saving a suicidal squirrel and an impassive fire hydrant. "Would you mind. . . ?"

"Sure, Senator. Hey, you don't mind if we talk politics just a little, do you? This uniform capitalization is making me crazy. I got to admit I can't figure out how to calculate my taxes this year. I thought you ole boys was going to simplify it for us ignorant fellows."

Having had some success steering the truck, I attempted to do the same with the conversation. "You're not ignorant, Arnie. We both know you're as sly as they come. After all, you followed instructions, didn't you?"

"To the best of my God-given talents," he said, watching me out of the corner of his eye. He pulled over to the curb and cut off the engine. "Back in a jiffy, Senator. Can I bring you anything?"

I shook my head. He bounced into a yellow brick building, and emerged a few minutes later with a white paper sack. "Day-old doughnuts," he announced as he got back into the truck. "Help yourself, if you're feeling a little hungry after a night in the slammer. I'm always ravenous, myself." He crammed one in his mouth, started up the truck, and blithely pulled back into the blessedly empty street.

"Now about these instructions," he said, reaching into the sack between us. "You could say I did, and you could say I didn't, depending on your where you stand on the issues. Now, I'll be the first to say I didn't drive the convertible like the parade chairwomanperson said I was supposed to, although we might not have been shot at if I'd been at the helm. Then again, I did fetch the convertible after the parade like I was supposed to."

"And head for the Dew Drop Inn?"

"I don't recall it was specified where I was supposed to go. All I was told—instructed, if you prefer—was to get the car and then get it and yours truly out of town for a couple of days. I was limited by my choice of destinations; I lacked the ready capital to make it to Florida, or even the racetrack in Hot Springs. So I said to myself, I said, Arnie, why don't you run out to the Dew Drop and see if anybody's interested in a friendly game of eight-ball? Worked out nicely, until old smoky showed up."

"Were these instructions given with any financial remuneration?"

"Why, Senator, do I look like the sort of man who'd accept a bribe?" He gulped down a mouthful and gave me an indignant scowl.

"Heavens no," I said hastily. "I'm terribly curious to know who gave you the instructions to snatch the car after the parade."

"Do I look like the sort of man who'd accept a bribe?"

"Yes, now that I look at you more closely, I see that you do." I opened my purse and took out my billfold, which was in no way bulging with bribes. "How about an easy ten, Arnie?"

"I've been eating day-old doughnuts so long I've forgotten what fresh ones taste like."

"Twenty will buy a lot of fresh doughnuts, Arnie," I said with more mildness than I felt. "Dozens and dozens of them. More than anyone could eat in one day. If you buy too many, you'll end up with day-old doughnuts, anyway."

"Ain't life ironic?" Chuckling, he stopped in front of the theater and offered the sack to me. "Last chance, Senator."

Thirty-one dollars and eleven cents bought me the right to take three guesses. I handed over the cash, then leaned back and considered the most likely instructors. In the interim, Arnie ate doughnuts and discussed his favorite game shows. He seemed confident he could take all their money and shiny new cars, given the opportunity, but it was too expensive to get out to LA to take a test, and besides, everybody knew they were more interested in minority contestants. Now if he were a black Chicano woman . . .

McWethy had fired the shot, I decided, and therefore might have wanted the evidence whisked away until everyone calmed down. "A tall, gangly man with a beard?" I suggested.

He beeped the horn and shouted, "Who was the sixteenth President of the United States?"

Rain began to splatter on the windshield in the ensuing silence.

"Ah, sorry, Senator," Arnie murmured. "No, it wasn't any tall, ganglious type."

While he hummed tunelessly and drummed his fingers on the top of the steering wheel, I tried to envision Cyndi in a conversation with Arnie. I reminded myself that she had blackmailed Mac into abetting her. She certainly wouldn't want the bullet examined before her round of television interviews and press conferences.

I gave Arnie a stern look, then said, "Was it the girl who rode in the back of the convertible? Pretty, with dark hair and long, thick eyelashes?"

His hand jerked toward the horn, but stopped with centimeters to spare. "No, it wasn't the beauty queen who kept yelling someone was trying to kill her. I'd remember that. That's two, Senator."

The rain increased, until it battered the roof of the truck and trickled through a crack in the windshield. The gutters along the street filled with bubbling brown water. Raindrops hurled down from the marquee and splattered on the sidewalk like ping-pong balls. I felt like the mendacious maiden in Rumpelstiltskin, which is to say I didn't have a clue to the unknown name. I wasn't sure it mattered, but at some level it seemed important. Vital. True to the fairy-tale premise, I ran through all the names of anyone remotely connected with the pageant, from the contestants and judges to Sally Fromberger. I was on the verge of admitting defeat and offering Arnie a check, when he abruptly switched on the engine.

"I've got to run along, Senator. I want to get home in time to watch 'Meet the Press,' just like you do. Really nice to have seen you; maybe we can have lunch some time. I hear the bean soup at the capitol dining room is wowsy."

"I have one guess left," I reminded him. "We agreed on the rules before I gave you every last cent in my purse. We are going to sit here until I make my third guess, and it may not be until 'Sixty Minutes' comes on tonight."

"You politicians know how to drive a hard bargain, don't you?"

You've got me over the ole porkbarrel, Senator. I don't know the lady's name, but she was attractive. Dark hair. No older than you. Nice manners. Better heeled than some. That's about all I can tell you. Now, if you'll pardon me, I would like to get home in time to whip up an omelette before my show comes on. You ever tried mushrooms and ricotta cheese, with just a pinch of oregano? Ciao."

He leaned across me and opened the door. I was eased off the seat with a gentle, unrelenting hand. The door slammed shut and the truck drove down Thurber Street. I realized I was standing in the rain, gawking, and moved under the marquee to gawk.

Sally Fromberger was a blonde. Feminist considerations aside, the pageant contestants were girls, not women. Eunice was not unappetizing, but I doubted she would be described as "attractive," and she certainly was older than I. I could think of two women who fit Arnie's criteria. I realized my shoes were filling with water and my nose was dripping in rhythm with the falling rain.

Cursing the desk sergeant for his lack of concern, I dashed down the sidewalk beside the building and around the corner to the alley. My car was gone. My comments were drowned out by the rain. I ran back to the protection of the marquee, clutched my purse to my chest for warmth, and gazed at the empty street. Taxis relentlessly cruise the streets of Manhattan, but they do not cruise anywhere in Farberville unless requested to do so. As I mentally reviewed the route to my apartment, the rain began to pour down hard enough to pockmark the concrete. Lightning snaked across the sky, and three seconds later thunder boomed. A gust of wind threw rain across my face—cold, cold rain.

There were pay telephones in front of the copy shop across the street. There were several valid reasons why they were of no damn help whatsoever. One involved whom to call, and another how to operate the machine without so much as a penny, Arnie having fleeced me with the adroitness of an Australian sheep shearer.

A second flash of lightning sent me to the glass door of the theater. I peered into the lobby, which was dark, deserted, and dry. Police seals were plastered along the edges of the doors, and a cardboard notice promised all sorts of official retribution to anyone who entered the premises. I took out my key and entered the premises. After all, the current situation was Peter's fault. I was cold and wet; one small telephone call and I would be out of there. Surely he would understand. Ho, ho.

"T"H"I"R"T"E"E"N"

It might have seemed expedient to make the call and get the hell out of the theater, but once I was in the office, I went to the bathroom and grabbed a handful of paper towels to dry my face. I took off my shoes, held them over the sink, and watched brown water dribble down the drain.

Despite a gloomy prescience, I went to the desk and dialed Luanne's telephone number. She did not answer. For a gimp, she was out quite often, I told myself as I slumped back in the chair and studied the ceiling. She was having an affair with Mr. Whoozit of tomato-growing repute, she worked for the CIA in her spare time, or she was involved in something she certainly didn't want me to know about. And doing an exceptionally competent job of it.

I noticed two broken pencil pieces on the desk. I decided it would not be tactful to call Peter, tell him someone had stolen my car, and ask him to give me a ride home from the same theater I'd illicitly broken into minutes ago. If I'd known Arnie's last name, I might have called him; an omelette sounded pretty damn good. The sociology professor who lived below me rode a bicycle. Caron was twelve months away from driving her mother anywhere except up the wall.

The light flickered as thunder echoed outside. I took my ever-ready flashlight from my purse and toyed with it while I contemplated my next move, which I was confident would prove to be brilliant. Things did not seem brilliant at the moment, however. I was stranded in a dark building which had housed two murder victims and had sheltered at least one murderer. If I stuck one toe outside, I would be struck by lightning, washed down the gutter with the litter, and arrested posthumously for trespassing.

On a more optimistic note, the office was reasonably warm and dry. I was the only inhabitant, and the police were not likely to drop by any time soon. The storm would end. I would then walk home, fix myself a hot cup of tea, and fall into my bed for six or eight hours. Eight or ten hours. Ten or twelve hours. The fantasy was so appealing that I went over to the couch and lay down, telling myself I would under no circumstances close my eyes for more than one second.

A jab in the rear woke me up a few minutes later. I felt the crack where the cushions met and found the perpetrator, a stiff corner of paper. I pulled it free and held it above my face. A sealed envelope, fresh and white rather than faded and yellow. It was thick enough to indicate it contained several sheets of paper. As I debated the delicate social dilemma of ripping open someone's mail to read the contents, I heard the front door open with a tiny click. Stealthy footsteps came across the lobby.

I scrambled to my feet, grabbed my flashlight from the desk, and hurried across the office to turn off the light. I used my flashlight to illuminate a path to the bathroom. I left the door open an inch and cowered behind the commode, feeling both inordinately silly and thoroughly alarmed. Police officers never sneak across anything. The first course at the academy is in striding, plodding, and stomping. At the moment, my heart was doing all three.

The office door opened and the light came on. Footsteps continued across the room. The chair squeaked. After a metallic click, a drawer was pulled open with a grating noise. Papers rustled.

My ears were right on top of the situation, but I couldn't see anything except the dusty plastic plant and one end of the couch. I suddenly realized I had the envelope in my hand; I folded it several times, and stuffed it down the front of my shirt in true heroine fashion. Then, frustrated to the point of recklessness, I inched around the commode so that I could see the desk.

Luanne, dressed in a raincoat and scarf, was taking something from the drawer. She let out a yelp of surprise as I stomped out of the bathroom. "Claire? What in heaven's—what are you—you doing here? Why were you hiding in there?" she said amid stutters and gasps.

I put my hands on my hips and glowered down at her. "My presence is a long and marginally entertaining story. What are *you* doing here—and more to the point, what are you taking out of the drawer?"

She closed the drawer with a bang. "Nothing of any significance. Just a few personal things I left here several days ago. I thought Mac was our resident phantom; I still can't believe you were hiding in the bathroom at seven o'clock in the morning."

"I am fed up with these evasions and digressions," I snapped. "If what's in the drawer is so darn insignificant, why did you risk the wrath of the police to come into the theater at—as you so accurately pointed out—seven o'clock in the morning? Why are the drawers always locked and what are you keeping in there?"

"I can't tell you," she said in a low voice. She looked down at her purse in her lap and sighed. "You'll have to trust me, Claire. I have a problem and I'm not ready to tell anyone about it. But it has nothing to do with the two murders and blackmail and all that crazy stuff. It's personal."

I went to the couch and sat down. Hating myself, I said, "How do you know there's been a second murder?"

"Peter called last night to tell me what happened. I'm supposed to go to the station and make a statement this afternoon."

"I called you last night right after Steve was killed, and you didn't answer the telephone."

Luanne covered her face with her hands, then jerked them away and gazed steadily across the desk at me. "I was home all night. You must have called while I was in the shower. Listen, Claire, I know my behavior has been pretty flaky this last week, but I didn't hurt anyone, much less decide to cut short the pageant by murdering Miss Thurberfest and the emcee."

"But you came here at an ungodly hour to get something from the desk drawer. Did Peter tell you to leave the drawer key at the police station when you went there?"

She nodded. "He wants to look through the contestants' applications, although I can't imagine what he's hoping to find—beyond whimsically creative bust measurements and inflated grade-point averages."

"Or a starchy white envelope?"

"I have no idea, Claire. He told me what happened, mentioning something sarcastic about Miss Marple-Malloy along the way. I said I'd appear at the station and drop off the key. That was the gist of it," she said with a look of bewilderment.

I slumped down and rested my head on the back of the couch. If the envelope wasn't Luanne's, then it was someone else's (Miss Marple-Malloy was again beginning to feel potential brilliance in the offing). It occurred to me that Steve's explanation for being in the theater involved some misplaced papers. The explanation hadn't held as much water as my shoes, but he certainly might have been looking for something. Something so vital that it warranted prowling around an inky theater.

Perhaps I'd disparaged Cyndi Jay too readily. She might have had enough sense to realize the inherent peril of chatting with her blackmail victim. The time-honored tradition was to keep the damning evidence in a safe place, and sneeringly inform the victim that he'd better not do anything rash. In fact, she'd been carrying an envelope before the parade. She'd been alone in the office afterward, and might have hidden it between the cushions of the couch.

Which led to the obvious conclusion that the envelope contained a detailed description of the affair. I could have ripped it open to confirm this, but, then again, it was still raining. Luanne didn't seem particularly comfortable behind the desk, but the couch was surprisingly devoid of springs poking through the plastic upholstery. And Super Cop might fail to be amused with torn evidence, which he would interpret as evidence of felonious interference on someone's part.

I dug around until I caught a corner of the envelope, then pulled it free and held it up for Luanne's inspection. "Do you know what this is? This is Cyndi's insurance policy. It's a lovely account of the blackmail ammunition she used on Steve for the last half-year, and was planning to utilize for the final payoff."

Luanne blinked. "It is? Is that why Steve came to the theater last night?"

"It makes sense," I said as I stretched out on the couch and closed my eyes. "She'd shown it to him earlier, minutes before the parade. After the parade, she was in this room, in her dressing room, and then at the hospital. The dressing room was too risky, since she knew the police would search for clues to her purported assailant. Steve must have been planning to check the greenroom or the audio booth when I appeared on the scene."

"Did he really confess to everything—just out and out admitting he was a philanderer, a blackmail victim, and a murderer?"

"Most amiably," I murmured. "So amiably that in retrospect I'm not sure I buy it. The affair is understandable; he was at the age when a lot of men lose their minds, and he sounded rather wistful when he talked about the grand passion." I thought of someone else who'd seemed rather wistful about beaches and happy-ever-afterness. "Do you think this midlife crisis is a male phenomenon they all go through—a rite of passage to pensions and middle-age spread? Whatever they've been doing suddenly seems inadequate, and they decide it's time to make a drastic change?"

"Didn't you go through one?"

"I haven't reached midlife yet," I said, raising my eyebrows. "That's why I was asking the opinion of an older woman."

The older woman sniffed. "I haven't qualified for a discount at the movies quite yet, but it's possible I'm somewhat precocious for my age. About two years ago, at the stroke of midnight, no less. I sat up in bed and looked at my second husband, who was happily snoring away like a freight train. I decided he was a great guy—sexy, cooperative, considerate, cheerful, trustworthy, loyal, obedient, et cetera. I then realized I didn't want to spend the rest of my life with a Boy Scout. Fred took the news well; he was a really nice man. My family, from my college-aged son to my dottery grandmother, all hit the ceiling of the family manor, and those babies are eighteen feet high."

"Sounds like a classic example of a midlife crisis to me."

"Well, I didn't start dallying around with the gardener's youngest son or the delivery boys from the market."

"Why not?" I asked through a yawn. "Too respectable?"

"The gardener's youngest son was nine, and the delivery boys were covered with zits."

"How old was the gardener?"

"Old enough to weigh several hundred pounds. And his fingernails were always so dirty; I don't know how Lady Chatterly stood for it. But now that we've explored the ramifications of the standard midlife crisis and found it genderless, if not senseless, what else did Steve say before he was killed?"

"He was terribly eager to admit his guilt, as if I'd already wrapped it up and stuck a bow on it. In reality, I was struggling with a lame story that would place a hypothetical key in his hypothetical pocket. He was a politician. Those guys can explain away a three-billion-dollar deficit—what's one little key?"

"Maybe he knew there was proof, once the police took off on the right tangent."

"If I hadn't taken a nap on the couch, no one could have proved he had an affair with Cyndi, much less that he tried to asphyxiate her twice. All he had to do was insist the theater door was unlocked when he arrived to look for his missing papers. Warren knew the truth, and Eunice had an idea what was going on, but—" I sat up so quickly I almost fell off the couch. "Patti knew, too. I heard her say something to Warren. At the time I didn't realize that she wasn't demanding an explanation—she was coaching him on his lines."

"Do you think she killed Steve because of it?"

"It ended six months ago, and I can't see her simmering for half a year while she went hopping down the campaign trail with him."

"Six months of luncheons with the Rotarians and I'd kill," Luanne said with a dry laugh. "Think of the menu: chicken à la something, green beans almondine, new potatoes, salad with thousand-island dressing, apple pie, and iced tea. The woman could get off on justifiable homicide."

I mumbled an agreement as I considered the significance of Patti knowing about the affair. No earthshaking conclusions rolled me off the couch. Four people knew for sure: Steve, Cyndi, Warren, and Patti. Eunice suspected. Mac had heard me tell Peter.

"Mac is involved in this somehow," I muttered. "He'd like us to believe that Cyndi had a mild bit of dirt on him, and that on her orders he gave her a key, ignored her peculiar behaviors, and fired at the convertible. She's not around to confirm or deny his story."

"But Peter said that Mac claimed he came to the theater to get the rifle before it was waved under a meddlesome amateur's nose, thus setting off all manner of questions."

I told her what Arnie had told me, which didn't take long. "So someone paid Arnie to snatch the convertible. It wasn't Mac and it wasn't Cyndi; Arnie may be a sot, but he's a credible sot. What if Patti were behind the shooting? She might have staged it for the same reason Cyndi was so frantically staging her pranks—publicity. The Senator didn't have the primary in the bag. His popularity would have shot up if he could stand tall against union thugs."

"You can't run around accusing her of that," Luanne protested. "She's the heiress apparent to a powerful political dynasty. She's not going to hire someone to fire a shot at a convertible simply to stir up publicity. She crosses her ankles when she sits down. She knows her linens. Her children wear petticoats and write thank-you notes."

"Okay, okay, she's not likely to have her photograph on the post office wall. But she is a political animal, perhaps more so than her good-looking, affable, manicured husband. Steve had more dimples than brains. Her father plotted out his career, saw him through an apprenticeship, and then patted his fanny and told him to end up in the White House. Everything was going quite well until Steve lost his mind over an eighteen-year-old beauty queen."

"You're fantasizing, right?"

"I haven't had anything to eat since five-thirty last night," I said as my stomach rumbled in unison with the thunder. "Low blood sugar, along with a night of interrogation, always makes me giddy." I heard the drawer open. Seconds later something landed on my lap. After a moment of fumbling, I discovered it was a cellophane-wrapped Twinkie. "Did a little truck with a tinkling bell just cruise through the lobby?"

"Elevate your blood sugar and continue with this theory."

"Yes, ma'am," I said. I polished off the Twinkie, licked my fingers, and then intertwined said fingers under my neck. "We've got hapless Steve Stevenson, destroying his career over a small-town girl. Warren covers for him, but when the affair is ended, the girl digs in her claws and demands money to keep quiet. Steve doesn't mind—until she ups the ante to an impossible level. He then feels obliged to silence her." I sat up and brushed the crumbs off the front of my shirt. "But suppose he wasn't the one who received the ultimatum? What if Cyndi assessed the perspicacity of the potential blackmail victims and realized Patti was the most promising?"

"You're beyond the curative powers of a single Twinkie. We need at least a half-gallon of Häagen-Dazs."

"This makes sense—sort of," I protested, licking a sticky lip. "Here's the scenario: Cyndi Jay decides to stage a few harmless pranks to get publicity. She acquires a key from Mac so that she can pull up a pertinent nail, saw the rope of the weight, and write a threatening message on her mirror. None of that works, to her chagrin. Unbeknownst to her, Patti Stevenson is playing the same game."

"How did Patti convince Mac to do the dirty deed?"

"Power and money, for starters. Now, if I may continue . . . When the shot is fired, Cyndi does her best to take credit as the victim, but that doesn't work, thus forcing her to pull the final desperate stunt with the space heater. Someone happens by for a chat, and locks the door on his or her way out."

"Patti wasn't in the theater," Luanne said heartlessly. "She couldn't have done it."

"Then she had help. Anyway, if you'll stop interrupting for a minute, I'll finish the story. Cyndi now realizes she has someone in the vise. She calls the hotel and arranges to meet Patti at the theater." I stopped. The very obvious became . . . well, obvious. "Cyndi didn't have her car at the hospital. She went there in the ambulance, and left under her own steam."

"Fascinating," breathed the devil's advocate, who was clearly enjoying herself.

"But it is fascinating. Think about it—who might have picked her up? Steve? No, he and Warren were at the Thurberfest. It's one thing to escape for a few minutes, but it's decidedly another to trot back to the hotel to fetch the car, drive across town to the hospital, drop Cyndi off at the theater, murder her, and then run the car back to the hotel. We're talking serious time-frame problems here."

The DA had to concede that one. "So it might have been a little awkward to bribe the pony man to cover for an hour. Warren and Steve couldn't have done all that, but Patti might have. You may resume."

"How really, really gracious," I said. "Patti's at her leisure long enough to do all of the above, and still be back at the hotel by midafternoon in time for tea. She accommodatingly arranges to pick Cyndi up in the hospital parking lot. They chat, Patti does the bit with the hair-dryer cord, and when Cyndi's thoroughly unconscious, she turns on the gas, locks the door, and drives back to the hotel to wait for Warren, hubby, and the kids to come home from the Thurberfest and tell her all about the clowns and pony rides. When the Feds decide to blame everything on Cyndi, it's confetti sprinkles on the cupcake."

"And she did all this to protect Steve's reputation? How very liberated of her. When I was younger, we used to fret about the girl's reputation—especially if she was seen in certain backseats after midnight."

"Well, he didn't have enough sense to do it, and she was keen to redecorate the Rose Room and hang the girls' photograph in the Oval Office. She had as much at stake as he did, if not a good deal more. All she had to do was keep him untarnished and dimpling, and White House here we come."

"That's tenable, if not terribly concrete. If she'd risked everything to protect Steve, who killed him?"

I rolled over and rested my cheek on the cool plastic cushion. "You can be very demanding at times."

"And how did he get the key to the theater last night? If he wasn't roaming the Thurberfest with the key in his pocket, having taken a quick break to murder Miss Thurberfest incarnate, how'd he end up with it? If he's so all-fired innocent, what's the point in shooting him? I hope you're not going to fall back on the maniac-off-the-street routine after all your whining and complaining about how you don't like that."

"Patti shot him. She gave him the key and told him to go to the theater and find the papers Cyndi hid. He obediently did as directed, but she must have had second thoughts about his ability to find anything, including the theater, and followed him."

"Weaker than the third cup of tea on one bag," Luanne said. "You were doing so well, Claire. I must say this is a letdown."

"If she didn't follow him," I mumbled to the cushion, "she followed someone. Mac was here; maybe she came to the theater to pay him for the sniping."

"Patti may be determined, but she's not demented. Why would she suggest they meet at the theater, especially when her husband was inside searching for a vital packet of evidence. Sorry, dear, it won't play in Peoria. The rain is letting up. Why don't you go home and call a certain cop to relate all this, as any civic-minded citizen would do."

"My car's been stolen," I said, sighing. "I guess I'd better report it. Then you can drive me home, and I will indeed call that man and offer my theory." I dragged myself up and across the room to the telephone. I called the police station and duly recited make, model, color, and license number. After a moment, I banged down the receiver. "My car wasn't stolen. The officer in charge of the investigation, one Lieutenant Rosen of the CID, had it impounded last night. Some goon towed it away to a fenced yard in the south part of town. The desk sergeant has no idea when it'll be released."

"He did that?" Luanne said, feigning dismay.

If I hadn't seen the smile, I would have been more impressed with her sympathetic tone. "Yes, he did, and he did it because he was angry with me. He then told the officers at the police station to refuse to give me a ride to the alley or even to my apartment. When it started raining, he must have been overcome with amusement." I went back to the couch and sat down, muttering under my breath. "He's not going to get away with this." I added when I could trust my voice.

"I'm not sure you can do anything to a police lieutenant," Luanne said dubiously.

"I'm not going to go home and tell him my theory," I said. "I may solve the whole thing and call a press conference in front of the theater. Certain police lieutenants will look rather foolish when a civilian solves the case for them."

"Oh, Claire," she said, shaking her head mournfully. "This may be your midlife crisis. Luckily, you can't prove any of your theory, and Patti Stevenson is not going to admit it to you so that you can show up the local CID."

I picked up the envelope and studied it. "I might not be able to prove my theory, but I can confirm it. Watch this," I went to the telephone, ascertained the number of the hotel from directory assistance, and dialed the number. While Luanne made disapproving noises, I briskly asked to be connected to Mrs. Stevenson's suite. The operator said no calls could be put through, but backed off readily when I said I was calling from the Governor's office.

"Mrs. Stevenson," I said, "this is Claire Malloy. I'm dreadfully sorry to disturb you, but I wanted to express my condolences for the terrible tragedy last night." Before she could mention the inappropriateness of the hour or the lack of gubernatorial connections, I added, "And I wanted to let you know I found something at the theater that I thought might interest you. I haven't called the police yet, but I suppose I ought to. However, it's of such a personal nature that I hate to involve them."

"Is this a cruel joke?" she demanded.

"I wish it were. I was napping on the couch in the office and discovered an envelope hidden between the cushions. It has your name written on it, Mrs. Stevenson."

"Did you—ah, open it?"

"No," I said truthfully, "that would be tampering with evidence, and the police take a dim view of that."

"Then how do you know it's of a personal nature? My husband often wrote out his itinerary for me and stuck it in an envelope. In fact, he mentioned that he'd lost the next week's schedule." She stopped, and after a melodramatic moment that would have done Caron proud, said, "That's why he went to the theater last night, Mrs. Malloy. He was looking for a few insignificant papers that I needed in order to arrange baby-sitting for the girls. My God, if we'd only known . . ."

"It's unfortunate that Warren couldn't have come in his place, but I suppose he was too devastated by Cyndi's death to do more than sit in a dark theater and watch dwarfs sing."

I was treated to another melodramatic moment while she decided how to field that one. I made a face at Luanne, who was shaking her head and clucking like a brooder hen. I covered the receiver and whispered, "I'm just checking on my theory. If she admits Steve was the one who had the affair, then we're back to first base. If she——"

"Yes, Mrs. Malloy," Patti said carefully, "Warren is very upset about the girl. We all were, of course, but he took it hardest. All the passions of youth, you know, and she was such an intense girl. Are you at the theater now?"

I said I'd had a bit of car trouble and was indeed stranded at the theater until the storm passed. We agreed it had been quite a storm. I offered to call the police and have them deliver the envelope to the hotel; she stumbled all over herself to say that was too much of a bother over a minor thing, a few sheets of paper with no intrinsic value. She added that she would run right down to the theater herself, because—well, she'd like to have the schedule as a keepsake. I said I'd be more than happy to wait for her, and replaced the receiver with a Cheshire cat smile.

"Good work, Marple-Malloy," Luanne said without enthusiasm. "You've just arranged to meet the alleged villainess of the plot in a basically deserted building on a dark and stormy morning. If she had no compunction about killing Cyndi, I doubt she'd evince any concern for your welfare. And if she shot her husband—why, she has a gun. Didn't you ever read any Gothic novels?"

I fluttered my eyelashes and clasped my hands together. "But I just have to go to the attic on the fifth floor to learn the truth about Baron von Nosepick's first wife. Why, whenever the wind blows across the moors, I can hear all those pitiful cries and the pitter-patter of feet around the turret. Every time I gaze in the mirror in her boudoir, I have amber eyes and raven hair. It's so very, very vexing. Whatever can it mean, my old and faithful nursemaid?"

"It means you've lost your mind, Veronica Angelica. You run along to the attic. I'll call Peter and tell him we've arranged to tête-à-tête with a possible murderer."

"I'll call him," I said, sighing. "But I hate to wake him up in the middle of a midlife crisis."

"F"O"U"R"T"E"E"N"

When Patti tapped on the glass door, I let her in the lobby and locked the door. She wore a tailored dress with all the right accessories, and despite the steady dribble of rain, looked fresher than a Junior Leaguer embarking on a charitable mission. Others of us were rumpled, frizzled, dusty, and tired. Accessories were out of the question. Patti studied me for a moment, politely disguising a grimace as a faint smile, and said, "I don't understand why you're here, Claire. There's a sign posted on the door that says the building is sealed until the investigation is completed. Aren't we trespassing?"

"Oh, yes," I said as I walked across the lobby and started down the corridor, forcing her to follow. I went into the auditorium and up the short flight of steps to the stage. Her heels clattered on the wood floor, and her breathing was audible. The houselights were on, but dimmed enough to keep both of our faces shadowed and the rear areas of the stage murky. I turned around abruptly. "The trespassing was inadvertent. I spent the night at the police station, making a formal statement, and then found myself stranded on the sidewalk."

"The sidewalk?" she said, bewildered. "But that hardly explains why you're in here."

"It all began on the sidewalk," I said with a wry chuckle (or what I hoped was a wry chuckle, having always felt the term ought to describe a visitor at a birdfeeder). "I was trudging toward Thurber Street when I managed to catch a ride with our mutual friend, Arnie. Wasn't that a stroke of luck?"

"I'm glad you didn't have to walk all that way, but I'm afraid I don't know anyone named Arnie."

"Of course you do, although you may not have heard his name. I'm sure you'd recognize him—short, black hair, red eyes."

She gave me the look that probably worked well when one twin accused the other of tie-dying the family cat. "Perhaps I have, if he's one of the myriad of loyal campaign workers. I meet so many people, but I simply can't keep them straight. Steve was very good at remembering names and faces." She stopped and took a lace-edged handkerchief from her purse to dab her eyes. I leaned forward to look for a weapon, but she snapped the purse closed and stepped back, her expression turning leery. "I do appreciate you taking the time to call me about the schedule. If you don't mind, I'm in a bit of a rush. The girls were asleep when I tiptoed out, but they may wake up any moment. The hotel manager is already perturbed about a broken lamp and some crayon scribbles on the wall."

"Surely Warren can control them," I said. "He seems quite efficient, even in his hour of grief over his loss of poor, poor Cyndi Jay. He's done a remarkable job of amusing your children all weekend. First the Thurberfest yesterday afternoon, and then the movies last night. You must appreciate the opportunity to be alone so that you can, as the kids say, do your own thing."

"I suppose all parents enjoy a few minutes of privacy. Now, if I could have the schedule?" Patti came forward, her hand outstretched. She was wearing suede gloves, which matched her purse, which matched her shoes, which may well have matched her underwear. The woman did accessorize. Although her smile was correct, her eyes glittered in the gloom and her hand shook. "I really must have the schedule, Claire."

"I'll get it for you in a moment," I said, retreating a few inches.

"I thought you wanted to know about our mutual friend, Arnie. He was nice enough to give me a ride to the theater. We even played an abridged version of Twenty Questions."

"How amusing for you." She didn't sound envious.

"Our game was called Three Questions, due to a lack of funds on my part and a feverish desire to watch 'Meet the Press' on his part. He's somewhat of a political buff, our friend Arnie." Wishing I had Caron's flair for theatrics, I forced myself to stop at the shore of the murkiness. "I was trying to guess who slipped him a few dollars to make the convertible vanish before the police got to it. Whoever bribed the chap made a mistake by paying him in advance, thus allowing him to stop by a bar before the parade, but it worked out. Arnie was supposed to be driving, but he did manage to repossess the car after the parade and abscond for the hinterlands."

"And you were permitted three questions?" she murmured. "I think I'd prefer three wishes. But this person you insist I know isn't exactly a magic fish, is he?"

"Three wishes," I repeated pensively. "Attorney general, governor, third star on the left and straight on till Pennsylvania Avenue? Steve might have been able to pull it off, had he not been killed. These days the voters hardly judge the candidates by intelligence, convictions, or the potential for decisive leadership. Dimples and affability seem to be the order of the decade."

"Steve was very popular with his constituents. He served them well and had an excellent reputation with his peers at the capitol. The governor was devastated when I told him this morning that Steve had been gunned down by union thugs. He swore he'd demand a federal investigation, and then asked me to complete the term." She paused to dab a few more invisible tears. "I told him I would, despite the pain of the tragedy and the hardship on the family. Staying busy will help me through the grief, I hope, and the girls will be able to stay with their friends at their little nursery school."

"And you won't have to worry about Steve's peccadillos, will you? Affability sometimes leads to situations that end up in a sticky mess—worse than cotton candy on a chin. However, you had things under control until the Miss Thurberfest pageant, when Cyndi decided her swan song would involve a final payoff that would sustain her career move."

Patti's smile faded. "I think you'll have to discuss the girl's problem with Warren. Steve and I had very little to do with her, beyond listening to Warren talk incessantly about her."

"That's unfortunate, since you and she had so much in common. Oh, I realize she was a small-town celebrity and you're the scion of a major political dynasty, but both of you were fiercely determined. She pulled her pitiful stunts for publicity, and you unwittingly were playing the exact same game to ensure Steve's victory in the primary." I shrugged as I tried to read her expression, self-preservation being dear to me. "Arnie admitted everything, I'm afraid. Mac tried to imply he shot at the convertible because Cyndi forced him to, but he'll name names rather than be parboiled in someone else's hot water."

"The girl's feeble little ploys inspired me. I realized I could assist my husband's campaign, and, if it fell apart, allow the blame to fall on the girl's back. She was a coldhearted tramp."

I heard a rustling near the area of the audio booth, but I kept my eyes on the Senator's widow, who was not smiling as she edged forward. Her fingers were white as she clutched her purse, and her shoulders more squared than a marine's. "Then why did Steve have an affair with her?" I asked.

"Warren had an affair with her."

"That's what everyone kept saying," I agreed amiably. "But Steve admitted to me in this precise spot that he was the one who had an affair with Cyndi. He even admitted he killed her when her demands became impossible and she threatened to expose him."

"He would have admitted to masterminding the Teapot Dome scandal, if you'd accused him of it. He had a whimsical sense of humor, and at times failed to consider the wisdom of speaking on impulse. We had to be quite careful at press conferences; he was inclined to say things that later proved regrettable. Warren and I tutored him nightly, although it was an uphill struggle." She gazed sharply at the shadows behind me. "Did you hear something? Is someone back there?"

"That's Luanne Bradshaw," I said. "She went to the prop room to see if she could find a revolver. My daughter had it late yesterday afternoon, but swore she returned it before the police finally permitted us to leave the theater last night. When Caron had it, it was loaded with blanks. Someone used real bullets last night to murder your husband."

She laughed. "Come now, I'm sure the police searched the theater for weapons all night long. They must have tried the prop room."

I laughed, although without her conviction. "I suppose you're right, although they did manage to overlook the envelope in the office—the one Steve implied was a schedule for the next week of campaigning. We both know you paid Mac to fire a blank at the car and Arnie to steal it afterward to prevent an immediate investigation. As long as you've established a rewarding financial pattern, you might as well pay me for the so-called schedule."

"I seem to have misjudged you," she said appraisingly. "I thought you were just one of these frustrated, busybody spinsters. The ones whose lives are so dreary that they feel obliged to stick their noses into everything in hopes of a vicarious thrill or two. I hadn't noticed this felonious stripe down your back."

"What can I say? I read the contents of the envelope, and it's a convincingly lurid account of the affair between Cyndi and Steve. She listed motel addresses, dates, possible witnesses, presents he gave her, and the dates she deposited blackmail money in her account. You're not the widow of a politician who sacrificed himself in selfless service to the public; you're the widow of a good-natured philanderer who carried on with an eighteen-year-old girl." I tilted my head and gave her a perplexed look. "Good-natured, but also a murderer. There's a problem with the portrait, isn't there? If he murdered Cyndi, then his posthumous reputation is tainted, to say the least. If he didn't, then someone else must have. And we still have the very real problem of who murdered him while he was explaining all of this to me."

"Union thugs killed my husband. As for the girl, we may never find out who realized the world might be a better place without her." Patti moved forward until she was less than a yard from me. She looked over my shoulder, then patted her purse. "I did bring some money, just in case you turned out to be an unscrupulous sort who's willing to destroy my dead husband's reputation. How much do you want?"

I gazed out over the rows of seats, rather aggravated with her eagerness to pay me off and toddle away to the state senate. I was trying to decide how best to provoke her when Luanne came out of the darkness, her crutches thudding softly.

She held up a revolver. "I found the weapon in the very back of the prop room, under the Arc de Triomphe, if you can imagine. At least I didn't have to climb the Eiffel Tower to reach it." She nodded to Patti, then offered the gun to me. "The police must have missed it, but it's most likely the murder weapon."

Patti's fingernails cut into her purse. "It's not the murder weapon. It's a damn toy. I don't know what you two are trying to pull, but I'm not staying here any longer. Give me the schedule. I'll pay whatever you say, as long as it's reasonable, and we can be done with this nonsense."

I pointed the gun at her. "Are you sure it's a toy? What if it's loaded with real ammunition?"

"It's a toy. The real gun is—" She caught herself and shook her head. "A prop is a prop is a prop. You can't kill someone with a prop."

I looked at Luanne. "She's right. It's not a real gun."

"Then she didn't use it to shoot her husband?" Luanne said,

scowling at me. "Then why on earth did you insist I poke around that filthy little room to find it? I snagged my stocking on a spear for nothing."

"I'm sorry. It seemed so logical to think she"—I gestured at Patti, who was observing us with a bemused look—"murdered Cyndi yesterday afternoon, then murdered her husband last night when she realized he was likely to implicate her if he continued babbling to me."

Luanne raised a crutch to point at Patti. "But we already decided she didn't kill Cyndi. She wasn't even in the theater Friday afternoon when the first attempt was made. She couldn't find a baby-sitter—remember? You really must stop making wild accusations, my dear."

I idly twirled the revolver around my finger as I said, "She didn't have a baby-sitter because Warren was here. In fact, I spotted him trying to sneak out of the auditorium that very afternoon. What's more, one of the contestants heard a male voice down in the dressing room. I'll bet you a case of Twinkies that Warren went to talk to Cyndi."

Patti's head had swiveled back and forth as she observed this Abbott and Costello routine. She stopped to stare at me. "Why would Warren go down there—if, as you claim, he hadn't had an affair with the girl?"

If I'd possessed dimples, I would have switched them on. "It's a matter of the old midlife crisis. Warren's too young, but it seems to be epidemic with those of us approaching forty. Steve told me that was the reason he took up with Cyndi. Was that the reason you and Warren—ah, found solace in each other's company when Steve was at Warren's apartment?"

"I fail to see the relevance," she snapped.

"It escapes me, too," Luanne contributed, blinking at me.

"Well," I said, "let's suppose that Cyndi called Patti from the office immediately after the parade and demanded money. Motherhood posed a problem, so Patti sent Warren down to talk to

Cyndi. He appraised the potential of the faked asphyxiation, locked the door, and went back to the auditorium. Everybody wandered away for dinner, but Cyndi was discovered before it was too late to revive her. She again called the hotel, and this time Patti came down to the theater and made sure things went more successfully. She was feeling quite confident until Steve mentioned the damning letter Cyndi hid in the theater. The two came down to search for it. I stumbled into Steve and began asking awkward questions. Patti, who'd been searching the light booth, realized he was about to slip and shot him. She then tried to shoot me."

Luanne gaped at Patti, who was decidedly displeased. "Did you really try to shoot Claire? I know she's meddlesome and occasionally infuriating, but she owes me money for lunch last week."

"She's meddlesome, all right—and wrong," Patti said grimly. "This story of hers is a fantastic series of lies, theatrics, and wild guesses. If she repeats one word of it, I shall instruct my attorney to file a libel suit. She can peddle her books from a little wooden cart in the future."

"Then you don't have a gun in your purse?" I inserted before the two indulged in further character assassination. "It's okay if we call the police and ask them to come down here right now to examine the contents of your purse?"

She stepped back, opened her purse, and took out the handkerchief to neatly touch the corners of her mouth. She then took out a nasty little revolver and pointed it at us. "It's really not convenient at the moment, I'm afraid. It would have been much easier on everyone if you hadn't insisted on playing detective, but what's done is done. I want the schedule. Once it's in my possession, we can discuss what else needs to be done."

I pointed my gun at her. "Put that away or I'll shoot," I said in the fine tradition of the Old West. I would have clinked my spurs had I been wearing any.

"My gun is real. Yours is not," she responded serenely.

I eased back into the shadows. "Are you sure?"

She advanced, looking somewhat tired of the scene. "Yes, I'm quite sure. Now shall we stop this silliness and deal with the situation like adults?"

At which time Luanne bashed her across the back with a right crutch. The revolver fell to the floor. Patti stumbled forward, waved her arms frantically as she teetered on the edge of the stage, then toppled into the orchestra pit. After what seemed like several seconds, we heard a thud and a muffled curse.

"Bravo," I murmured as I went to peer down into the black hole. "I'd give her at least a five-six for technical merit. Do you think we ought to call an ambulance?"

"In a minute," said a male voice from the back of the stage. As Luanne and I looked up, startled by the intrusion, Warren appeared from the shadows. He bent down to pick up Patti's gun and aimed it in our general direction. He looked around until he located her purse, which he then opened and dug through until he found a key chain. "If you don't mind, I think I'll engage in a sudden and unexpected career move myself. I'd like to commend both of you for the calmness you displayed. She's crazy, a political animal afflicted with rabies. She probably would have shot you dead without a moment's hesitation."

"Thank you," I said, eying him cautiously. "It wouldn't have saved her. We've already called the police."

"She'll have a lovely time trying to explain away the blackmail evidence, but I think I'll take the revolver with me." He raised his voice to include the woman in the pit. "If she keeps her mouth shut, however, there won't be any evidence to involve either of us in the homicides. Her father can call in the lawyers, and the whole thing will eventually blow over. It's been a pleasure, ladies, but I must run along now."

"You're not leaving me, you swine," came a growl of outrage from the pit. "This was your idea, not mine."

He went to the edge of the stage and leaned forward. "No, darling, it was your idea. Do you honestly think anyone would believe that I wanted to have an affair with someone old enough to play bridge with my mother? I merely assumed it was in the job description somewhere."

"How dare you!" she called, recovering rapidly from the unexpected exit from the stage. "You seduced me, you pimply little frat boy!"

"I hate pimples," Luanne said under her breath. She then lifted a crutch and poked Warren in the back. His exit was almost a five-eight.

Somewhere from the back of the auditorium came the sound of applause. The houselights came on more brightly, and policemen scurried in from the corridors on either side of the auditorium. The spotlights suddenly bathed us in a puddle of pink. The single member of the audience, one David McWethy, continued to clap. I took Luanne's hand, and we bowed together.

"F"I"F"T"E"E"N"

"Climb every mountain," warbled a voice from the center of the stage.

Peter's hand tightened around mine, as if he were resisting the urge to clamp it over an ear to drown out the sound. "How many of them are going to sing this?" he hissed. "We've climbed every mountain in the Alps. Do we have to tackle the Himalayas, too?"

"Only these two," I whispered back. I noticed the judges (Mayor Avery, Ms. Maugahyder, and one Sally Fromberger) were doodling on their legal pads and less than entranced with the strange tremolos coming from one of the Lisas. Said girl came to a merciful stop, curtsied to the judges, and trotted offstage as the audience clapped dutifully, if not enthusiastically.

The emcee offered his congratulations, then peered myopically through red-rimmed eyes at the card in his hand. "Wasn't that wowsy? Now our next contestant has the cutest little pooch you folks are likely to see. Let's have a big welcome for Heidi and Chou-Chou!"

"Heidi's the tall one," I whispered to Peter as two pink-clad performers came onto the stage. One had a hula hoop and an optimistic expression; the other had beady black eyes and a defiant glower. To the audience's surprise (and perhaps disappointment), the former coaxed the latter through the hoop without a single drop shed on the stage.

Once the applause faded, Heidi put her hands on her hips and glared at the light booth above our heads. "See?" she snapped. "The only reason Chou-Chou had problems before was that one of the contestants was so jealous she kept feeding peepee pills to poor little Chou-Chou. It wasn't his fault at all, Mr. Meanie!" She snatched up the dog and stalked offstage.

"Peepee pills?" Peter said incredulously.

"Diuretics. Dixie, the clarinetist, wasn't supposed to be in the theater after the parade, so she couldn't admit that was when she heard a male voice in Cyndi's dressing room. She called me last week and we had a long talk. She cried, and I tried very hard not to laugh."

Luanne was on the other side of me. She caught my eye and tried very hard not to laugh. We were both snorting away as Julianna came on stage and flashed shiny teeth at the judges. In the wings, Eunice Allingham watched with a satisfied expression, her eyes on the contestant but her mind fifteen hundred miles away at the Big One. I could almost hear her humming.

The awesome display of talent subsided, and while the contestants changed into evening gowns, the emcee told several off-color jokes that would have played better at the Dew Drop Inn. In the more sedate confines of the Thurber Street Theater, the silence was eloquent. Mayor Avery's ears turned pink, and Ms. Maugahyder's hand froze in middoodle. A bray of laughter floated down from the light booth.

"What's going to happen to Mac?" I asked Peter.

"Not nearly enough. Although he could have been of great assistance to the prosecution, it seems someone has rekindled his political aspirations. We'll try to peg him for obstruction and a few pesky charges, but we're getting a lot of pressure from the Governor's office and higher powers that be to stay away from him. Patti Stevenson's father carries a very big stick. Not big enough to protect her entirely, but adequate to keep things very quiet. The prosecutor has hourly migraines."

The girls swirled back onstage to field demanding questions from the emcee. Julianna said in a steady voice that she wanted to speak for her generation, fight poverty, and help make the world a better place. Dixie admired Mother Teresa and Madonna. Lisa I and Lisa II both aspired to spread understanding and love throughout the country via modeling. Bambi wanted to feed all the underprivileged people, and then model. Dixie also wanted to be the spokesperson for her generation, thus bathing us all in peace and understanding and brotherhood and that sort of thing, you know. Heidi wanted us to know how really much this all had meant to her and Chou-Chou.

After more swirling and simpering, the girls huddled in the center of the stage while the judges scribbled, passed notes, whispered, scribbled, and looked up every now and then at the would-be queens. The audience wiggled around restlessly. The emcee turned his back, but I saw the flash of a flask moving from pocket to mouth and back to pocket. A faint howl came from the green-room.

I poked Luanne. "You're going to the therapist every day, right? If you let me down, you know how hard I'll blotch."

"Every single day," she said in a low voice. "I had the bulemia licked for years, but the pageant set it off again. I haven't binged since the morning after the second murder. I'm doing heavy-duty vitamin therapy, and following the shrink's orders down to the last stalk of celery."

"Will you swear to that on your neighbor's vine-ripened tomatoes? As much as it would interfere with my long hours of inertia at the Book Depot or my ever so cheerful chats with my accountant, I will find you three times a day to make sure you're following orders. Damn it, Luanne, I care about you. Bulemia's serious. It can do dreadful things to your stomach, throat, and mouth. It plays havoc with your body chemistry. How will Caron Malloy run around in inappropriate black cocktail dresses if you're not there to clothe her over her mother's protests?"

"I know, I know," she murmured. "It's a dangerous, potentially fatal compulsion. I started when I first began participating in the beauty pageants, where one's body is everything and every ounce of flab is an enemy. After a while, my body became my enemy. It's going to take intensive therapy to work that out, but I do intend to hang around if for no other reason than to cloth over protest."

"I feel guilty that I didn't figure out what you were doing behind locked bathroom doors, but I associate bulimia with younger women. You've already had your midlife crisis, my gray-headed friend. You should be fighting an urge to overdose on Mah Jongg or lithe young gigolos with sunlamp tans."

"While you, of course, are decades away from a midlife crisis?" she whispered tartly.

Before I could respond, Mayor Avery gave the emcee the envelope. While the audience held its collective breath, we worked our way from sixth runner-up to first runner-up. Julianna shrieked, burst into tears, and was swarmed by her court. Caron Malloy, a child of many talents, appeared with a crown and stuck it into Julianna's upswept hair. Eunice's arms remained crossed as she gazed at her gal, but her eyes glittered more brightly than all the Vasolined teeth on the stage.

Miss Thurberfest reigned supreme.

"What was all that muttering about midlife crises?" Peter asked once we were on the sofa in my living room.

I poured two glasses of wine and handed one to him. "It's an excuse adults use for behaving in an adolescent manner. A rationale for irrational behavior. Teetering on the brink of middle age doesn't give one a license to abandon responsibility for a few cheap thrills."

"Oh," he murmured, trying to sound wise. "Then we're too old to change our ways, huh? We'll just trudge along in our respective ruts until we drop?"

"Who's in a rut? A lifestyle isn't necessarily a rut. It's order and continuity. It's a sense of comfortableness, of knowing what you want from life and how best to acquire it."

"Not even one little cheap thrill?"

I looked at the broad grin, the hint of gray in the curls over his temples, the deceptively mild color of his eyes. "Can I help it if I have reservations?" I said, shrugging.

"I know you have reservations," Peter murmured, moving in with great charm. He nibbled here and there, then added, "I suppose I'll have to trudge along in the rut until I wear you down."

"For these reservations, you need a passport."